PRAISE FOR ISABE

T0244823

A Forgo

"Maldonado's years of law enforcement experience continue to add grit and texture to the series, and she supplements those details with a barn burner of a climax. Readers will clamor for the sequel."

—*Publishers Weekly*

"Maldonado's expertise in the criminology field really shines through in her books . . . She covers her bases, does her research, and creates a realistic investigation and chase that is compelling and engaging!"

—Shelf Reflection

"Filled to the brim with suspense and danger, *A Forgotten Kill* is one of those great reads that crackles with nervous energy from start to finish. A book that urges you forward with a desperate desire to learn the outcome as quickly as possible."

—Best Thriller Books

"Dani Vega is the kick-ass heroine we've all been waiting for! Former Army Ranger, current hard-core FBI agent, she can outthink, outfight, and just plain outclass any opponent around. Welcome to your next favorite series!"

—Lisa Gardner, #1 *New York Times* bestselling author

A Killer's Game

"Maldonado keeps the plot boiling and the bodies dropping to the end."

—*Kirkus Reviews*

"Intense, gripping, and compulsively readable, *A Killer's Game* goes from zero to ninety on page one and never slows down. FBI agent Dani Vega is a heroine to cheer for—tough, inventive, and highly capable. A winner."

—Meg Gardiner, #1 *New York Times* bestselling author

The Falcon

"Another great read from [Isabella Maldonado]! I'm a Nina Guerrera fan, and this book is the best of the series so far. Don't miss it!"

—Steve Netter, Best Thriller Books

A Different Dawn

"A horrifying crime, cat-and-mouse detection, aha moments, and extended suspense."

—*Kirkus Reviews*

"Maldonado expertly ratchets up the tension as the pieces of the puzzle neatly fall into place. Suspense fans will be enthralled from the very first page."

—*Publishers Weekly*

"A thrill ride from the very start. It starts off fast and never lets up. It's one of the best thrillers of the summer."

—*Red Carpet Crash*

"*A Different Dawn* is a heart-stopping journey on parallel tracks: police detection and personal . . . Isabella Maldonado has created an unforgettable hero in Nina Guerrera."

—Criminal Element

"A killer of a novel. Fresh, fast, and utterly ingenious."

—Brad Thor, #1 *New York Times* bestselling author

The Cipher

"The survivor of a vicious crime confronts her fears in a hunt for a serial killer . . . forensic analysis, violent action, and a tough heroine who stands up to the last man on earth she wants to see again."

—*Kirkus Reviews*

"[In] this riveting series launch from Maldonado . . . the frequent plot twists will keep readers guessing to the end, and Maldonado draws on her twenty-two years in law enforcement to add realism. Determined to overcome her painful past, the admirable Nina has enough depth to sustain a long-running series."

—*Publishers Weekly*

"*The Cipher* by Isabella Maldonado is a nail-biting race against time."

—POPSUGAR

"Maldonado does a superb job of depicting a woman who's made a strength out of trauma and an even better job at showing how a monster could use the internet to prey on the vulnerable. Maldonado spent twenty-two years in law enforcement, and her experience shines through in *The Cipher*."

—Amazon Book Review

"A heart-pounding novel from page one, *The Cipher* checks all the boxes for a top-notch thriller: sharp plotting, big stakes, and characters— good and bad and everywhere in between—that are so richly drawn you'll swear you've met them. I read this in one sitting, and I guarantee you will too. Oh, another promise: you'll absolutely love the Warrior Girl!"

—Jeffery Deaver, *New York Times* bestselling author

"Wow! A riveting tale in the hands of a superb storyteller."

—J. A. Jance, *New York Times* bestselling author

"Intense, harrowing, and instantly addictive, *The Cipher* took my breath away. Isabella Maldonado has created an unforgettable heroine in Nina Guerrera, a dedicated FBI agent and trauma survivor with unique insight into the mind of a predator. This riveting story is everything a thriller should be."

—Hilary Davidson, *Washington Post* bestselling author

A KILLER'S
CODE

ISABELLA MALDONADO

A KILLER'S CODE

THOMAS & MERCER

Published by Thomas & Mercer, Seattle

www.apub.com

Amazon, the Amazon logo, and Thomas & Mercer are trademarks of Amazon.com, Inc., or its affiliates.

ISBN-13: 9781662515835 (paperback)
ISBN-13: 9781662515842 (digital)

Cover design by Shasti O'Leary Soudant
Cover image: © Miguel Sobreira / ArcAngel; © KPegg / Shutterstock

Printed in the United States of America

For J.A. Jance,
who is the embodiment of true grit.

With an indomitable spirit,
she overcame countless obstacles
to rise to the top of her profession
among the greatest crime fiction authors.

I am forever grateful for her generosity
in taking time from her demanding schedule
to offer her hard-won wisdom
and her friendship.

PROLOGUE

Five months earlier, Thursday, May 9

The priest had blessed the last parishioner and was about to emerge from the confessional when the door opened again. A slight creaking sound told him a penitent had knelt.

He adjusted his rotund frame on the cushioned seat and reached up to slide open the panel. The dark screen prevented him from seeing who had entered the other side of the booth, but he observed a silhouette making the sign of the cross.

"In the name of the Father, and of the Son, and of the Holy Spirit. Amen."

He responded with a blessing. "May God who has enlightened every heart help you to know your sins and trust in His mercy."

"Amen."

Aware such unburdening could not be rushed, the priest waited in silence.

"Bless me, Father, for I have sinned. It has been more than ten years since my last confession."

Clearly, this was not an AdLenitent. He'd invented the term for parishioners who came to church only during Advent or Lent to make penitence. He also privately referred to those who attended Mass only on Christmas and Easter as Chreasters.

The supplicant now before him had chosen this day, and this church, for relief from over a decade's worth of guilt. Confession was, indeed, good for the soul.

"These are my sins." Another long pause. "I have killed people."

"People?" He deliberately maintained a calm tone, hiding his shock as he sought clarity. "As in . . . more than one?"

"A lot more than one."

The priest had been at his vocation long enough to have heard thousands of confessions. Including admissions of murder. But never anything like this. He considered himself a good judge of character, and these words had the ring of truth.

This was no joke, and he responded with gravity. "You don't know how many?"

"Never kept count. Plus, there are people whose death I caused indirectly. I'm not sure how to add those up."

It was not his place to pass judgment. Only God could do that. Nothing could be done to bring back the lives that had been cut short, so instead he dealt with the situation at hand.

A killer had come to confess. "I sense deep pain and remorse."

"You have no idea, Father."

He'd learned never to make assumptions, so he asked, "Why are you here?"

"I seek the sacrament of Reconciliation."

"First, you must do penance," he said, laying out the path to what would no doubt be an arduous spiritual journey. "Then, I will hear your act of contrition. Finally, if you have truly repented, you will be granted absolution. Once you are reconciled, go forth and sin no more."

"I can repent for what I have done, but I will almost certainly kill again."

"I don't understand."

This time, the silence stretched so long the priest wondered if there would be any response at all. Then, finally, "It's the nature of my work."

"You need to find another job. You cannot be reconciled if you are not truly contrite. And you are not if you have no intention of changing your ways."

"I see." The kneeling bench creaked again as the silhouetted figure rose. "Thank you for hearing my confession, Father."

His heart lurched as he sensed the moment slipping away. "Please keep coming to Mass. Keep praying. Don't give up on your immortal soul," he pleaded. When he heard no response, he heaved a weary sigh. "Peace be with you, my child."

"And also with you."

The priest remained in the dark confessional for the next half hour, praying fervently. Only divine intervention could save that particular soul.

CHAPTER 1

Present day, Monday, October 7, 8:00 a.m.
Bellevue Hospital, Manhattan, New York

She shouldn't say it. It wouldn't help. Might make the situation worse. Then again, tact had never been Daniela Vega's strong suit.

So she said it. "Maybe my mother would be ready to leave if you weren't overmedicating her."

Dr. Ashley Maffuccio was Camila Vega's treating psychiatrist and had overseen her care during the decade she had spent in the secure psych ward at Bellevue Hospital.

"Excuse me," Dr. Maffuccio said coolly. "I wasn't aware you had a medical license. Or a board certification in psychiatric medicine."

Yep, Dani should have chosen her words more wisely. She had come to Bellevue to take her mother on her first outing since her incarceration ten years earlier. Dr. Maffuccio had nixed the plan, explaining that even a short trip away from the controlled environment of the hospital grounds put someone in Camila's fragile mental state at risk of sensory overload.

"You changed her prescription," Dani said. "You told me it would help make her more lucid so she can understand what's going on better."

Her mother had been catatonic for years, only recently regaining the ability to communicate in anything other than disjointed fragments of Bible verses.

Dr. Maffuccio nodded. "And she's improved. She still quotes scripture, but it's less random now, and she's been able to have meaningful conversations with the staff." She rested a hand on her hip. "But she's not ready to stroll through Central Park."

"Look, I just want her out of here. Not forever, but for an hour or two. How else are we supposed to work toward getting her discharged if she never takes the first step?"

"She's no longer on lockdown," Dr. Maffuccio said. "She has free run of the campus, but she chooses to stay in her room most of the time."

Unlike Dani, Dr. Maffuccio knew how to hold her tongue. Still, the unspoken words cut all the way to the bone.

Camila Vega had been remanded to Bellevue ten years ago based on Dani's testimony. At seventeen years old, Dani had come home from school to find her mother kneeling beside her father with a bloody knife clutched in her hand.

No one else was in the apartment, the knife had come from their kitchen, and the door had been locked when Dani entered. Her mother was in shock and totally unresponsive. Dani had been left to give the only account the NYPD homicide detectives would ever get.

But it had been wrong.

And Camila Vega had been incarcerated for a crime she didn't commit. She'd lost ten years of her life as well as her husband and Dani, who had rarely come to visit.

Worst of all, a murderer had been free to kill again for a decade. Dani felt every bit as responsible for those deaths as she was for the lives she had personally taken during her military career prior to joining the FBI. At only twenty-seven years old, she had plenty of blood on her hands.

Dr. Maffuccio paused to regard her, then softened her tone. "I understand that you want to set things right, but rushing the process will set your mother back. She's made a lot of gains in the past few weeks, but you must be patient."

Another virtue Dani did not possess. She turned to look through the wide picture window that overlooked the courtyard. Camila had a sketchbook in her lap. She dug through a container the size of a cigar box and selected a colored pencil, scrutinized it, put it back, then chose another.

Dr. Maffuccio followed her gaze. "I've been meaning to talk to you about her drawings."

Until recently, Camila's sole form of expression was thousands of random words scrawled in regular pencil on sheets of paper. She'd taped the pages to all four walls of her room, creating an unsettling display.

Two weeks ago, Camila had requested a set of colored pencils. Dani rushed to an art store and got her the best set she could find, along with an easel and a quality sketchbook. Her mother had lifted the items reverently out of Dani's arms and immediately began drawing intersecting lines using every hue in her new pencil set. Soon, the lines formed geometric shapes, which coalesced into vivid designs in a kaleidoscope of colors.

Dani picked up on the note of concern in the psychiatrist's voice. "What's up?"

"The sketches are increasing in complexity," Dr. Maffuccio said. "We've only seen something like this once before, and it's not an exact match, so we're conducting some tests."

Never the words you want to hear from anyone with an MD attached to their name.

"I'm not following."

"We believe your mother may have a rare condition called acquired synesthesia." Dr. Maffuccio seemed to notice her alarm and added, "There's nothing to worry about. In fact, many people consider it a gift."

"A gift?"

"Synesthesia is when two or more of the five senses overlap. Some people can see sounds or hear colors. Others can feel colors or see flavors. There are many types of synesthesia. Some people can smell the notes played in a symphony or see different words as having specific colors."

Dani blinked. "You think my mother has this . . . why?"

"When Camila is creating her art, she's made comments about how the colors and shapes sound when she puts them together." Dr. Maffuccio shook her head. "Actually, that's not right. She says she composes the shapes. Like composing music. She's referred to herself as a conductor."

"And this is when she's clear, right?"

Camila still spent much of the time in silence, occasionally blurting biblical scripture. She had become lucid only within the past month, but those stretches had been increasing in length.

Dr. Maffuccio nodded. "Only two to five percent of the population has this condition, and most of those are born with it. They're called synesthetes." When Dani continued to stare, she elaborated. "Some incredibly talented artists have spoken openly about how it has affected their art."

Dani raised an inquisitive brow.

"Billy Joel said he could see different hues in melodies versus rhythms. Vladimir Nabokov wrote about his synesthesia in his memoir. Duke Ellington perceived musical notes in terms of color as well as texture. He described a D as a dark-blue burlap. Pharrell Williams says he couldn't compose music without what he refers to as his gift. Lady Gaga said her hit song 'Poker Face' had a deep amber color. Marilyn Monroe tasted colors, and Nikola Tesla was—"

"Stop." Dani held up a hand. "I get it. Lots of amazing people are synesthetes. But my mother never mentioned this before, and you said she 'acquired' it."

"Exactly," Dr. Maffuccio said. "We aren't sure why, but sometimes people's neurons form new connections due to physical, psychological, or emotional trauma."

Camila had always been emotionally fragile, but she had never shared details about her upbringing in Puerto Rico. Her husband and Dani's father, Sergio Vega, had been her rock. When he died a violent death, it seemed her final tether to reality had snapped. Now that she was recovering, had that trauma caused a structural change in her brain?

"What kinds of tests are you talking about?"

"We'd like to do an MRI to confirm the diagnosis, but getting her into one of those tubes with all the noise has been a total nonstarter so far. We're looking into an open MRI."

"I'll put in for a leave of absence at work," Dani said, coming to a decision. "I'll help her get through the testing. Maybe if I spend more time with her, she'll get better faster."

She had come to visit her mother early in the morning as soon as visiting hours began. If things worked out, she'd come back tomorrow with her younger brother and sister, both in college. They had visited their mother more often over the years and seemed to have less trouble than Dani did with the environment. Then again, they hadn't presented evidence against Camila.

Dr. Maffuccio smiled. "She'd like that."

Dani made the trek down the corridor toward the courtyard. She could at least spend some quality time with her mother even if they couldn't go anywhere.

Her cell phone buzzed in her pocket. She reflexively pulled it out. And came to a halt.

The head of the FBI's New York Counterterrorism Division, Special Agent in Charge Steve Wu, was calling her. He was several layers above her in the chain of command at the New York field office. Which meant he would not contact her directly unless something important was going on.

She raised the phone to her ear. "Agent Vega."

"Drop whatever you're doing," he said, not wasting time with pleasantries. "Report to the briefing room at 26 Fed immediately."

The FBI's New York field office was located at 26 Federal Plaza in Lower Manhattan. Fortunately, not far from Bellevue.

It felt as if fate was testing her resolve. She had just vowed to take a leave of absence to help speed her mother's recovery.

But duty called.

She glanced at her mother, lost in her art, serenely sitting in the quiet courtyard.

"Agent Vega?"

SAC Wu was rock solid. Always calm under pressure. But she detected a note of strain in his voice. Her mind flashed back to her time in the military.

Her commanding officer had given her marching orders and needed acknowledgment that she had received them loud and clear.

When she was in the Army, there would have been no hesitation. A crisp salute followed by "yes, sir" would be her only response.

Duty had always come first, but now, things had changed.

Or had they?

"Agent Vega?" A brief pause, then, "This is about Gustavo Toro."

She closed her eyes and pinched the bridge of her nose. "On my way, sir."

CHAPTER 2

Five months earlier, Wednesday, May 8, midnight

The blade Gustavo Toro had brought to slit Simon Buckwald's throat glinted in the moonlight.

He readjusted the hunting knife, not wanting to give away his position. The forest surrounding the cabin was dense, a faint rustling of the trees around him the only sound in the darkness. Buckwald should arrive any moment, unless the information given to Toro was wrong.

Which it never was.

His employer for this particular contract did not make amateur mistakes. The boss had tasked his top lieutenant, Denton Foley, with coordinating the hit. Two days ago, Foley had texted Toro's burner phone with the kill order. Upon learning Toro was at his main residence in Monaco, Foley sent a private jet to fly him to the US for the job.

During the flight, Toro reviewed a digital file with all the data he needed about the target. Buckwald was planning a trip to his cabin in the woods. It was the perfect opportunity to take him out.

According to Foley's surveillance team, Buckwald often escaped to his secluded hideaway with his mistress. He always arrived at the cabin an hour before his guest to prepare the place and left an hour after she departed so he could clean up any evidence of their liaison.

Tonight, Buckwald would never make it inside.

Foley had dropped Toro off outside the property so he could maneuver into position to ambush Buckwald between his vehicle and the cabin's front door. After dispatching the target, he would run through the woods to meet Foley at the rendezvous point. Foley would drive him back to the airport so Toro could return to Monaco on a commercial flight under a different name, as he did after most of his contracts.

But this time, Toro was going someplace else. And Foley could never find out where—or most importantly—why.

The distant rumble of a Land Rover's engine caught Toro's attention before its headlights cut through the night. Buckwald was right on time.

He edged out from behind the trunk of a towering oak tree when the vehicle slowed to a stop and the engine cut off, plunging the woods back into darkness.

The target got out and slammed the door shut, then started for the cabin. Knife in hand, Toro raced toward Buckwald.

Only it wasn't Buckwald.

And he wasn't alone.

The silhouetted figure he mistook for his target aimed a pistol in his direction as three men in black camos leaped from the back of the SUV.

Toro instinctively ducked before the first round flew over his head. He spun and sprinted back toward the massive oak. Out of the corner of his eye, he saw something that made his blood run cold.

Partially cloaked by darkness, a group of men were swiftly leaving the cabin. Outfitted in black, with rifles trained in his direction, they fanned out to surround him.

Was this a police SWAT team?

He could worry about how Buckwald had found out about him later. Right now, he had to get to the woods. It was his only hope of hiding from the gunmen coming after him. Once he'd lost them in the forest, he could circle around to the meeting point so Foley could extract him.

He plunged a hand into his tactical vest and pulled out his pistol as another shot rang out from behind him. The round grazed his left shoulder, bringing the sensation of a hot sting. He veered right as he aimed his muzzle over his shoulder to get off a quick shot.

He was firing blind. His only intention was to back his pursuers off long enough to make it to the tree line.

The team after him had other ideas.

A cacophony of shots exploded around him. The riflemen had engaged. He made a sharp course correction and turned his body enough to take aim this time. A couple of quick rounds from his gun bought him an extra second, but he'd exposed himself in the process.

Three red dots materialized on his upper body.

Running on a mixture of pure instinct and adrenaline, he tucked and rolled. Another round grazed his thigh as he sprang up and sprinted, allowing the momentum to carry him closer to the woods.

Moments later, he plunged into the trees. Curses behind him told him they were charging in after him. He figured they would assume he'd head deeper into the forest, so instead he turned to his right and ran parallel to the tree line, which seemed to work.

Until it didn't.

His only warning was a glint of metal, giving him a split second to literally dodge a bullet. Again, he chose to do the unexpected. The muzzle flash gave away the man's position, and offered a target for Toro, who immediately fired on the spot.

A grunt of pain followed by a thudding sound. Shouts from others in the forest, now crashing their way toward him. Apparently, they had spread out to cover more ground in their search and the man who fired on him was alone.

He approached the man, now lying on the ground clutching his thigh, his weapon just out of reach. Toro did not waste time or ammo. He quickly pulled out his knife and plunged it into the man's throat, cutting off his ability to call out to his comrades—or to breathe.

One down.

He picked up the man's pistol and snatched an extra magazine from a pouch on his webbed belt. Now carrying a gun in each hand, he retreated behind a nearby tree and waited for the others to come to the aid of their fallen colleague. He picked off three more as soon as they got close. From this vantage point, he could snipe at them virtually at will. He was starting to like his odds.

Until a bullet slammed into the middle of his back.

Unlike in the movies, a small projectile—even traveling at 1,200 feet per second—didn't send a human body flying through a window in a shower of shattered glass. Depending on the shot placement and type of round used, however, it could cause massive internal damage leading to a quick death.

When Toro's knees buckled, he made no effort to remain standing to take another bullet. He fell onto his stomach and rolled over, bringing both guns up to return fire. The shooter went down, as did another one rushing to join him in the fight.

Toro sat up and took stock of his situation. The man who'd shot him in the back had not been among the ones equipped with rifles. Fortunate for Toro, because a rifle round would have penetrated the layers of Kevlar in his vest.

His ears were ringing from the deafening gun blasts. He went to the firing range often but always wore ear protection. It would be anywhere from minutes to days before his keen hearing fully recovered. For that reason, he had to rely on his sight.

Surveying the area, he detected no movement. Had he gotten them all? He did a quick count but couldn't be certain. Either way, the mission had been thoroughly compromised, and it was time to evacuate.

He struggled to his feet, fighting through the pain that radiated from the center of his back. For a moment, he wondered if swelling from the impact might cause nerve damage along his spine. Then he decided not to worry about a potential injury when every second he remained carried the risk of immediate death.

He picked his way through the woods as quickly as he could with only scant moonlight not blocked by the canopy of trees to guide him. He tripped over roots and rocks, falling to his knees twice, before finally reaching the meeting place.

But Foley wasn't there.

He checked his watch. Despite the gun battle in the woods, he had arrived within the assigned window for a pickup. Had Foley heard the shots and taken off?

He dug out his cell phone. No incoming texts or missed calls. If Foley had changed plans, he would have used his burner to send a coded message directing him to another location.

And then it all suddenly made horrible sense. Foley wasn't here because he didn't expect to pick up Toro. After all, why wait at the rendezvous point for a dead man?

Foley had planned the hit. He knew when and where Toro would be. He told Toro to use a knife rather than a gun for the job, knowing that any backup weapon Toro carried would be tucked away and not easy to reach. That mercenary team had switched places with Buckwald and then lay in wait for him inside the cabin and in the back of the Land Rover. They could do that only if they knew he'd be there . . . because someone told them he was coming.

Denton Foley had set him up. But why? Toro was the best. He had never failed to complete an assignment.

And then he recalled one contract that had ended badly. But that was years ago. Why would Foley care about it now? He could think of only one answer.

After all this time, Foley must have finally figured out Toro had double-crossed him, which meant the boss knew as well.

The critical question was, Did they know the true motive behind the betrayal?

CHAPTER 3

Present day, Monday, October 7, 9:00 a.m.
26 Federal Plaza, Manhattan, New York

Even from beyond the grave, Gustavo Toro was causing trouble. Toro was a stone-cold killer. A hit man who sold his services to the highest bidder.

Or so Dani had thought until she'd gone undercover on an assignment as his partner several months ago. She'd barely survived. Toro hadn't been so lucky.

As he lay dying, he shared things that made her believe he wasn't the soulless mercenary she'd thought. Her heart ached at the memory, and she'd grieved him in her own way, putting him firmly in the past.

But Toro had refused to stay put.

After arriving at the Javits building in Lower Manhattan, better known as 26 Fed, she had taken the elevator to the thirty-fourth floor.

She'd walked into the small conference room adjacent to Special Agent in Charge Steve Wu's corner office. Seated beside the SAC was Sanjeev Patel, a civilian analyst who specialized in cybercrime and all things tech. Whip smart and younger than most FBI employees, Patel was as far away from starched white-collar shirts and Hoover-blue suits as anyone could get. One of many reasons she liked him.

Wu had provided a brief overview of the situation, explaining that she was here to decrypt a digital cipher to unlock the contents of a flash drive allegedly belonging to Toro. She still had trouble understanding how it had taken so long to come into Wu's possession.

She glanced at the small device jutting out of the port on Patel's laptop. "You're saying this came from France?" Then realization hit. "Toro's primary residence was in Monaco."

Wu nodded. "Our Paris legat was coordinating with the Monaco police to go through Toro's residence. There was quite a bit of red tape involved."

The FBI had legal attachés in countries around the world, and the Paris office covered Monaco. When Toro died, he took his secrets to the grave, including the identities of many former clients. After learning one of those clients was very high profile, FBI Director Franklin had ordered an investigation to uncover the rest. Naturally, that involved searching Toro's apartment in Monaco.

The timeline still didn't make sense. "But Toro died in late May."

"Toro gave the flash drive to his attorney in Paris," Wu said. "They rarely spoke, so it took months for the lawyer to learn of his death. When he did, he took the drive to the Paris legat and conveyed Toro's strict instructions that it was for the FBI director's eyes only, and that it had to be hand carried to him."

"Seems extreme," Dani said. "He could've encrypted a digital file and had his attorney give it to the legat to transmit through our secure server."

Patel's dark brows furrowed. "Must have been worried about a hack. And he didn't trust snail mail or a regular courier service either."

"That's what his attorney told us," Wu said. "Toro's instructions were to ensure the flash drive went straight to the top. Claimed it was too sensitive to risk with anyone else. That wouldn't ordinarily work, but Director Franklin was personally following the investigation, so he went along with it. The legat had a tech team check for toxins or explosives in the device before flying to DC to hand carry it to the director."

"This is wild," Patel said. "Whatever's on this thing must be damned important."

"I previewed the opening statement, and Toro sounds deadly serious," Wu said, then gestured to Patel, who tapped the screen with his fingertip to open a video file.

Dani recognized the familiar laptop, which was decorated with stickers of a Jolly Roger flag, a stop sign, and a biohazard emblem. Patel used it to open outside files, programs, and drives because it wasn't connected to the secure FBI server. There would be no Trojan horse malware infecting the Bureau on his watch.

They all turned to look at the laptop as the screen flickered to life.

A handsome man with wavy dark-brown hair, a three-day growth of beard, and intense brown eyes seated himself at a desk facing the camera.

Dani's breath caught at the sight of Toro alive and healthy, looking better than she'd ever seen him. "When was this recorded?"

"There's a date stamp in the bottom corner," Wu said.

She squinted. "April twenty-fourth. That's five and a half months ago."

She barely had time to process the fact that he'd been killed a little over a month after making the video before Toro began to speak.

"If you're watching this, I'm dead. And others will be soon if you don't act fast."

CHAPTER 4

Five and a half months earlier, Wednesday, April 24
Monaco

Gustavo Toro settled into the black leather chair and focused on the camera's lens. He had taken the time to adjust it on a tripod. He didn't want a view of the ceiling or an odd angle that put half his face out of the frame. No, he wanted to do this only once, so he'd made sure everything was set up right.

"If you're watching this, I'm dead," he began. "And others will be soon if you don't act fast."

He paused to let that sink in. Having dealt with the FBI during his career, he understood that they would need a good reason to spend time, money, and resources on a case brought to them by a solution specialist—a term he'd come up with for what he did. He wasn't just a killer. After all, sometimes the problem person needed to remain alive after they were persuaded to cooperate.

The Bureau was like a steam engine, though, and once they got going, they were an unstoppable force that would plow ahead until they reached their destination. He didn't like them, but he respected them in the way a diver respects a shark.

"This video is for the director of the FBI," he continued. "And by now you know who I am and what I do."

He assumed the flash drive his attorney provided would end up on the director's desk accompanied by a dossier. After all, he'd done his own research on the one who currently held that position, Thomas Franklin, and figured him for an all-business, no-bullshit kind of guy. Not fun to have a beer with, but exactly what this situation needed. He'd also learned Franklin was in his second year of a ten-year term of office. If Toro lived that long, he would have to evaluate the next director and adjust his plans if needed. But for now, Franklin was at bat.

The camera's glowing red light brought him back to the task at hand. "I've got information to share with you, but you'll have to earn it."

Part of his research had been to find the right bait for his hook, and Franklin seemed the type to rise to a challenge. What Toro was doing now was pure manipulation, but he was out of options. If he was dead, the FBI was his only shot.

"In my line of work, you can't be too careful." He gave his head a small shake, aware of the irony of the situation. "The fact that you're watching this means I wasn't careful enough."

For an instant, Toro wondered who would be the one to kill him. The list of possibilities was long, but at the top were Denton Foley and his boss—*if* they ever found out what he'd done.

Toro had heard a few whispers that Foley was jealous of him, but he hadn't taken it seriously. Foley was the boss's top enforcer and most trusted employee, yet somehow, he had come to view Toro as a threat.

As he prepared to make a case for his unseen audience, he reflected that it wasn't Foley but an entirely different set of circumstances that had prompted him to set up this desperate scheme. A totally unanticipated situation had thrown his life into chaos as it brought everything into sharp focus. And now his top priority was recruiting the FBI with bait they couldn't resist. To do that, he would have to bare his soul, admitting ugly truths about himself.

"Over the years, I created my own form of insurance. I made secret recordings of conversations, kept digital copies of financial transactions, including codes for overseas banks, and physical evidence. Basically, it's a treasure trove you can use to close a lot of unsolved crimes."

He should have the director hooked by now. Time to reel him in.

"Some of the people who hired me are powerful enough to make victims, witnesses, and evidence all disappear. They would literally kill to find what I've stashed away and destroy it. So I had to set up some safeguards. I couldn't just give it all to my attorney for safekeeping or put it in a safety deposit box. Banks can be robbed, and attorneys can be forced to talk."

He didn't bother to add that he knew this from personal experience.

"I've set up a kind of treasure hunt. The pot of gold at the end is my entire stash of evidence. And you'll be surprised at some of the people you'll be arresting. The other file on this drive is encrypted, but not with software. You can't just plug it into your bat computer or use some fancy AI to decode it. You'll need a human mind. Choose your best team to work on this. Agents you would trust with your own life, or your family's life."

He hoped the director got his meaning. He'd never been in a position where his goals aligned with those of law enforcement, and it felt odd to pass the baton to his enemy.

Perhaps it was best that he wouldn't live to see the day he depended on the Feds to finish what he'd started.

"If you succeed, organizations will crumble, powerful people will fall, others will die, and secrets will be revealed. Once you start looking under these rocks, invisible adversaries will find out and use all their resources to stop you. Put your best agents on this, ones who can stand up to sabotage, blackmail, and professional killers."

He stared into the lens and for once allowed his emotions to show in his normally tightly controlled features. "Now that I'm dead, the clock has started ticking. Time's running out. If you're up for the challenge, click the button."

For the thousandth time, he reflected on his plan. There was a ton of risk, but he couldn't see a better way to go about it.

A dead man's options were few.

CHAPTER 5

Present day, Monday, October 7, 9:05 a.m.

Dani watched Toro's image fade as he spoke his final words. "If you're up for the challenge, click the button."

Patel glanced at Wu, who nodded, before he moved his cursor to a red square and clicked.

The screen went dark, then two words appeared in bold white text.

CHALLENGE ACCEPTED

"That unlocked the second file," Patel said, frowning. "I don't understand. It was supposed to be encrypted."

"Can you connect that laptop to the wall screen without hooking it into our server?" Wu asked.

Dani and Wu waited while Patel hurried to grab a connector cord from one of the workstations lining the wall of the conference room. A minute later, they were all studying an enlarged picture of an ancient stone statue.

"I've seen this before," Wu said. "On a trip to Mexico."

Dani recognized it too. "That's Quetzalcoatl, the feathered serpent god." When they both looked her way, she shrugged. "When I was in the Army finishing my bachelor's degree, I took a course in Mesoamerican studies."

Wu made a note of the information and assigned them tasks in their skill areas. "Pull the image apart down to the pixels," he told Patel. "See if there's any sign of digitized steganography or hidden visuals."

"On it," Patel said.

He turned to her. "Look for patterns, find something to decrypt. Basically, do whatever the hell it is you do to break a code."

She nearly smiled, aware her training gave her skills others considered one step removed from sorcery, even though she downplayed her abilities.

Wu and Patel began to discuss the apparently unconnected bits of information while she processed things in silence. The data points appeared random on the surface, but she searched for patterns. Her subconscious mind was picking up something that remained frustratingly beneath the surface.

"I've got something." Patel looked at Wu. "You were right. There's stego in the image."

Wu gestured to the screen. "Show me."

Eight numbers appeared. "That's all," Patel said. "And without anything to go with it, I've got no clue what it means."

They all turned to Dani, as if she would instantly understand what 4, 17, 32, 49, 28, 3, 12, and 6 meant. She focused her gaze, willing herself to find meaning in the numbers. They continued to hold their secrets, so she refocused on the image, which called to her somehow.

"Hello?" Patel was waving his hand in the air. "Where are you at, Vega?"

"What?"

It had come out a little sharper than she'd intended, but she was in deep. When she'd been on missions with the Rangers, there had been times when she'd been required to let her mind roam to free-associate solutions to puzzles and codes. This was a vulnerable condition for her, limiting her situational awareness. Her sergeant assigned someone to cover her while she worked through the problem. It allowed her to access both sides of her brain, enabling her to be incredibly creative and intensely logical at the same time.

It also put whoever was guarding her at extreme risk.

"You've stopped contributing to the discussion," Wu said. "I'm assuming because you're working through the problem."

Of course she was. "I have a theory, but I want to check it first."

"Give us your best guess," Wu said. "I'll decide if it's worth pursuing."

She had finally realized why the image had seemed vaguely familiar. "When I was in the regiment, one of the guys on my team got married in Las Vegas between deployments. He showed us pictures when he got back from his honeymoon." She felt herself blush at the memory of some of the pictures. "The ceremony was at a hotel called the Toltec. It's shaped like a step pyramid and decorated with a Mesoamerican theme."

"I see your point," Wu said. "You figure Toro would be more likely to stash something in the US, and this is probably the biggest place with Quetzl-whatever on it."

She nodded. "We can check other sites later, but this one feels right."

"What about the numbers?" Wu asked.

"Not sure about those, but we might spot something in or around the hotel that'll make another connection for us."

Silence filled the room when Dani finished talking. She glanced at each of her colleagues in turn. Her eyes lingered on Wu, the one who called the shots. She tried to read his expression but could detect nothing in his steady gaze. To call it unsettling would have been an understatement.

After a long moment, Wu turned to Patel. "Get us a schematic of the Toltec. I want to see the entire layout."

Patel retrieved another laptop, this one with full access to the Bureau's databases, and propped it open on the table. Moments later, he'd shared it with a second wall screen beside the first. She watched in awe as he rapidly accessed archived information about the construction of casinos, which was probably a closely guarded secret.

She had other concerns. "Will you ask agents at the Las Vegas field office to check it out?"

Wu shook his head. "Director Franklin called me personally this morning. He wants this circle to be as tight as possible. No other agents will be involved unless it's strictly necessary."

She exchanged a surprised glance with Patel. The director oversaw thirty-eight thousand employees and dealt with the most sensitive national security issues. To hear that he'd reached down through many layers of the hierarchy to tap Wu came as a shock.

"Does Hargrave know?" she asked, unsure how secret this mission was.

Most FBI field offices were run by special agents in charge, like Wu. Three of them, however, were so large and handled such complex investigations that an assistant director in charge managed their daily operations. The New York field office was the largest of these, and ADIC Scott Hargrave was at the helm.

Wu pursed his lips. "He knows."

When her boss offered nothing further, Dani recalled the contentious meeting in Hargrave's office after her most recent assignment. The ADIC had been ready to discipline her for coloring outside the lines when Wu came to her defense. She had the distinct impression the two men were often at odds. As in the military, she observed occasional infighting among the upper ranks as an observer, grateful not to be in the mix.

Her combat experience had also taught her the difference between leaders. Some were what was known as "stripe heavy," wearing their official rank as a license to bark orders at everyone around them. Others, like Wu, were quiet, solid, and intelligent, with a healthy respect for those above and below their position, considering input from all sources before rendering a decision.

In short, she would follow Wu into battle. Hargrave, on the other hand . . . well, she might consent to lead him if he would deign to follow. Otherwise, she had little use for him.

"Got it," Patel said. Moments later, the screen shifted to a blueprint of the Toltec. "Look what's in the center of the structure."

They all studied the concentric squares that depicted the step-pyramid shape of the building.

"That's the main casino," Patel went on. "But directly below that is the hotel vault."

Dani felt the familiar tingle that told her they were on the right track. "If he's hidden something for us to find, it's got to be in the vault, but if we're not sending local agents out, that means we have to go."

Wu nodded. "Those hidden numbers could be the number of the box or the combination, but we need confirmation before we go rushing halfway across the country." He glanced at Patel. "How does the security in their vault work?"

Patel split the screen and pulled up detailed security protocols for the hotel. Scanning the information, Dani gathered that a team of armed guards used a state-of-the-art audiovisual system to monitor the entire area, which was four levels underground. The vault itself was similar to what she had seen in banks, with reinforced blast-proof steel doors. Inside, hundreds of security boxes were in rows lining each wall.

Patel moved his cursor to indicate the final paragraph. "Security boxes can be rented indefinitely as long as regular payments are made."

Interesting. Toro could have set up an autopay to keep the box for years, maybe decades. She was impressed at his foresight, especially when she read the next clause. "A box can only be opened by entering the renter's code while the manager's key is turned in the lock."

"A double fail-safe," Wu said. "Can you tell how the security boxes are numbered?"

Patel pulled up photographs of the vault's interior. "They're in sequential rows starting with 0001 and ending with 9999."

Dani checked the other screen with the numbers 4, 17, 32, 49, 28, 3, 12, and 6 still visible. "If we're right, that would mean the number of the box is 4173. The rest of the digits must be the combination."

"One way to find out," Wu said. "Call the manager and request a copy of the rental agreement for that box."

She picked up one of the designated outgoing landlines and tapped in the number Patel called out to her. She was routed to the assistant manager, Ethan Polk, who explained that his boss was meeting with a client about booking a rock concert at the hotel.

National security couldn't compete with the prospect of millions of dollars in revenue.

She forged ahead. "Could you shoot us a copy of the contract for security box 4173?"

She heard the familiar clacking of a keyboard in the background for a few seconds, then, "I'm sorry, Agent Vega, but that box is flagged in the system. I can't send anything out without verification in person."

She wasn't ready to give up. "But you do have a box with that number, and you can provide the name of the person renting it?"

There was a long pause. "Yes, there's a box with that number. It's rented by Geraldo Trujillo. I can't say more than that."

He didn't have to.

She thanked him and disconnected, then turned to Wu and Patel. "That's Toro's box."

Patel frowned. "How do you know?"

She recalled interrogating Toro after arresting him. "He used a lot of aliases, but he had a trick for remembering them. He always chose names with his real initials."

"Geraldo Trujillo," Patel said. "G. T. Gustavo Toro."

Wu seemed satisfied. "Director Franklin authorized a jet and a pilot for this assignment." He gave them their marching orders. "Go home, pack a go-bag, and meet me in the garage in two hours."

CHAPTER 6

9:30 a.m.

SAC Steve Wu sat in Assistant Director Hargrave's office, doing his best to maintain his composure. He had no intention of letting his immediate supervisor know how much he annoyed him.

He avoided Hargrave whenever he could, but it wouldn't be possible to fly halfway across the country without letting him know.

"Las Vegas?" Hargrave said, as if he hadn't heard the explanation Wu had just provided. "Seems like a lot of expense to check out a hunch."

"It's not a hunch." Wu kept his tone calm and measured. "It's a logical conclusion drawn from a careful analysis of the facts at hand."

"Maybe we should have Crypto double-check."

Hargrave was trying to pull him in, but he didn't take the bait. "We're supposed to limit this investigation to our team."

He avoided mentioning Director Franklin by name, denying Hargrave the opportunity to confront him about the phone call that had bypassed him to go straight to Wu.

Which meant Hargrave had serious heartburn about it.

"Of course," Hargrave said. "I was just thinking about how it would look for you if it turned out you wasted a lot of time and money on a dead end."

The ADIC had just put him on notice that he would track the team's expenses and hold him accountable for every penny. Wu didn't waste his breath protesting the unfairness of the situation when they both knew some leads didn't pan out.

Instead, he focused on the real point of contention.

Agent Daniela Vega.

When Wu briefed Hargrave about the call from the director early this morning, the ADIC had not even wanted Vega to see the video. He was concerned that she'd been hopelessly compromised by her under-cover assignment with Gustavo Toro, hinting that she had been all too ready to sink to Toro's level under the stress of deadly confrontations. She had shifted from federal agent to special forces soldier far too readily for his liking.

Wu had argued that the very nature of that assignment afforded her greater insight into Toro's mind than any other agent. He'd finally convinced Hargrave that Vega should be treated as any other asset, and using the most effective tool for the job was not only efficient but also their duty.

He had won that skirmish but was now back for a larger battle. For some reason, Hargrave had a problem with Vega, and he couldn't tell why. Was it her unconventional way of thinking, her physical presence, or perhaps the fact that she could kick any of their asses in a fair fight?

Wu didn't have a problem with strong, intelligent, beautiful women. He had been raised by one.

He understood that Hargrave's comment had been an attack on his own judgment as much as on Vega and handled it as such. "I have no doubt Agent Vega's solution to the clue is correct," he said, bringing the debate into the open. "And I'm prepared to take the consequences if her assessment proves to be wrong."

Hargrave raised a brow. "You seem very . . . taken by Agent Vega and her abilities. Perhaps that has clouded your reasoning in—"

"Agent Vega has had advanced training in cryptanalysis," Wu cut in. "And she's had to crack codes in the field. With bullets flying around her. We don't have anyone like that in Crypto."

Hargrave's thin smile told Wu his response had been a few degrees too heated. He ratcheted down his next remark. "I stand behind her."

"Fine," Hargrave said. "Since you're taking point on this investigation, if you want to tie your success to Agent Vega, so be it."

Hargrave's smug expression told Wu he'd walked into a trap. But it also led to another conclusion. His boss viewed him as a threat.

He probed the sensitive underbelly Hargrave had inadvertently revealed. "You're upset that Director Franklin contacted me directly." He made it a statement rather than a question.

Hargrave reddened. "I have regular communication with the director. He could've contacted me first to inquire about your availability."

Wu concealed a smile. Until this moment, he wasn't sure Franklin hadn't called Hargrave first. The fact that the director had bypassed the ADIC who ran the New York field office was unprecedented. And telling.

It went without saying that anything the director needed done would take priority over other assignments, so Wu made no response, letting an awkward silence stretch between them.

Hargrave visibly puffed up. "You seem to have an affinity for headline-grabbing cases," he said, effectively eliminating all doubt that he felt threatened.

If Hargrave had any leadership skills at all, he'd understand that his own reputation would be enhanced, not diminished, by the success of his subordinates. Wu had given statements about several high-profile cases recently, but he didn't relish news conferences, which were like minefields.

"I don't seek the press," he said evenly. "They come to me."

"You want this office?" Hargrave said, motioning around him. "There's more to being an assistant director than talking in front of cameras."

Hargrave thought he was after his job. Wu could have reassured him, could have explained that he would never elbow his way past others to get ahead. But Hargrave—who had the sharpest elbows in the Bureau—deserved no such consideration.

Instead, Wu took the accusation as a dismissal and walked out.

CHAPTER 7

Five months earlier, Thursday, May 9

Toro stomped the pedal to the floor but only managed to make the engine of the battered VW Bus whine louder.

He glanced in the rearview for the hundredth time but still saw nothing suspicious on the sparsely traveled freeway. Instead of bringing him comfort, the lack of an obvious pursuit vehicle made him edgier.

He was certain Foley had set him up on the Buckwald contract last night. All had gone according to plan until he was ambushed by the kind of private security that cost a fortune and carried serious firepower.

He had a nasty bruise on his back from the fiasco but counted himself lucky he wasn't dead. Despite what had to be a high body count, he hadn't heard anything in the news about a gun battle. The cabin had been on fifty acres of private property in a remote area, so once the bodies were disposed of, no one would know what happened. The kinds of mercenaries who performed such operations understood they might not survive, and they obeyed strict confidentiality protocols. They were chosen because they were unattached, and no one would miss them.

Toro understood this because he was the same.

When Foley didn't show at the pickup point, Toro had been forced to jog ten miles to get to the nearest city, where he caught a Greyhound bus to Las Vegas. He'd used the travel time to come up with a new plan, calling Foley during the trip, pretending he had no idea he'd been set up. As expected, Foley faked shock at the ambush.

Toro played along to see how much Foley and his boss knew. From their conversation, and a bit of his own digging, Toro concluded Foley was acting on his own. The boss had ordered the hit on Buckwald, but that was all.

Toro figured Foley had warned Buckwald about the hit, then offered the services of a private security force to protect him. Of course, the men were Foley's and would ensure neither Toro nor Buckwald survived.

That plan had gone to hell, but Foley capitalized on the disaster. When the team was killed, Buckwald would believe they had died trying to protect him. Even if he'd gone into hiding, Buckwald would trust Foley and willingly meet with him. It would be a fatal mistake for Buckwald and the perfect opportunity to carry out the original hit for Foley.

Now convinced Foley wanted him dead, and knowing the kind of resources he could access through his boss, Toro was suspicious of everyone around him. Which was why he'd taken a cab to a sketchy used car dealer in a lot on the outskirts of Las Vegas for today's mission.

He explained to the dealer that he needed a vehicle old enough not to have GPS, cellular connectivity, or any other technology that could be used to track it or remotely shut it down. In less than an hour, cash exchanged hands, and Toro became the owner of a vintage VW Bus complete with Grateful Dead stickers and macramé hemp seat covers.

Flashing lights drew his eyes back to the rearview. A state trooper was closing fast behind him. Was it a fake cop Foley had hired to execute him on the side of the road after pulling him over?

"Shit."

He looked at his speedometer. He wasn't over the limit. Hell, he was driving a brick on four wheels. He couldn't even speed, much less outrun the cops.

He slowed, steering the VW Bus onto the shoulder. Maybe the trooper caught a whiff of the cannabis fumes flowing in the hippie mobile's wake. Toro was transporting a stash all right, but it was far worse than marijuana.

Heart pounding, he began to formulate a plan. And then the trooper flew past him, lights still flashing, evidently on the way to handle an emergency.

Toro mopped the sweat from his brow with the back of his hand. He couldn't afford delays. He'd told Foley he was heading to Vegas to hit high-roller tables all over the Strip for the next few days. If Foley was watching, he'd see that Toro was living it up in Sin City after his brush with death.

He'd chosen to stay at the Toltec after researching their policy on security boxes. The only ones who could access his box would be himself or the Feds, which was fine with him. He also paid five years in advance on the rental fee to keep the contract in full effect.

He eased the Bus back onto the dusty desert highway as his pulse slowly came down from stroke range. If the trooper had stopped and investigated, things would have gotten awkward. In the back of the vehicle was evidence of blackmail, extortion, arson, and multiple murders. All of which implicated Toro.

As well as the people who had hired him over the years.

A young trooper could earn a gold shield with that kind of bust. Fortunately, Toro was spared the burden of making sure that didn't happen. Fate was strange that way.

The only question left on his mind was whether he could reach his hiding place, stow the evidence, and make it back to the Toltec before anyone noticed he was missing.

CHAPTER 8

Present day, Monday, October 7, 4:00 p.m. local time
Las Vegas, Nevada

Dani stood beside Wu and Patel in front of a towering Mesoamerican step pyramid. The juxtaposition of the Toltec Hotel and Casino along the same part of the Las Vegas Strip as Caesars Palace, Bellagio, Paris, and the Mirage was visually jarring. And yet, somehow, also appropriate for the landscape of fantasy blooming like an oasis in the Nevada desert.

"Check your watches," Wu said. "If they're analog, you'll need to set them three hours back."

Dani glanced down to see that her digital watch had automatically adjusted to the local time, which was four in the afternoon. What would have normally been over a six-hour flight from LaGuardia to Harry Reid International Airport on a commercial airline was cut down to under four hours in the Gulfstream, allowing them to continue their investigation immediately. The car service from the private terminal to any hotel on the Strip had been an added bonus since they didn't have a Bureau car.

They walked inside and headed for the security desk, where the assistant manager had told them to ask for him.

"We're here to see Ethan Polk," Wu said to the clerk. "He's expecting us."

The clerk lifted a handset and murmured into it. In less than a minute, a pale, slender man close to Dani's age emerged from shiny gold elevator doors and approached.

They exchanged greetings, and Polk escorted them back through the same gleaming elevator doors he'd just come from.

"The manager is waiting for you," Polk said as he pressed one of the buttons on the control pad. "I filled her in on your request, but she has . . . certain procedures."

Dani noticed they were descending four floors down, where the schematic Patel had found indicated the vault was located.

They followed Polk from the elevator into a wide-open space that was modern and high tech, in direct contrast to the eleventh-century decor on the hotel's main level.

An attractive woman with a chic blond bob, wearing a Chanel suit, crossed the tile floor and extended a hand. "I'm Maddie Pimentel."

Wu, who was standing in front of their group, shook her hand and introduced them. "We appreciate you assisting us with our investigation."

Dani appreciated the unspoken message in what appeared to be an innocuous greeting. Wu's comment presumed the manager's cooperation while underlining the importance of their visit.

Pimentel hesitated, then said, "The security box you referenced was rented out five months ago. The guest paid a substantial fee to add extra safeguards in his contract—which he paid five years in advance, so it's still very much in effect."

"What are the safeguards?" Wu asked.

"The box is only supposed to be opened by the renter or the FBI." She looked apologetic. "There was a concern that impostors might try to access it, so I need to see all of your IDs and verify your employment."

While they all opened the small leather folding cases containing both their badges and credentials, Pimentel pulled out her phone and tapped in the general 800 number for the Bureau.

Dani appreciated that the manager hadn't asked them for a number to call, which could have been part of a sophisticated ruse. Instead, she was going directly to the source. Wu's grim expression told her he wasn't happy about having their presence shared outside their circle, but he held his tongue. Apparently, there was no other way to get what they wanted without applying for a court order, which would have meant describing the details of their investigation in an affidavit filed with the Nevada Supreme Court.

What kind of enemy had Toro made? Impersonating a federal agent could result in a steep fine and a three-year stretch in a penitentiary. Yet he was afraid someone would risk it to get whatever he'd hidden.

Pimentel finished her phone call and smiled at them. "I'll take you back to the vault."

They followed her past a pair of armed guards and down a short corridor. She raised her hand and pressed her palm, fingers splayed, against a screen set into the wall.

A light flicked from red to green. Pimentel leaned forward, angling her right eye toward a lens. A beam glowed from the lens, then a loud click echoed through the passageway.

The dense steel door opened with a hydraulic hiss, and Pimentel stepped inside, beckoning them to follow.

Dani peered around the vault, which was exactly as the schematic had indicated, yet much more impressive in person. Rows of identical boxes lined all four walls, surrounding a clear melamine table with steel legs that occupied the center of the room.

Dani navigated around the table to meet Pimentel in front of box number 4173. The manager inserted a metal key embedded with electronics, and one of the lights flashed blue. Now it was Dani's turn. She would have the correct combination, or she wouldn't.

She looked at Pimentel, who took the cue and turned her back to Dani. Taking no chances, Dani crowded in close to the box and used her left hand to cover the pad while she used her right to enter the code.

A second blue light flashed, and the small rectangular door clicked slightly open.

"I already know there's only a flash drive inside," Pimentel said. "I personally rented the box out to Mr. Trujillo."

Dani did not correct the manager. Toro must have had excellent identification backing up the Geraldo Trujillo alias. Which meant he didn't want anyone to know his real name.

Pimentel glanced at Patel, addressing him for the first time. "I see you have a laptop, and you seem to be in a hurry. You're welcome to review the drive here where it's private. I'll tell the guards not to let anyone else back here until you're finished." She started to leave, then paused. "I'll have that copy of the contract you requested ready when you come out."

Patel was already booting up his laptop on the glossy table by the time the manager left. Dani slapped the flash drive into his outstretched hand, and he plugged it into the port.

Moments later, he clicked on a digital file and Toro's face appeared on the screen.

CHAPTER 9

Twenty seconds earlier
Undisclosed location

Denton Foley clicked the mouse to zoom in on the laptop resting on the clear rectangular table in the middle of the vault.

His boss was craning his neck and squinting. "Can you get a better angle? It's hard to see Toro's expression."

"The cameras are all concealed in the ceiling," he said, still fiddling with the focus. "They don't rotate, but I'm recording this so our video techs can enhance it later."

"That will do," the boss said.

Toro's face appeared on the screen, bringing back a familiar wave of resentment that hadn't been cooled in the slightest by the man's death.

"This information is for the FBI," Toro said. "You saw my first video. You know what's at stake . . . at least, part of what's at stake. Leaving this drive here is the best I can do to make sure the treasure doesn't fall into the wrong hands."

Treasure? What the hell was Toro talking about? Foley glanced at his boss, who appeared equally baffled. This was, quite possibly, worse than either of them had thought.

Toro shrugged in a way that had always irritated Foley. The gesture was meant to convey carelessness, but he'd learned through bitter experience that Toro was never careless.

"But I've learned to be cautious, so I'm putting one more obstacle in your way." An insolent grin lifted the corners of his mouth. "Okay, maybe more than one, but when you find all that evidence, it'll be worth it."

So Toro was handing evidence to the FBI. That confirmed something they'd heard through back channels recently.

Gustavo Toro was a snitch.

Worst of all, he was the kind of informant who couldn't be threatened, killed, or silenced in any way. Now that he was dead, he was totally beyond their reach.

"Every client I've ever had," Toro continued, "every payment, and every target. All there for you to find. As a bonus, I'm throwing in any collaborators or contacts I had along the way. Some might surprise you."

Foley had personally given many contracts to Toro. His name would be at the top of the list. His gaze drifted back to the boss, who gave orders through intermediaries. Would his name appear?

Toro laid a hand on his chest. "What can I say? People who believe in superstition think I have a heart of stone. That I'm lost. But the answer is really just personal taste." He dropped his hand and leaned forward, suddenly intent. "Your next step is to contact Tina Castillo. You'll want to keep her safe, because she has the last piece of the puzzle."

The screen went black.

Foley shot to his feet. "I knew it."

The boss sank back into his chair, stunned. "The bastard double-crossed us." He shook his head. "He was lying to us all this time."

A stream of expletives resounded through the office. His boss, filled with impotent rage, could do nothing more to the man who had betrayed him.

As far as Foley knew, no one employed by the company had ever so much as disobeyed his boss, much less actively undermined him. He seemed to have trouble coming to grips with the concept.

It was hard for Foley to fathom as well. Five years ago, he'd dispatched Toro on what he considered a standard assignment. But somewhere along the way, Toro had changed the parameters of his mission.

His boss, who must have also recalled the contract, suddenly rounded on him. "You should have known." His deep blue eyes narrowed to slits. "Toro answered to you. He was your responsibility."

He offered the only acceptable response. "I'll fix this."

"You'd damned well better. Or you'll join Toro."

The threat wasn't necessary, and it irked him that his boss felt it was. Hadn't he proven himself loyal? Hadn't he shown he could manage disasters?

"Sir, we wouldn't even have this video if it weren't for me."

He'd always been suspicious of Toro since the botched hit on Buckwald five months ago, which was actually a botched hit on Toro. But the boss didn't know that. Foley had explained that Toro screwed up, and that he'd personally cleaned up the mess. In the end, Buckwald had lived only one week past his original expiration date, and Foley had taken Toro's reputation down a notch.

Foley suspected Toro believed the ambush was a setup at the time. Aware Toro was the type to get even, he watched him covertly for a month.

The trip to Las Vegas could have been a way to blow off steam after literally dodging a bullet, but Foley thought there could be more to the short vacation. When Toro checked into the Toltec, Foley discreetly followed him. Then he did what he did best.

Cultivated a source.

The manager was poised and confident, not a good target. But the young, eager assistant manager was an easy mark.

Ethan Polk had carefully studied the photo Foley showed him and called the next day to say the man in the picture had rented a security box under the name Geraldo Trujillo.

Polk couldn't open the box and said the manager couldn't either. She also kept the contract locked in her personal safe, so he couldn't read it or make a copy.

The information had partly confirmed Foley's fears, but at the time, he didn't know what Toro had stashed away. Maybe some of the uncut diamonds he'd been paid with. Who knew?

He'd paid Polk to notify him whenever anyone accessed the box. A precaution that had been well worth the expense when Polk called several hours ago to tell him FBI agents were on the way.

Fortunately, that had given Foley enough time to have the company's video tech squad work with Polk, instructing him how to allow them to hack into the vault's live security feed.

But instead of congratulating Foley for his ingenuity, the boss was issuing threats. He tamped down his frustration. "We have an advantage over the FBI. We know where to start looking for her and they don't."

"They have a ton of resources. They'll figure it out in a matter of hours."

He lifted his chin. "That's all I need."

CHAPTER 10

Dani felt the frustration that always overtook her when there was no forward momentum.

She looked at Patel. "Can you find out anything about Tina Castillo?"

"Toro sure as hell didn't give us much to go on," Patel said, shutting the laptop with a snap. "I brought my Bu-box, but it could take a minute with nothing but a name to go on."

Dani caught his meaning. A Bu-box was a Patel-ism for his FBI-issued laptop, as opposed to his freestanding unit. And "a minute" meant a long time, especially considering the current US population hovered around 337 million. If Toro was referring to someone in another country, the search would expand to over eight billion. Tina Castillo was not an uncommon name, so they'd have to sort through thousands of people.

"We can't stay in their vault all night," Wu said. "We'll set up camp somewhere where we can work uninterrupted." He led them out and down the corridor where the manager was waiting for them.

"Here's a copy of the contract," Pimentel said, handing a sealed manila envelope to Wu. "I know you all flew in from New York, so you've got to be hungry and tired by now."

Clearly used to dealing with people from time zones around the world, Pimentel understood that their bodies thought it was 9:30 p.m. Past time for dinner.

Pimentel regarded them. "I'm not allowed to talk about it, but I can say that I've had occasion to work with the FBI."

Dani took that to mean the Toltec had been targeted by organized crime in the past. She hadn't personally investigated such cases but had heard other agents talk about crime bosses that tried to muscle their way into casinos, beginning with their construction.

Pimentel smiled at Wu. "I'd be happy to comp your team a suite. You can order room service and make it a working dinner, then feel free to spend the night."

Dani glanced at Patel, whose eyes were focused on Wu as if he were willing the boss to consent.

"Actually, our pilot isn't supposed to fly again until tomorrow," Wu said. "We're stuck here anyway. May as well get some work done."

Pimentel said, "I'll put your team in one of the presidential suites. It isn't booked until next week."

Wu agreed, then watched her head toward the elevator to make the arrangements at the front desk on the main level before turning to the others. "We'll go back to the private jet terminal and get our go-bags."

The team had left their overnight duffels on the plane, unaware they'd be spending the night in Las Vegas.

Dani had developed a fondness for their pilot, who seemed determined to get them where they needed to be in the shortest time possible. "While we're there, can you ask our pilot to see if she can stay with us for the duration of the assignment?"

Wu nodded. "She's in demand, but I'll do what I can." He gave his team a considering look. "We'll come back to the hotel and make it a working dinner. Once we get a lead, we can hit the ground running tomorrow."

He was making it clear he expected a breakthrough tonight. Dani shared his determination, but Toro had promised to throw obstacles in their path. How long would it take to overcome this one?

CHAPTER 11

7:00 p.m.

Wu had invited the pilot to their suite, but she preferred the accommodations at the terminal. Apparently, private pilots were treated to first-class amenities at Harry Reid International.

She might have changed her mind if she'd seen the sumptuous four-bedroom presidential suite at the Toltec.

Wu had never been inside a six-thousand-square-foot hotel room, which was four times larger than his Lower Manhattan apartment in Chinatown. He thought the baby grand piano was overkill, but the gourmet kitchen, full bar, and laundry room seemed practical for anyone who needed a home away from home. Of course, at more than $10,000 a night, he wasn't surprised the suite also boasted a pool table, sauna, and private massage room.

He had just dropped his bag in one of the bedrooms when he came out to see Patel stalking through the living room, holding a black device about the size of a whiteboard eraser with two stubby antennae jutting up from the top.

Vega emerged from a different bedroom. "I didn't know you brought a bug sweeper," she said to Patel.

He responded without taking his eyes off the detector's glowing lights. "I helped investigate a ring of people who installed cameras in hotel rooms a couple of years back. They took videos of unsuspecting people and sold them on the black market. Customers could buy footage of people undressing, having sex, taking showers—even going to the bathroom. Whatever their kink was, they could watch it." He shuddered. "I had to shower, like, five hundred times during the course of that case, and I've never stayed in a hotel room without sweeping it since."

Wu had been briefed on that case, as well as several others that involved vacation rental properties. Some of the videos included children. As head of counterterrorism, he didn't normally oversee those sorts of investigations, but he appreciated the agents who did.

Vega moved closer to Patel, watching his progress. "You pick anything up?"

Patel shook his head. "Nothing so far. This baby detects WiMAX, Bluetooth, 2.4- and 5-hertz Wi-Fi, DECT, LTE, GSM, and RF."

Patel often slipped into technobabble when he was in the zone, so Wu let his cyber expert have at it while he accepted a room service food delivery and tipped the server. After a brief discussion, the group had agreed on Greek cuisine. Vega helped him spread out containers of souvlaki, moussaka, and tzatziki sauce with triangles of warm pita on a glossy black table in the dining room.

Patel ended the sweep by passing his detector over the food and dishes before he declared the space bug-free.

Wu was hungry, but he was also anxious to get down to business. Since it was a working dinner, he didn't stand on ceremony. Patel had both of his laptops open on the table, with the one connected to the FBI server providing full access to the many databases they routinely used.

Wu opened the discussion. "Toro told us to keep Tina Castillo safe because she has the last piece of the puzzle. Any suggestions on how to narrow the parameters of our search?"

Vega was quick to respond. "We can eliminate anyone who's not an adult. I think we should keep it to the United States for the first pass, then expand to other countries if we don't get any viable hits."

"Agreed," Wu said, thinking about the fact that they were in Las Vegas. "We'll play the odds."

Patel was keying in the parameters as they spoke. "Toro mostly lived in Monaco, and he traveled all over the world, but I won't go there for now."

Something occurred to Wu. "Toro made both recordings back in April. Maybe Tina Castillo got married over the past five and a half months. If so, many American women change their last name to their husband's."

"But the last name Castillo is Latin," Vega said. "Depending on how traditional she is and what her culture is, she might keep her surname and hyphenate it with her husband's last name."

He glanced at Patel. "Can you check for that?"

Patel nodded. "It's going to widen the search again, though."

Wu sighed and picked up a triangle of pita bread, then put it back down. "I haven't had a chance to review the contract. Maybe there's something there."

He reached across the table and grabbed the sealed manila envelope Maddie Pimentel had given him. He slid a knife under the adhesive, wondering why the manager had left it unopened. Had that been part of the directions Toro had given her?

He pulled out what appeared to be a boilerplate three-page contract for a security box. Until the area at the bottom of the last page where special instructions included verifying that anyone coming to open the box was with the FBI.

Again, he was struck by how Toro had relied on an agency he must have viewed as an enemy to carry out his wishes. Perhaps "enemy" wasn't accurate. Maybe Toro saw the Bureau merely as an adversary.

But an adversary he respected.

He focused on a photocopy of the driver's license. Toro's face appeared with the name Geraldo Trujillo. He glanced at the address, aware that Toro might simply have chosen a random house in a city he'd never even visited, but it was worth checking. He showed it to Patel. "Let's see who's connected to this address."

Patel began typing, then stopped. He took the paper from Wu's hand and squinted at the bottom right corner. "This is weird. It says 'form,' but the characters next to it aren't a form number—and they're printed by hand."

"Show me." Wu took the sheet back as Vega stood and circled the table to peer over his shoulder. When she leaned in close, her long hair swung down, and he caught the scent of vanilla and almond shampoo.

"It looks vaguely familiar," Vega said. "It could be a code."

Wu figured she'd studied thousands of code variants during her training. He looked at the characters again.

[ )€I\II/[-I?

Patel grabbed the paper back and stared at it. "I just remembered where I've seen this before." His face split into a wide grin. "It's hacker-speak."

Wu recognized the term but hadn't seen it used.

Patel was in his element. "Instead of trying to decipher or calculate, you view the shape of the text." He angled his laptop so they could see the screen. "Here, let me show you." He navigated to a calculator app, punched in 5508.14, and looked at Wu expectantly.

"I'm not getting it."

Patel flipped the laptop upside down. From that perspective, the numbers spelled out "hI.B0SS."

"I remember playing around with calculators in elementary school." Wu tapped the code on the paper lying on the table between them. "But this isn't that."

"This is a bit more sophisticated, but the principle's the same." Patel pointed to the numbers and characters neatly printed on the contract. "It starts with a left bracket, then a right parenthesis. Together, they form the letter D. Next is the symbol for the euro, which looks a lot like a capital E."

Wu was starting to see it now.

Patel continued, "Then take the next three characters together, a pipe symbol—or vertical bar—followed by a backslash and another pipe symbol. What does that look like?"

\|\|

He tilted his head. "The letter N."

"Bingo. Now connect the bottom of the two characters, which are a pipe symbol and a backslash."

\|/

Wu saw it quickly. "That's a V, but I'm not sure about the next one."

"I'm assuming Toro wrote this, because it doesn't require any advanced math or crypto skills. It's really just intuitive. But he's playing it safe, so he made the next letter in a different way." He cut his eyes to Vega. "That way, a codebreaker wouldn't spot a pattern right away."

She raised a brow. "Except that I have a brother who's into all things computer. I've seen him use symbols like these."

Wu had met Vega's brother, Axel. The young man was gifted in many ways. He wondered if unconventional thinking ran in the family, or if their shared tragedy made them perceive the world differently.

"The left bracket followed by a hyphen resembles a capital E," Vega said. "And, yes, not repeating the euro symbol prevented obvious pattern recognition. Pretty clever."

That left the last two characters, and Wu wasn't sure if they formed a letter together or if there was actually supposed to be a question mark at the end.

|?

He sensed Patel and Vega watching him. He wasn't fluent in hacker-speak, but he could manage deductive reasoning.

"The last letter must be an R," he said. "I can sort of see a resemblance, but mostly it's the next logical letter after D, E, N, V, and E." He glanced at Patel. "There may be other places with the same name, but let's start by checking for Tina Castillo in Denver, Colorado."

"Already on it."

Wu felt confident they'd arrived at the correct answer, but it was getting late. With their pilot grounded until morning, even if they got a lead, it wouldn't make sense to pursue it tonight. Part of his job was looking after his team, and they were tired.

Patel blurted, "Found her." Then he frowned. "But there's a problem."

Of course, there would have to be a problem. "What is it?"

Patel looked up from his screen. "I can't find any sign of her for the past five years. It's like she vanished off the face of the earth."

CHAPTER 12

Dani took a moment to process the new information. "Why would Toro send us after a dead person?"

Under Colorado law, people who disappeared for five years could be legally presumed dead, so she made the same assumption. If Tina Castillo hadn't surfaced by now, she likely never would. At least, not alive.

"Can you find a death certificate for her?" Wu asked.

Patel shook his head. "No, but her landlord filed a missing person report with the Denver police."

"Her landlord?" Dani said. "Not her family?"

Patel was scrolling through various databases on his FBI laptop. "The address on her Colorado driver's license comes back to an apartment downtown. The landlord must have filed the report to establish a claim so he could put a lien on her property. He sold her furniture to pay off her lease when she vanished."

"And her relatives didn't step in?"

"Let's see what I can dig up in her background."

Dani was confident Patel could dig up a hell of a lot.

"She never married and had no living relatives in the US. She was an only child of parents who emigrated from Mexico three years before Tina was born. Her father died of a heart attack six years ago, and her mother passed a year later from the flu."

Wu craned his neck to peer at the screen. "Going by her date of birth, she was twenty-seven years old when she went missing, and she'd be thirty-two now—if she's still alive."

Dani was still grappling with her initial question. "Toro made the video over five months ago. Tina had already been missing four and a half years at the time. He made the video for the FBI, and he wants us to locate someone no one else can find. Why?"

"More than that, he asked us to keep her safe. If she was already dead, he wouldn't have said that. It's like he's telling us she's alive, but she might not be if we don't track her down."

"As they say, follow the money. Is there a trail?"

"She withdrew most of the funds from her bank account and cashed her final paycheck, then there was no activity. She never used her credit cards again. So if she was still alive, did she start living off the grid?"

"Who issued that last payment?" Wu asked. "What did she do for a living?"

"She grew up in New York City, but she never worked there," Patel said. "Oh, wow, this is interesting. She won a scholarship to Caltech, where she got a bachelor's, a master's, and a PhD."

Dani was impressed. The California Institute of Technology was among the most prestigious STEM universities in the nation. "What did she study?"

"Quantum physics," Patel said. "She might have learned a few things from her dad before he passed away. He was a physicist and tenured professor at the University of Mexico before he came to the States. Actually, it looks like he was recruited by a research lab in Manhattan. He went straight into their tech development division."

"Where did she go after getting a doctorate?"

"She was hired by Exmyth Technologies in Denver at the end of her final semester and worked there right up until her disappearance."

"So the last people she regularly saw were there," Dani said. "Maybe she made friends and confided in a close colleague about what was going on in her life."

"We can make contact with them," Wu said. "It's not what I'd call a hot lead, but at least it's a starting point. We might learn something that will point us in the right direction."

"According to their website, the CEO is Richard Sterling," Patel said. "There's a main number listed."

"Make the call from your laptop," Wu said. "Block the ID."

Patel's laptop was equipped with software allowing him to place a wireless call. If needed, he could spoof any location or caller ID. Since Wu hadn't given Patel instructions to pretend to be Mo's Dry Cleaning in Aurora, Dani assumed he simply wanted to get general information without alerting anyone the FBI was doing the asking.

While Patel set up the call, Dani checked her watch. "It's after business hours," she said to Wu.

He gave her a look that said he was well aware of the time and had his reasons.

After an electronic version of a ringtone, a voice sounded through the speaker. "Exmyth Technologies, how may I direct your call?"

Wu responded in a crisp, businesslike manner. "Richard Sterling, please."

"Mr. Sterling has gone for the day. I can connect you to his administrative assistant's voicemail."

Wu spoke quickly, before he could be redirected to the fathomless black void where his message may or may not ever be received. "This matter is time sensitive. When will he be in tomorrow?"

"He usually comes in at nine," the voice said. "His admin comes in at eight. You can mark your voicemail as urgent. I'll connect you now." This time, the click was immediate, allowing no time for further discussion.

Wu drew his index finger across his throat, and Patel disconnected the call. She understood his reasoning. They had just confirmed Richard Sterling would be in tomorrow morning without letting him know they were coming.

"I take it we're headed for Denver."

"First thing in the morning," Wu said. "I'll contact our pilot and let her know so she can file a flight plan."

The day, including the travel and jet lag, suddenly caught up to Dani now that their work had ended for the moment. With luck, tomorrow's investigation would yield some leads.

But for now, Dr. Tina Castillo remained an enigma.

CHAPTER 13

The following morning, Tuesday, October 8, 8:00 a.m.

Dani inhaled the heavenly aroma of strong black coffee. Since her days in the Army, it was the only thing she had for breakfast.

Wu added cream from the suite's well-stocked refrigerator to his, while Patel dumped in what looked like five packets of sugar and stirred it vigorously with a spoon. Her suspicion that he had a sweet tooth was confirmed when he pulled a square of baklava from the dessert box that came with last night's Greek dinner and ate it in two bites.

"You'll get the handles of your bag all sticky," she warned him.

He licked the honey from his fingertips and grinned. "Problem solved."

They had gotten up early and packed their go-bags. The shower and fresh clothes were welcome, and worth the extra time.

"We should get going," Wu said. "Polk is waiting for us."

The assistant manager, Ethan Polk, had called half an hour ago to inform them someone had just requested the presidential suite. He offered to send a bell person up for their bags, a not-so-subtle hint that it was time to vacate the suite to make room for guests who were willing to pay $10,000 a night.

Five minutes later, when they emerged from the elevator and started across the lobby, Polk materialized beside them. "I hope you enjoyed your stay at the Toltec."

"It's no Quonset hut," Dani said, deadpan. "And I had trouble sleeping without a mosquito net over me, but I suppose it was okay."

He frowned briefly, then smiled at her. "You were in the military, Ms. Vega?"

Wu stepped forward. "*Agent* Vega's background isn't your concern. We have a flight to catch. Is the transport vehicle here?"

Polk kept his eyes on Dani and extended his hand. "Thank you for your service to our country."

She shook it reflexively but reiterated Wu's point. "We have to go."

He hesitated before dropping her hand, then stooped to pick up her go-bag. "Will you be returning to Las Vegas?"

Whether Polk was being chivalrous or flirtatious, she was unaccustomed to the behavior.

Wu, who seemed to share her discomfort, cut in. "We'll contact the manager if we need anything further from the Toltec." He scowled. "And Agent Vega is more than capable of carrying a duffel bag."

A flush spread through Polk's cheeks, and he handed the bag back to Dani. "I was trying to be helpful."

"Thank you," she said, not unkindly. She had no problem with gallantry, even if she hadn't experienced it often. To her, the spirit of the gesture mattered.

They left through the main entrance and found the courtesy car from the private terminal waiting nearby.

She started to get into the car but sensed someone watching. She turned to see Polk staring at her. She couldn't explain why, but something about the intensity of his gaze sent a ripple of unease through her.

CHAPTER 14

Denton Foley tightened the rope around the man's neck. The braided nylon bit deeper, purpling his victim's face as he strained against the restraints binding him to the chair.

Foley bent down. "Tell me where she is." His lips nearly touched the man's ear. "And I'll let you go."

Strangulation was far more intimate than shooting, and far cleaner than stabbing. As an expert in his craft, he also knew it had the potential to be staged as something else.

When the man's blue-tinged lips tried to form words, Foley eased up a fraction, allowing him to speak.

"You don't have to do this," he said in a barely audible rasp.

What his captive failed to understand was that Foley did have to do this. It was, after all, his job.

"If you want to keep breathing, you'll tell me where she is."

"I don't know," he said, reduced to tears. "I swear I haven't heard from her in years."

This was always the tricky part of an interrogation. He had promised to spare the target's life if he gave up his secrets. And the man had responded by swearing he had none to give.

Foley was lying, of course. The only way this guy would leave his house was in a body bag. But if he knew he was about to die, he'd never talk, not when spilling his secrets would get someone else killed as well.

So were they both lying to each other?

He'd had similar encounters with his victims over the years. After the pleading that usually ended in groveling, acceptance sometimes followed. Not unlike a condemned prisoner on his way to the death chamber, there was no sense trying to escape the inevitable. But some individuals were determined to hold on to the last bit of control they possessed.

Defiance.

In this case, noncompliance would most likely take the form of deception. To prevent that, Foley had to convince him there was still hope. People without hope did strange things. Sometimes even heroic things. Better squash that.

"I won't hurt her," he whispered. "I just want to . . . talk to her."

The man's red-rimmed eyes narrowed in suspicion. "Even if I believed you, I don't know where she is."

"Then I'm genuinely sorry for you." Another lie.

Foley didn't relish his job. It brought him no special pleasure. He was a tactician skilled in his craft. He moved to resume his position behind the target he'd been sent to extract information from. The outcome would not be good for either of them.

His victim's troubles would end shortly, but Foley would have to face his boss and admit failure. Again.

CHAPTER 15

10:00 a.m.
Exmyth Technologies, Denver, Colorado

Wu was a patient man, but his tolerance was being severely tested today.

First, Polk had done everything short of asking for Vega's phone number when they left the Toltec. Instinctively, he didn't like Polk. No, it was more than that. He didn't trust the man either. Wu was good at reading people, especially their body language, and Polk radiated deception.

Or was he just annoyed that the assistant manager had openly flirted with Vega? If so, why did that bother him? He decided not to examine that thought too closely.

Instead, he turned to the second source of frustration this morning. Namely, Richard Sterling. The CEO of Exmyth Technologies was being less than cooperative, despite the insincere smile plastered on his administrative assistant's face.

So far, their flight into Denver International Airport had been the only thing that had gone smoothly today. After arriving at Exmyth, they'd been put off for an hour by Sterling's assistant, who came up with a string of excuses, arousing Wu's suspicion. In his experience, executives who were told FBI agents had arrived would rearrange their schedules to cooperate, or at least find out what was going on.

Executives who had something to hide, on the other hand, delayed the visit as long as possible. Was Sterling on the phone with his attorney? Was he frantically shredding documents in the back room? Was he in the bathroom tossing up his Wheaties?

Hard to say, and unfortunately, they had no warrant to wave around forcing the CEO to grant them access immediately. This had started out as an investigative long shot. They were chasing the only lead they had—and it was a stale one from five years ago. What Sterling failed to realize, like many others, was that his reluctance to meet with them only served to pique their interest.

Wu was done playing nice. "Tell Mr. Sterling that we're leaving," he said to the assistant. "We'll be back with a federal warrant. Since he won't answer our questions, the warrant will have to cover every physical document, digital file, and financial record."

He turned away and beckoned Patel and Vega to follow him. He was bluffing. They had zero grounds for any warrant, much less such an invasive one. His colleagues knew this, of course, and Vega asked to use the restroom before they left.

As intended, the assistant paused to direct Vega to the bathroom before scurrying off to convey Wu's message to the boss.

Earlier, Wu had made sure the assistant took his business card to Sterling. The fact that the special agent in charge of the largest Joint Terrorism Task Force in the country had traveled from New York to speak to him should have prompted an immediate response.

If Sterling wasn't familiar with his position, a quick Google search would make him aware that Wu was in the upper echelon of the Bureau. Someone of his rank didn't go out in the field except under very serious circumstances. And yet, Sterling still hadn't seen him.

Unless . . .

"Special Agent Wu?"

He turned to see the assistant waving at him from inside the elevator she'd disappeared into a couple of minutes ago.

"Mr. Sterling will see you now."

Shocker.

Right on cue, Vega came from the hallway where the restrooms were located. "I'm ready to go, sir," she said to Wu.

He didn't trouble to hide his sarcasm when he replied, "Mr. Sterling has managed to squeeze us into his busy schedule."

Vega gave him a tiny wink before they filed into the elevator, and the assistant pressed the top button.

Minutes later, he was seated at a small conference table in the corner of the spacious office, flanked by Patel and Vega. They had deliberately moved their chairs to sit on either side of him so all three faced Sterling. A common tactic they wouldn't have used if the CEO hadn't acted so evasively.

Sterling addressed Wu. "What can I help you with?"

Wu took in Sterling's drumming fingers, dilated pupils, and the perspiration that added a gleam to his balding scalp. He hadn't disclosed the purpose of their visit so he could personally observe any reaction. Now that he had a baseline, it was time to elicit a response.

He said, "We're looking for Tina Castillo."

A vein along Sterling's temple, visible beneath his pale skin, began to throb. He licked his lips, an indication his mouth had gone dry.

"I haven't seen her in five years."

With that one answer, Sterling had given himself away. He didn't say that he hadn't heard from her in ages, or that he'd lost contact with her years ago, but he specified an exact number of years. Combined with his obvious physical signs of stress, Wu concluded that Sterling had been alerted in advance that they were coming to ask about Castillo. Whether he knew her whereabouts now, he was certainly hiding something about her disappearance.

He didn't challenge Sterling right away. Instead, Wu came at him with an unexpected question he wouldn't have prepared for. "When was the last time you heard any mention of Dr. Castillo?"

Sterling's gaze swung up and to the left, indicating he was trying to quickly construct a story. "When did I last hear mention of her?"

Repeating the question to buy time while he scrambled for a response.

"I'm not sure, but I think it was maybe around a month or so after she stopped coming to work."

After being specific and direct with the first answer, Sterling hedged and qualified the second one. Wu simply stared at him, allowing an awkward silence to form. Soon, Sterling felt compelled to fill the void.

"That's when our payroll clerk sent out her last paycheck. And then, well, I don't know. I suppose the guys on her team talked to me about it, but . . ." The words died on his lips. He had the stricken look of someone who realized he'd said too much.

Wu pounced. "Her team? Who was on her team, and what were they doing?"

Sterling dug a finger into his collar and cleared his throat. "Castillo was in a group of three scientists. They were researching new propulsion technology."

Interesting.

"That's a sensitive area," Wu said, thinking about potential national security ramifications if this CEO had been compromised. "Was this for a contract?"

When he posed the question, Wu didn't specify a US government contract in case the research was underwritten by a foreign nation or private business. Sterling was hiding something and couldn't be given any leeway to respond with half-truths.

"I'm not at liberty to say."

Even more interesting.

"We'd like to see your data."

Sterling shook his head in an exaggerated show of regret. "I've tried to be helpful, but that research involves proprietary formulas, privately funded studies, and patents. I'm going to need a warrant to turn over that information."

"I'll be sure to get one," Wu said. "In the meantime, we can speak to the other two scientists who were on her team."

Another shake of the head accompanied by an apologetic expression. "I'm sorry, but they're not available. Dr. Morton Wallace is on his way to Miami right now. He's taking a Caribbean cruise tomorrow, but he'll be back next week."

"And her other colleague?"

"Dr. David Easton. He was the lead scientist on the team, but he left our company a few years ago. He went to work for a lab in New York City."

The first piece of good news. They could head back and interview Dr. Easton on their own turf without any interference from Sterling.

"We'll need his contact information."

"My assistant will give you the last phone number and address we have on file."

They really didn't need his help finding Easton, but he was testing for cooperativeness on that front.

Sterling got to his feet. "If that's everything, Agent Wu, I have a busy schedule, and I've already pushed back a meeting to speak to you."

"This isn't over, Mr. Sterling." He stood and lobbed a parting shot designed to provoke a reaction. "I believe you were directly involved in Dr. Castillo's disappearance, helped cover it up, or know what happened. Whatever the case, you're holding out on us."

Sterling's face reddened. "I categorically deny that."

Wu exchanged a glance with Vega, who gave him a knowing look. People who used the phrase "I categorically deny" were often lying. The only thing that would have made Sterling look more guilty would be to swear on his mother's grave.

It was hard not to laugh when Sterling added, "I swear."

CHAPTER 16

One hour later
Denver International Airport

Dani had been watching an artist at work. Steve Wu was a skilled interviewer. He had methodically trapped Richard Sterling, who was not as skilled, in several lies.

Per protocol, the team had remained silent after leaving Exmyth until they could speak freely. In this case, that meant commandeering one of the executive lounges in the private jet terminal at Denver airport.

Now behind closed doors, Dani opened the discussion with the point that had nagged her most. "Who tipped off Sterling?"

"I know, right?" Patel said. "He was vague about a lot of things, but he remembered exactly how long ago Tina Castillo left. Then he lied his ass off about when he'd last talked about her."

Patel had clearly picked up on the same issue. Wu hadn't mentioned the purpose of their visit. Sterling would have no reason to believe the FBI was on his doorstep asking about an employee who by all accounts had walked off the job years earlier.

But he'd kept them waiting. And it appeared that he'd taken the time to check company records on Castillo. Which meant he'd been warned.

She glanced at Wu. "If I had any doubt Sterling knew why we were there, it disappeared when you mentioned her name and his sweat glands went into overdrive."

Wu nodded. "My last question was dead serious. I'm convinced he knows something, but I can't tell if he's covering for himself or someone else." He turned to Patel. "Sterling's admin gave us the last contact info they had for all three members of the team. Were you able to confirm?"

"Obviously, the address and phone for Castillo was useless," he said. "But Morton Wallace and David Easton's data checks out."

"Sterling told us Wallace is traveling to Miami," she said. "He may not be reachable right now, but Easton's in New York City, which I'm assuming is where we're headed next. Why not start with him?"

"Agreed," Wu said, then gestured to Patel's laptop. "Let's give him a call, but this time, make the caller ID show up as FBI. If it's his home number, he might not answer if it shows a generic blocked number."

Dani concurred. They had no reason to hide their identity and didn't want to risk getting screened as a potential telemarketer.

Wu jerked his chin at her. "You're on point for this one."

She didn't question him. The boss had a reason for everything he did, and she'd come to trust his logic. She waited while Patel set up his laptop and routed the call through the special software, then listened through several ringtones until someone answered.

"Hello?"

They had called his home, which turned out to be located in Queens. Perhaps he didn't have caller ID. A rarity, but possible. She hastened to identify herself.

"This is Special Agent Daniela Vega with the FBI. May I speak to Dr. David Easton?"

"I'm Dave," the voice said. "What's going on?"

"We got your number from Richard Sterling at Exmyth Technologies. We're looking for Tina Castillo, and we were hoping you might have a way to get in touch with her."

"I remember Tina. She was always so nice," Easton said, then hesitated. "Not in trouble or anything, is she?"

"We're concerned about her safety, but we can't reach her."

A long pause.

"Look, Agent uh . . ."

"Vega," she supplied.

"Agent Vega," he said. "Tina left suddenly. I was never sure what happened. It was a long time ago, but I might have kept a number or an address or something. I just can't remember."

"Anything you can tell us could be helpful."

"Truth be told, I'm a bit of a hoarder. Got a basement office in my house with boxes of files and papers. I might've jotted down an email address or a cell phone or something, but I'd be hard pressed to find it in this mess."

She pictured teetering stacks of boxes. "We can help you look."

"Sure. I'm about to head out, and I'll be busy most of the day, but you can come by tomorrow. Nine in the morning is the best time. I've had enough coffee to be awake, and I don't have to be in the office until noon."

She thanked him and disconnected. "Looks like we might be busy awhile sorting through a mountain of boxes," she said. "I've seen a few hoarders' houses, so I'm hoping he's serious about being 'a bit of a hoarder.'"

"Our pilot's already filing a plan for LaGuardia," Wu said. "We don't have enough for a search warrant for Exmyth, but if we ever do, I'll be back with a whole team of agents."

CHAPTER 17

Thirty seconds earlier

Foley hung up the phone and swiveled to face Dr. Easton. "Do you think I sounded like you?"

"Mmmf!"

He couldn't be sure what Easton was trying to say through the gag, so he answered his own question. "Doesn't matter. It's not like they know what you sound like anyway." He shrugged. "Sure, they're the FBI, so they could dig up a recording of you and do a voice analysis, but they've got zero reason to suspect you're not who they talked to. At least not yet. And by the time they do, I'll be long gone."

He walked over to Easton and leaned down. "The question is, Where will you be?" He saw Easton's face purple as he thrashed against his bindings.

Message received.

He was about to give Easton a final chance to talk when his cell phone buzzed in his pocket. He slid it out, checked the caller ID, then tapped the screen.

"What's up?"

"The Feds just left," Sterling said. "How did you know they'd come?"

"The same reason I called you." He didn't hide his impatience. "You and her team were the last ones to see her. It's the only lead they've got. It's also the only one I've got."

"I followed your instructions. Didn't tell them anything."

"Obviously, you did." Foley called him out on the lie. "Or they wouldn't have tried to contact Dr. Easton."

"I meant that I didn't *volunteer* any information. They brought their boss out. He was grilling me like nothing you've ever seen. Did everything but waterboard me."

He smelled the pure unadulterated bullshit right through the phone. Sterling had the backbone of a weasel. "I'm sure it was a brutal interrogation, but the point is that in the end, you must have put them on to Easton somehow."

"I-I might have mentioned that she was part of a team."

Foley wished he were in Denver so he could give Sterling the beating he deserved. If the fuckwit had blurted something about her team, the FBI would want to interview both of her former colleagues.

He continued over Sterling's sputtered excuses. "The only thing I need to know right now is if you told them what the team was working on."

"No, I refused. Insisted they had to get a warrant."

Foley scrunched his eyes shut and silently counted to five. Once his blood pressure came down from stroke level, he asked the next question with forced calm. "Do you know what a subpoena duces tecum is?"

A long pause, then, "A search warrant for documents."

"They can look through any damn documents they want." He spoke through clenched teeth. "That includes digital files. And guess what? They can access things like contracts, patent filings, and sales records."

Sterling swallowed audibly. "I didn't think—"

"No, you damn well didn't." He fought the urge to shout into the phone. "They have agents who are attorneys, forensic accountants, and financial crime experts. If they come back with papers, they'll crawl up your ass with a magnifying glass." He was breathing hard. "Have you ever had a body cavity search? Because you're about to get the FBI equivalent."

"I'm sorry." Sterling sounded near tears. "I was trying to think of a way to put them off."

"You did, but in the process, you gave them a reason to come back at you. Hard."

"What are you going to do?"

Foley gave Sterling a response that would make him understand exactly how much of a mess he'd made. "Clean up loose ends."

CHAPTER 18

Dani smiled at her tía Manuela. "Really, I'm stuffed. I can't eat another bite."

Her aunt, an excellent cook, was going out of her way to treat Dani to some amazing Puerto Rican cuisine, or cocina criolla.

Dani had group-texted her brother and sister to see if they'd like to join her for a visit with their mother. Erica responded to say they'd both just left Bellevue and that visiting hours had been shortened for facility maintenance. She added that they were headed to their aunt and uncle's Bronx apartment for dinner, insisting that Dani come.

More than a little leery after previous encounters with her tía, Dani required extra prodding before she agreed. As it turned out, she needn't have worried. Manuela seemed determined to make up for her past treatment of Dani and went out of her way to be kind and respectful from the moment she arrived.

The meal featured arroz con gandules, a classic rice-and-beans combo that included pigeon peas. The side of mofongo, made from mashed plantains, was the perfect accompaniment. Now, Manuela was trying to get Dani to have a second helping of tembleque for dessert.

The coconut pudding was rich and delicious, but Dani wasn't used to eating that much food in one sitting.

"You have to keep your strength up," Manuela said in a slight Nuyorican accent Dani had heard from her father growing up. The sound brought back pleasant memories. "You're working on a case."

Dani shot an accusatory look at Axel. Her brother had ways of snooping into her business.

"What?" His innocent expression fooled no one. "Dr. Maffuccio told us you cut your visit short after getting a phone call."

So that was the leak. Her siblings had visited their mother regularly over the years, becoming friendly with the Bellevue staff.

Unfortunately, the reminder that she hadn't gone through with her commitment to take a leave of absence brought on a wave of guilt.

"Don't blame yourself," Axel said, reading her expression correctly. "It's not like you've got a nine-to-five job or anything." He narrowed his eyes. "So what are you up to, anyway?"

Axel was always curious about her work, and now that he'd turned twenty-one, he was old enough to join the FBI. Patel had suggested he would make a fantastic civilian analyst, and she agreed. The two had met because of a previous operation, and she now wondered if they'd stayed in touch.

"I've got some news," Erica said. She had the air of someone bursting to share a secret. "I got accepted into Grossman."

For an instant everyone stared at her, then the whole apartment erupted into shouts of joy and congratulations. Erica had been working part-time as a medical assistant while she applied to New York University's Grossman School of Medicine. Admission was extremely competitive because every student received a full-tuition scholarship.

Dani had secretly set up an educational investment account for Erica once she learned her sister wanted to attend med school. The cost was staggering, and she still would have needed student loans. Now, none of that was necessary.

This bit of news was truly life changing.

She pulled Erica into a hug. "Are you thinking about a specialty?"

"I'm going to be a neurologist," Erica said. "I want to help Mom."

She should have guessed. Erica had the heart of a healer. She'd often remarked that Camila could get better under the right conditions and with the right treatment. Dani had overheard her having in-depth discussions with Dr. Maffuccio about her prescriptions and therapy regimen.

Axel grinned. "Maybe she'll figure all of us out too."

He had a fair point. Each of Camila's three children had a mind that worked differently from most. They had inherited some tendencies and developed other traits on their own, a combination of nature and nurture that came with unique advantages and challenges. At times, it felt like they were the only ones who really understood and accepted each other.

"How's it going with you?" she asked Axel, not wanting him to feel left out.

He ducked his head. "Oh, I've got some ideas. Nothing for sure yet, though."

She raised an inquisitive brow.

"Can't talk about it," he said. "Might jinx it."

She rested her hands on her hips. "You know I don't believe in any of that—"

Axel raised a placating hand. "I know, but just trust me on this . . . you don't want to know."

CHAPTER 19

The following morning, Wednesday, October 9, 9:00 a.m.
En route from Brooklyn to Queens, New York

Wu navigated the black Bureau-issued vehicle through morning rush hour traffic. Due to his position, he'd been offered an SUV, but he preferred the maneuverability of a sleek sedan in the busy streets of the nation's largest city.

He braked for a bicycle courier who had turned directly into his path without so much as glancing his way. After screeching to a halt, he looked over at Vega, who was in the front passenger seat.

She smiled and held up a steaming cup of coffee. "All good."

He'd been worried some of the piping-hot brew might have sloshed out and scalded her but realized he shouldn't have been concerned. She had excellent reflexes, as he'd seen on more than one occasion when the stakes were considerably higher.

When he'd texted to say he'd pick her up on his way from 26 Fed to Dr. Easton's house in Queens, she had responded with the mapped location of a Starbucks on the corner of her block. It had given him a much-needed chuckle after his meeting with Assistant Director Hargrave.

Wu accelerated back into the flow of traffic as the bicyclist pedaled away, oblivious to the near miss. "That guy's not going to last long if he doesn't watch where he's going."

Vega lifted a shoulder. "Maybe he's going for a workman's comp claim and a lawsuit. Could be part of a master plan to retire in his twenties."

"Except that he might be a bit too dead to enjoy it."

They lapsed into silence.

"How was your meeting with Assistant Director Hargrave?" she asked after a while.

He'd called his boss to brief him during the flight back to New York yesterday, but Hargrave had insisted on meeting in his office first thing in the morning. Looking back, it seemed that the ADIC had wanted the chance to interrogate him in person.

"He had a lot of . . . concerns," he said, downplaying the fact that Hargrave had taken the opportunity to second-guess everything Wu had done. "But I addressed them."

She cut him a knowing look but didn't press for details.

He made his way along the Brooklyn–Queens Expressway as they each contemplated their own private thoughts. He often wondered what Vega was thinking about. Her mind worked so differently from anyone he'd met. Well, anyone besides her younger brother. She was more like Axel than she probably realized. Always humble, she called him brilliant but would never say the same about herself.

She took a sip of coffee and started a new discussion. "What's Patel up to this morning?"

"I asked him to do a deep dive and dig up anything he can find on Exmyth Technologies and Tina Castillo's past while we help Dr. Easton try to find any contact info for her."

"Speaking of which, I'm not looking forward to ferreting around in Easton's basement. He claimed to only have slight hoarding tendencies, but that could be an understatement. If it is, we could spend days hunting for a scrap of paper."

He agreed. Adding an extra layer of difficulty would be the fact that they couldn't sort through the piles quickly. They'd have to scrutinize everything before ruling it out.

They were now on Queens Boulevard and would find out what they were up against soon. "Let's hope it's not that bad," Wu said, turning onto a smaller street. "We're supposed to keep this low-key. We can't send an entire team to go through his place."

She raised a brow. "Which means you can't send an entire team to Exmyth Technologies either."

"Not until this investigation is over or we get enough evidence. But I do intend to go back at some point."

"Over there." Vega pointed at a brick single-family home that looked like it had been constructed in the postwar era.

He had to wait for someone to leave before he could find a spot to parallel park along the street two blocks down from the house. They got out and took the sidewalk to a cracked cement path that led through the tiny front yard. The midcentury brick home was modest in size, but its location in Queens made the property far more valuable than it would have been elsewhere.

A quick glance up and down the block showed the classic American street, with rows of cookie-cutter structures lining both sides. The front of each residence held similar decor, and Wu imagined a family of four with a golden retriever living inside. Would he ever have such a life?

He made it onto the front stoop before realizing Vega had slowed her pace. He turned to her.

She stopped, frowned, and cocked her head to one side. "Something's off."

She had the demeanor of a gazelle sensing a predator in the tall grass nearby.

He glanced around but saw nothing. "What is it?"

Rather than respond, she tilted her head in the other direction. She was picking up on something, but he didn't get it. "You hear noise inside the house?"

"Not a noise." She wrinkled her nose. "A smell. It's familiar, but I can't place it."

He sniffed the air but caught no scent. Her comment brought a disturbing thought to mind. "A dead body?"

Had she picked up on the odor of decomp? Were they too late? When she didn't elaborate, he waited for her to step beside him before extending his arm to ring the doorbell.

Without warning, Vega grabbed his wrist. "Don't."

Wu noted the alarm on her face but couldn't understand the reason behind it. "I don't follow."

"No time to explain. We need to go." She tightened her grip. "Now."

She whirled around, pulling him along as she began to run.

She was strong, and he'd been caught off guard. He stumbled a few steps, trying to get his footing. She didn't wait for him. In fact, she was yanking hard enough to wrench his shoulder.

He'd never seen her act like this. For the first time, he was on the receiving end of her unexpected brute force.

He had two choices. Either stop resisting and start running beside her or use his own strength to restrain her and calm her down before one of them got hurt. Vega was tough and well trained, but he worked out regularly and had plenty of muscle to back him up if he needed to use it. An image flashed through his mind of a passerby streaming a video of two FBI agents fighting each other on the front lawn of a neighborhood in Queens.

Hargrave would have a conniption. And then he'd be on a mission to get them both fired.

Wu decided on the first option, but he never had the chance to fully regain his balance before he was knocked off his feet by a ground-shaking, window-shattering, bone-jarring explosion.

CHAPTER 20

One hour later, 10:00 a.m.
Queens, New York

Dani sat beside Wu inside one of the NYPD's gargantuan mobile command vehicles. They were both coated in dust and had squares of gauze taped over various cuts and abrasions.

She figured they had gotten off easy in what the city was now officially calling a major incident. Dr. Easton's tidy brick home in Queens had been reduced to charred rubble by a natural gas explosion.

When the fire department arrived, Wu had insisted they check her out first. The ambulance crew found no serious injuries but wanted to transport them to the hospital for more tests. They both declined.

The NYPD was next on the scene, stringing up perimeter tape, diverting traffic, and evacuating the neighborhood.

Dani and Wu had given preliminary statements to NYPD Crime Scene Unit detectives, Evidence Response Team technicians from the FBI, NYFD arson investigators, bomb techs from the NYPD's Explosives Ordnance Disposal Unit, and K-9 handler teams to sniff out accelerants—and cadavers.

Dani had insisted that the explosion was no accident, but her attempts to explain her thought process drew skeptical looks. Wu was the only one who seemed ready to accept her account at face value, but then he'd seen her operate in the field.

Rounding out the first responders was a team from Consolidated Edison, the local gas company known as Con Ed. Their personnel had shut off the gas main and were working with all the others to determine what had happened.

By the time Dani and Wu finished answering the first round of questions, the police had set up a command post, and a horde of investigators from every imaginable city, state, and federal agency had begun checking in.

A cluster of reporters had already descended on the area, parking their news vans and raising boom antennae all along the street outside the perimeter tape. When her cell phone vibrated, she realized she should have anticipated the text message that appeared.

SAW U ON TV @ EXPLOSION. R U OK?

She let out a groan.

Wu glanced at her. "What's up?"

"My brother, Axel. He must have seen me on the news walking to the command bus. He's worried about me."

"He loves you," Wu said simply.

She reflected on her conversation with her family last night, thinking of comforting words to send back that also didn't reveal too much.

ALL GOOD. WILL CALL SOON.

She sent the message and turned to Wu. "You were on camera too. Do you need to notify anyone that you're all right?"

He looked away. "No."

The one-word answer was so blunt that any further discussion died on her lips. She didn't know much about Wu's personal life. He'd mentioned an older brother who was a successful businessman with a beautiful wife and two children. Wu had never come out and said it, but Dani got the sense his older brother was the favorite son.

Perhaps his parents wanted more grandkids, but Wu seemed married to his job. Was he even in a relationship at all? She pushed the thought away. His personal life was none of her concern.

"So much for keeping things low-key with all this media," she said, getting back to the previous subject.

"At least the juiciest part hasn't leaked."

She had also been listening for any mention of Toro and his so-called treasure. "I doubt it'll stay that way once they find a detonator."

Wu gave her a sharp look. "Did you see something?"

She would have laughed if the situation weren't so grim. Her boss was beginning to think she had superpowers. "I made a deduction." When he merely frowned, she went on. "You never pressed the doorbell. We never got inside to flip a light switch. So if we didn't activate anything, that means someone else did."

Wu leaned back without comment, apparently considering her theory.

Dani glanced around. Inside the bus felt like a beehive buzzing with activity. She and Wu, the only ones not sitting at a workstation, talking on the phone, or going in and out to visit the scene, seemed to be inside a bubble by themselves.

She could tell that Wu, used to running critical incidents, didn't like finding himself in the role of victim-witness. She didn't either.

"Have you heard any updates about the body?" she asked him.

Early on, they'd gotten word that human remains had been found in what used to be the basement.

"Fortunately, Dr. Easton had worked on a few government contracts over the years," Wu said. "He voluntarily entered his DNA profile into the database."

With rapid DNA testing technology, that meant they'd soon know if Dr. Easton had died in the explosion. If not, she wondered who else might have been there. Patel had learned that the scientist lived alone.

She'd formed a conclusion, but wondered what her boss thought. "If you ask me, this was murder. What do you—"

"Did someone say murder?" a deep voice to her left said.

Startled, she glanced up to see a familiar face. NYPD Detective First Grade Mark Flint had just entered through the doorway in the middle of the bus. He was a homicide detective who worked out of the headquarters building at One Police Plaza.

"I didn't expect to see you here." She shook her head. That had come out wrong. "It's just that you're not assigned to Queens . . . um, normally."

The last time she'd seen Flint in person was in the hospital. He was recovering from a near-fatal gunshot wound sustained during an operation with her. She'd felt responsible, as she always did when partnering with someone in the field.

She'd been extremely grateful he survived that mission. In the past, there had been some who didn't, and their deaths weighed on her heart.

Wu gave her a sympathetic look, then shifted his gaze to Flint. "Thank you for coming, Detective."

Flint smiled. "I could hardly say no to the chief of detectives."

So Wu had found a moment to route a request through the top brass at the NYPD. She shouldn't have been surprised. Flint had proven himself in the past when he'd been assigned to the JTTF on a temporary basis.

He was a welcome addition, but his presence carried certain assumptions with it. "This incident is now being treated as a homicide?" she asked him.

"Our homicide detectives go out on suspicious deaths," he said. "And this one is about as suspicious as it gets."

"I knew they'd send someone," Wu added. "And I wanted to choose."

Greetings over, Flint got down to business. "I checked out the scene and spoke with the people working it before I came to the command post, but I still have a few questions." He eyed her. "Lemme get this straight. You smelled natural gas when you were still outside the house." He shifted his gaze to Wu. "And you didn't detect any unusual odor at all."

"I've never had a great nose since it was broken during an arrest years ago," Wu said. "But Vega's had lots of field experience."

"Part of my military training involved detecting noxious substances," she said. "Sometimes the enemy set up crude traps, sometimes they hid IEDs, and sometimes they deployed poisonous liquid, powder, or gas. Our instructors taught us to catch the slightest scent even when we were distracted."

Flint followed up with another question. "Okay, I'll go with the good nose and all, but how did you know not to let SAC Wu ring the doorbell?"

This was the part she'd tried to explain to the first responders without success. Now, she decided to be blunt. "I've seen fellow Rangers blown to pieces. My father barely survived an IED that left him physically and mentally damaged for the rest of his life. When you've seen up close the aftereffects of explosives, you make it your business to learn everything you can about how they work, where they're hidden, and what triggers them."

Flint was well aware of what had happened to her father. "I didn't mean—"

"No." She held up a hand. "You asked a valid question. I'll answer to the best of my ability." She drew in a deep breath. "In my unit, we called it the Hink. It's like a sense that something isn't right. That danger is nearby. The closest thing I can give you is when you feel someone watching you, but it's more than that. Sometimes it's specific and sometimes it's vague. But it's real."

She struggled to convey something completely intangible. Those who had experienced it would understand. Others would either believe her or they wouldn't.

She went deeper into her past to illustrate her point. "When one of us thought the shape under a blanket was a bomb, or the TV remote was a detonator, or the light switch closed a circuit when it was flipped on, we learned not to question it. We got the hell out of the kill zone and figured it out from a safe distance. Today, the smell of gas put me on high alert. After that, when I got the Hink, a mental picture of pressing a button to close a circuit flashed through my mind, and I acted on pure reflex."

Flint nodded, prepared to move on, whether he accepted her account at face value or not.

She had her own questions. "Was I right? Was the doorbell rigged to set off an explosion?"

"It's preliminary," Flint said. "So don't repeat this, but the bomb tech found signs of wiring attached to what's left of the doorbell. The arson investigator is working with a team from Con Ed. They think someone tampered with the gas line in the basement to make sure it filled the place with fumes. They didn't tape the windows and stuff towels under the doors, so their working theory is that whoever did this wanted it to look like an accidental gas leak that resulted in an explosion."

Dani was always amazed at how much physical evidence could be forensically recovered, even after a raging fire or a massive explosion.

"Did you get the results from the rapid DNA test?" Wu asked.

Flint nodded. "Dr. Easton was killed in the blast."

She wasn't surprised, but the news still unsettled her. "He took whatever he knew to the grave."

Wu scowled. "And whatever information was in the house went up in smoke too."

"I'm seeing a bigger problem," Flint said. "You two never rang the doorbell, but the house still went boom."

Wu tipped his head toward Dani. "She explained her theory about that before you came."

Flint raised one sandy-blond brow.

"I came to the only logical conclusion," Dani said. "Someone had us under observation. When we started running away instead of pressing the doorbell, they used a remote detonator to set off the device."

"And I realized that could only mean one thing," Wu added. "Someone had a backup plan to make damn sure we died too."

CHAPTER 21

Dani and Wu had come up with a theory about what happened, but she couldn't share it with Flint.

The NYPD detective did not have the benefit of knowing all the background on their current investigation, and the case was classified, so she gave him the broad strokes without going into detail.

"Dr. Easton might have had information pertinent to an ongoing investigation. Rather than ask him to come to 26 Fed for an interview, we went to his house because he told us he was a bit of a hoarder. He invited us to help him search through all his stuff to help him find what we needed."

"I've investigated cases involving hoarders," Flint said. "A search could take weeks."

She framed the concept in military terms. "Whoever did this achieved multiple objectives. They permanently cut off all communication from Dr. Easton, employed a scorched-earth policy to prevent us from using anything we found, and attempted to maximize casualties."

"So demolishing the whole house was the only way to prevent anyone from finding something inside." Flint's expression darkened. "Only I think you two weren't intended as collateral damage. I think you were targeted." He turned to Wu. "You and Vega are into something deep. I can't investigate this properly unless I've been read in."

Flint was asking the boss to give him access to classified information. Fortunately, his past assignments on the JTTF required him to have a security clearance, which was still active.

Wu regarded Flint for a long moment. "We're going to need someone from the PD involved going forward. That's one of the reasons I requested you for this case. I'll contact your chain of command and ask for another temp . . . if you're up for it."

Flint gave him a wry smile. "A doorbell bomb, a scientist working on something mysterious, and a classified investigation. Are you kidding? I live for this secret squirrel shit."

"Speaking of doorbells," Dani said, "that was damned reckless. Hell, Girl Scouts could have been going around selling cookies."

Wu scowled. "Which means we're dealing with someone who'll do anything, kill anyone, take any risk to get what they want."

"That's a good starting point for me," Flint said. "According to the fire department and Con Ed, it looks like the perp opened the gas valve sometime yesterday and let the house fill with fumes overnight. By the time you two showed up this morning, the place was ready to blow. There's not enough left of his remains for an autopsy, but if he wasn't dead already, the gas would have likely killed him."

Dani glanced at Wu, who was the only one present with the authority to authorize her to speak freely about the investigation.

He inclined his head briefly. "Go ahead."

"The only person outside of law enforcement who knew we were coming to see Dr. Easton this morning was Richard Sterling," she said to Flint. "He's the CEO of Exmyth Technologies in Denver."

"Could he have told someone else?"

"Certainly, but the point is that he'll know exactly who he told. And that person will know who they told."

Flint pounced. "You think this Sterling guy is behind it?"

"That, or he's the one who set us up. Either way, we need to talk to him. Sooner rather than later."

"We've got every kind of phone you need right here," Flint said, clearly anxious to make progress. "We can call him any way you want."

Meaning the NYPD had the same spoofing and blocking capabilities Patel had used. If Sterling had something to hide, he might avoid a call from the FBI.

Wu stuck his hand out. "Hand me the unit."

Minutes later, Wu had connected with Sterling's office number. Given the time difference, he should have been getting in by now. The call was automatically routed to the front desk, then forwarded to his admin assistant.

A smooth feminine voice responded. "Richard Sterling's office, how may I—"

"I need to speak to Mr. Sterling. It's urgent."

"I'm sorry, but Mr. Sterling isn't in yet."

Wu frowned. "Doesn't he come in at nine?"

"Yes, and it's not like him to be late. I'll be happy to take a message and pass it along to—"

"As I mentioned, it's urgent." Wu switched to a tone that would intimidate most people. "This is Special Agent in Charge Steve Wu of the FBI. What's his home number?"

A long pause, then, "I'm sorry, sir, but I can't give you that."

"Is it a state secret? Because I assure you, I've got clearance to hear those."

"Uh . . . no . . . it's company policy."

Wu didn't give her a moment to think. "Is it company policy to prevent the FBI from conducting an investigation?"

"No, sir, I just—"

"Thank you," he said dismissively. "I'll get it myself."

He disconnected and punched in the number Patel had provided. They waited through many ringtones before it went to voicemail.

"I don't like doing this long distance," Wu said. "But we're halfway across the country."

"This is where being a cop comes in handy," Flint said. "I can make a call to the Denver PD and ask them to do a knock and talk."

The idea was sound. Dani knew a DPD patrol officer could be at Sterling's door in five minutes, but it would take a lot longer to get an agent from the FBI's Denver field office briefed and sent out. The police wouldn't need a lot of background on the case to simply knock on Sterling's door and provide a number for him to call the task force.

If he didn't answer, they could walk around the outside of his house to make sure nothing looked suspicious.

"A preliminary contact," Wu said thoughtfully.

She looked at Wu. "You know that if you call the Denver field office, they'll demand a lot more information."

Wu sighed. "Do it," he said to Flint. "But tell them not to ring the doorbell."

CHAPTER 22

Two hours earlier

If you wanted a job done right, you had to do it yourself.

Foley had set everything up with careful precision at Dr. Easton's house. Unfortunately, he couldn't be in two places at once, so he left a subordinate in charge of the final phase of his plan.

Foley had to get to Denver and meet with Sterling, so he couldn't see the job in Queens through. The operative he'd called to help him only had to press a damned button. Seriously, how hard was that?

And yet, somehow the fuckwit had managed to screw it up.

Foley pulled his thoughts away from devising elaborate punishments for the man and back to the problem at hand, which required his full attention.

"What's in the lockbox, Richard?"

Sterling shifted his feet. "Nothing important."

"If it wasn't important, you wouldn't put it in a lockbox." He dragged out each point for emphasis. "Behind stacks of files. Inside a hidden wall safe. In your private office. With a door that has a separate security code from the rest of the building."

Did Sterling think he was stupid? Foley's fingers itched to snatch the weasel by his throat and choke the answers out of him. But the search would go a lot faster if Sterling was conscious and cooperative.

"I meant to say that it wasn't important to you, or to anyone else for that matter." He swallowed. "It's, um . . . personal."

He was getting an idea about where this might be going. "Open it." He reached into the wall safe and lifted out a heavy-gauge steel container the size of a shoebox. "Now."

Sterling accepted it with trembling hands. He punched in a code on a keypad in the front. Then opened the lid.

Foley peered inside. As he'd suspected, dozens of Polaroid photographs were piled on the bottom. Sterling himself appeared in some of them. There were also several old-fashioned videotapes and a small camcorder. Judging by the subject matter in the photos, the videos were the kind Sterling wouldn't want to upload onto a computer.

Foley felt his lip curl. "I never figured you for a pervert, Richard."

Sterling stared at the floor.

Foley closed the lid. "I had to make sure I got everything."

They'd spent the past two hours going through every computer file, every document, and every video feed. Everything that linked Exmyth Technologies to Foley, his boss, or the company in any way had been deleted, shredded, or destroyed. Sterling had thought Foley didn't know about the wall safe concealed behind the recessed fish tank in his office. Thanks to his own surveillance technology, Foley knew that—and a lot more.

He hadn't found out about Sterling's odd fetish, however, which bothered him. Not because he gave a rat's ass what the man did in private but because that was precisely the kind of dirt he liked to obtain about those he dealt with. Blackmail was a powerful incentive to cooperate. If he'd known about it five years ago, things might have gone a lot more smoothly.

Head still down, Sterling muttered, "Are we done here?"

He nodded. "It's all good. I don't want to leave on bad terms. Who knows? We may do business again in the future." He gestured to a crystal decanter and four highball glasses sitting on a credenza. "How about we knock one back before I go? That looks like some good bourbon."

"It's scotch. And it's excellent."

"All the better."

Sterling hesitated, as if an inner battle was raging. He obviously resented sharing his best hooch with someone who had just humiliated him. On the other hand, he looked like he could use a drink.

Shrugging, Sterling crossed the room and poured two fingers for each of them.

Foley accepted the glass and raised it in a silent salute before lifting it to his lips. Sterling, on the other hand, took an enormous gulp.

Foley gave him a sardonic smile. "That's not how you're supposed to drink fine spirits."

"These past two days have been a fucking nightmare," Sterling said. "And it ended with you looking at my . . . my . . . private business." He took another swig. "I might just polish off the whole decanter."

Foley swirled the amber liquid around in his glass, reflecting on his current situation. His boss had been furious that the operation in Queens had only partially succeeded. Foley had to remind him that the most important things were done. Easton couldn't talk. There could be no autopsy to prove he'd been murdered before the explosion. He admitted that he hadn't forced Tina Castillo's address out of Easton, but at least the FBI couldn't find anything either.

His boss was especially concerned that Agent Vega and her supervisor were not only still breathing but also making steady progress. Foley explained how he could track their movements in real time without their knowledge. That seemed to satisfy the old man, but not much.

The boss had ordered him to find Castillo before the FBI did and make her talk. Toro's comment made it sound like she knew where his stash of evidence was. In the end, the boss had told Foley not to come back until he'd recovered it.

The sound of shattering glass pulled Foley from his dark musing. He glanced at Sterling, who was clutching at his throat.

"You okay?" he asked.

Sterling's eyes bulged as his blue lips opened wide. Only a gurgle came out.

"Of course you're not okay. How could you be after such a massive overdose of your heart medication." He smiled. "They're quick-dissolve pills, so they disappeared seconds after I slipped them in the decanter when you were opening the wall safe. Didn't you notice that I never took a sip of my drink?"

Sterling tried to stand but fell to the tile floor, still gagging.

"I went by your house and emptied the bottle in your medicine cabinet." He leaned back to watch the show. "Clever, right? Everything will match up at the autopsy."

He despised Richard Sterling and took full advantage of the opportunity to torment the weasel while he was down but before he was out.

"Here's what's going to happen. The FBI agents who were here yesterday will quickly realize you must have given Dr. Easton's address and phone number to someone else—and then he ended up dead. They'll come back to ask who you talked to. Sadly, they'll find you dead."

Foley gave him a mock pout.

"Tragically, you realized the Feds would find out about your illegal dealings. Not with my company, because that evidence is all gone now. You knew they'd figure out you kept two sets of books, fudged your scientific research, and cheated on your taxes."

Sterling's movements were slowing. He wouldn't last much longer. Time to deliver the final blow.

Foley stood and retrieved the lockbox, which he'd closed without relocking it, and opened the lid. "They'll find you in here with your photos spread around. It seems you wanted to get one last look at your own private freak show before you overdosed. The world is going to know your dirty little secret, and that's how you'll be remembered."

He waited through Sterling's death throes, then started the tedious process of cleaning and staging the scene, something he would entrust to no one else on such a critical assignment.

As he'd been thinking earlier, if you wanted a job done right . . .

CHAPTER 23

Dani kept circling back to the underlying problem that had sent them looking for Dr. Easton in the first place.

"We're no closer to finding Dr. Castillo." She looked from Wu to Flint. "In fact, I think we're farther away."

She and Wu had spent the past twenty minutes bringing Flint up to speed on the investigation. It helped that he'd met Gustavo Toro and was familiar with his background.

"I understand that the case is classified," Flint said. "But if we don't have any better options, we could use her Colorado driver's license to make a BOLO and send it to law enforcement. Hell, maybe we should just put it out to the media. I'll bet somebody's seen her—if she's still alive."

Dani didn't like the idea, but she didn't have the detective's experience, so she waited to hear what Wu had to say before posing her objections.

"Based on what just happened, and on Toro's comments in the video, Tina Castillo is in grave danger," Wu said. "If someone spots her, I'm worried we couldn't reach her fast enough to protect her. For whatever reason, she hasn't gone to law enforcement yet, so she might not trust us."

"And we're not totally out of leads yet," Dani added. "There's still the third scientist, Morton Wallace."

Flint nodded. "Ah, yes. The one currently sailing in the Caribbean."

"Excuse me, Detective Flint?"

They all turned. A woman in a police uniform approached from the communications center in the rear of the command bus.

"A Denver PD lieutenant is asking for you." She held out a sat phone.

Flint took it and tapped one of the buttons. "Flint here, you're on speaker. Thanks for calling me back so—"

"This is a real shit show. What the hell did you get us into?"

Flint tensed. "What did you find? Is anyone hurt?"

Dani saw the color drain from Wu's face and knew he was feeling the same dread she was. They had been anxious to make headway, but not at the expense of anyone's life. The lieutenant plainly felt he should've been given more information.

"None of my officers if that's what you mean," the voice on the other end snapped. "But I can't say the same for this Richard Sterling character you asked us to contact."

She was relieved no one on the PD had been harmed, but her mind reeled at the new development. Things were accelerating, and she couldn't make out any patterns in the situation, except that they always seemed to be one step behind.

They spent the next fifteen minutes getting a blow-by-blow account detailing how a patrol unit had tried Sterling's home first and, finding it secure, went to his office to see if he'd gone in early. Security let them in, and they'd gotten an eyeful when they entered the CEO's corner office.

Wu provided his cell number for the lieutenant to transmit photos of the scene as he briefed them. Dani edged close to him as he opened the file. Nothing stood out about the crime scene . . . until Wu began swiping through the images of the Polaroids found scattered around.

She had witnessed many things in her rather eventful life, but what she saw unsettled her. "That's Sterling." She pointed at a naked figure on the left side of the small screen.

Wu slid his index finger to the left, bringing up the next photo. "It's safe to say the man had some issues."

The lieutenant interrupted their analysis to offer his conclusions about what happened. To him, it looked like Sterling was drinking when he collapsed and died beside the broken glass. From his experience, the lieutenant said Sterling's coloring made it seem like he might have ingested some kind of toxin or poison in the alcohol.

Wu advised the lieutenant the FBI would respond to assist in the investigation and asked him to treat the scene as a possible homicide. They agreed to collect and preserve the evidence and coordinate with the Bureau.

After the call ended, Dani offered her take. "No way did Sterling suddenly decide to kill himself."

"I've seen a hell of a lot and I'm no prude, but those Polaroids . . ." Flint grimaced. "The man was twisted."

"Doesn't mean he's suicidal," she countered. "We'll have to get out there to see what else he might have been hiding besides compromising photos."

Wu shook his head. "We're being pulled in too many directions."

"I can run point on the case in New York," Flint said. "Makes the most sense. That'll free you two up to head back to Denver."

Dani recalled what they'd been discussing before the DPD lieutenant called. "Wait. What about Morton Wallace?" She looked at Wu.

"There's nothing more we can do for Easton or Sterling, and we can't locate Castillo. Wallace is the last one standing."

Wu gave it some thought. "Patel already checked the cruise itinerary. The ship set sail out of the Port of Miami yesterday. They're scheduled for two days at sea before they reach the Port of San Juan."

She'd been to San Juan, where both of her parents were born, many times. Like most large cities, it was beautiful, lively, and, in certain places, dangerous.

"Someone could be waiting for him in Puerto Rico," Dani said. "Once he gets off the ship, he'll be vulnerable walking around. They could set up a hit to look like a street crime."

Wu got to his feet and headed for the rear of the bus.

She followed. "What are you doing?"

"I'm calling the captain of that ship. Now."

Dani wasn't sure what the procedures were for calling a vessel floating in the Caribbean, but the communications center in the command bus rivaled anything she'd seen in the field. In a surprisingly short time, they were patched through to the ship's bridge. The NYPD communications specialist laid the groundwork, explaining that this was an urgent safety matter and that a senior official from the FBI needed to speak with the captain immediately.

That did the trick, and moments later a male voice with an accent Dani couldn't place sounded over the speaker.

"This is Captain Radek Skála. How can I help you?"

"This is FBI Special Agent in Charge Steve Wu. We are making a formal request that you assign a security detail to a passenger named Morton Wallace," he said. "I can't go into specifics, but there's reason to believe he may be in danger."

There was a long pause, then, "Excuse me, but did you say Morton Wallace?"

"That's right. I'd like to speak to him personally."

"I'm sorry, Special Agent in Charge Wu," the captain said in precise English. "That won't be possible."

Wu frowned. "Why not? We need to warn him about—"

"Morton Wallace went overboard last night," Skála cut in. "He's been declared lost at sea."

CHAPTER 24

3:00 p.m.
The Caribbean

Dani wasn't sure whether the initial crash would kill her or if it would be the fireball that followed.

She peered down from the side window as the helicopter hovered above the ship's massive bow. The pilot was aiming the struts for the gigantic letter H painted on the heaving deck, but he'd have to time the landing just right to avoid coming down at the wrong moment.

These types of landings were among the most challenging, especially in choppy seas, but she and Wu had been assured this pilot had plenty of experience in his prior Navy career.

She glanced at her boss, whose jaw was clenched, and knew he shared her doubts. Wu had split up the team, sending Patel to Denver to oversee the collection of whatever data they could scrape from Exmyth's computer system, and Flint was back in New York leading the investigation in Dr. Easton's case.

Their speed-addicted FBI pilot had taken less than two hours to fly the Gulfstream G550 jet from LaGuardia to Miami International Airport, where Dani and Wu were greeted by agents with the FBI's Miami field office upon arriving.

They hadn't wanted to expand the investigative loop, but Wu's urgent request for a helicopter with an experienced pilot had necessitated contacting the Tactical Helicopter Unit. Again, Wu's rank and reputation had worked in their favor. Few agents could have gotten a Black Hawk for a landing at sea.

Wu had made another call during the flight, asking agents from the Denver field office to check out Morton Wallace's home. With notification of his presumed death, they had spent a large portion of the flight securing a search warrant from a federal magistrate. With luck, they would find contact information for Tina Castillo, and maybe other useful info about the case.

With all other bases covered, Dani and Wu were left to head to the ship, since the death of a US citizen in international waters fell under the jurisdiction of the FBI.

She shifted her gaze to see several crew members in crisp white uniforms, standing behind barriers that blocked off the landing zone. Farther back, rows of passengers were crowded along the railings with their cell phones held high.

Well, at least their fiery deaths would garner plenty of clicks and views.

The copter continued its descent, rotating just above the landing pad, as the pilot realigned it with the motion of the ship.

Seconds later, the skids hit the big H with a thump. Not bad considering the conditions. Dani made it a point to thank the pilot before she clambered down onto the deck.

The show was over, and at first she couldn't understand why passengers were still pointing their phones at them. Then she understood. A helicopter landing aboard a ship was a rarity. If a medevac was absolutely necessary, pilots preferred to lower a basket on a rope for the ship's crew to strap the patient in rather than put the bird down on the pad.

Dani had rappelled out of a Black Hawk on a fast rope plenty of times, but Wu had never done it. And now wasn't the time to learn.

Wu had exercised all his considerable authority to arrange for a special transport to the ship, and everyone was watching. While still on the flight to Miami, they had discussed their options. Ordinarily, agents from the FBI's San Juan field office in Hato Rey would meet the ship when it came into port. But she and Wu had all agreed that, whatever the ship's crew believed, Wallace had likely been murdered. Whoever was responsible was currently trapped on board, and they couldn't allow Wallace's killer to escape.

Captain Skála had explained that the ship would be delayed getting to Puerto Rico because of the passenger-overboard procedures the crew had undertaken last night.

They had not been able to learn much about Wallace's fall from the captain, who was reluctant to provide details over the phone. Concerned about liability, media coverage, and other issues, he insisted on seeing them in person and inspecting their credentials before allowing them access to the investigation his security team had conducted.

Now they would have the opportunity to do exactly that. The helo's whirring blades were winding down, and by the time Dani and Wu reached the waiting crew members, they could exchange shouted greetings.

A tall man with chiseled features and close-cropped brown hair under a white officer's hat stepped forward and extended a hand to shake each of theirs in turn, then spoke in a deep voice. "I'm Captain Radek Skála, commander of this vessel."

Dani had anticipated someone with gray hair and weathered skin, but Skála was far younger than she'd expected and looked like he belonged on the cover of a fitness magazine. She still couldn't place his accent. A quick glance at the bottom edge of his nameplate told her he was Czech.

Captain Skála glanced around at the crowded deck. "I'll take you to the security office, where we can talk in private."

Dani put her creds away. Evidently, a government helicopter had been identification enough.

After passing through a series of corridors, they waited while Skála passed a sensor in front of a scanner to open a secure door. When they followed him inside, the glitz and glamour of the passenger area seemed far behind them. They had entered the working zone in the heart of the ship, where only the crew went.

Minutes later, they entered a vast control center rivaling any Dani had seen at the Bureau. Dozens of screens covered the walls, along with hundreds of switches, lights, and alarms.

"This is our main security area," Skála said. "I wanted to bring you here first because there's something you need to see for yourselves. Something I couldn't tell you over the phone."

He turned to one of the security officers. "Bring up the video of Dr. Wallace going overboard."

Dani and Wu exchanged glances. They had hoped the incident would be caught on camera but had learned that many ships had blind spots in their monitoring systems.

"Is the image clear?" Wu asked. "Can you identify the person who pushed him?"

"Pushed him?" Skála tilted his head in confusion. "Dr. Wallace jumped."

CHAPTER 25

Dani could not accept what she'd just heard.

"Were your cameras functioning properly?" she asked Captain Skála.

He gave her a knowing look. "You do not believe." He gestured to the monitor. "See for yourself."

Dani and Wu drew closer to the screen. The night sky above the ocean was a moonless black, but the deck was sufficiently lit to see that the video was in color with high resolution. They would have a good view of whatever had happened last night.

She recognized Morton Wallace from his driver's license photo and other pictures Patel had culled from an internet search. He stepped unsteadily into the frame from the left, lurched toward the railing, and paused. In khaki pants and an aloha shirt decorated with parrots and palm trees, he appeared to be a tropical tourist who'd had too much to drink.

Wallace spun around, peering in every direction. He seemed to be searching for something, but he never fixed his gaze on any one spot. He grasped the railing, and Dani noted that his hands were empty. He put a foot on the lowest rail, then hoisted himself up two more rungs until he could swing both of his legs over.

Now seated on the railing, facing the sea with his back to the deck, he darted a glance over his shoulder. This time, Dani read abject terror in his expression. He immediately turned back toward the water and jumped, pushing off from the railing with his feet with such force that he sailed off into the darkness before dropping out of view.

He had not slipped. He had not fallen by accident. The captain was correct. Morton Wallace had jumped.

But . . .

"He looked scared," Dani said to Skála. "Do you have any other cameras that show more of the deck in that area?"

"Of course." Skála signaled the security officer, who ran through four different feeds with the same time stamp. That entire portion of the ship was completely deserted. No one was anywhere near Wallace.

"This makes no sense," Wu said, echoing her own feelings. "He was unsteady on his feet, as if he might have overindulged, but he didn't stumble and fall overboard. He put effort into climbing over the railing, and he intentionally launched himself off it."

"And what was he looking at over his shoulder?" Dani added. "It was like he was trying to get away from someone . . . or something."

"We wondered the same thing," Skála said. "A check of his passenger card showed he ordered two glasses of wine with dinner and then had a cocktail at the bar three hours later before going back to his cabin." He lifted a shoulder. "That is not much for a man his size."

"Was he drinking in his cabin?" Dani asked.

"He did not order anything, and we do not allow passengers to bring alcohol aboard the ship unless they purchase it during one of the excursions. But our first port of call is not until tomorrow, so that is not possible."

"Did he have any visitors?"

"Dr. Wallace was traveling alone, and no one entered his room at any time except the steward and housekeeping staff."

Wu said, "We'd like to see the cabin."

They followed Skála through a warren of passageways in the interior section of the ship. Curious about the inner workings of such a massive vessel, Dani quickened her pace to walk beside him. She peppered him with questions, and learned the ship carried over six thousand passengers and two thousand crew. It was like a floating city, with its own fire and police departments, a hospital, and even a morgue.

Without warning, Skála reached out and pulled her against him. "Look out."

She had reflexively begun to push away, then froze as a motorized forklift stacked with containers zipped past them.

Where the hell had her situational awareness gone? She'd nearly been crushed because she was so engrossed in the details about the ship. Or had she been distracted by the captain himself?

Skála glanced down at her. "We call this the superhighway. Food is taken from cold storage to the galley for meal preparation. Supplies are transported all over the ship at all hours."

A cart whizzed by, the driver snapping a quick salute to Skála without slowing down.

"It is one of the most dangerous places on the ship, which is why passengers are not allowed here without an escort to keep them safe."

She could see why. The forklift driver's view had been partially obstructed by the towering load. Clearly, the crew knew to keep an eye out.

"We'll keep that in mind." Wu's gaze fell on Skála's arm, which was still around Dani's waist. "I think Agent Vega's out of danger now."

Skála took a step back and cleared his throat. "Of course."

When he turned to lead them across the superhighway, Dani noticed the backs of his ears had reddened.

After what felt like an hour but was probably less than ten minutes, they were standing in front of a stateroom on the fourteenth deck. Skála had contacted the steward, who was standing at attention beside the door when they arrived.

He saluted Skála. "The door is sealed as you ordered, sir." He glanced at them. "I am Tommy, Dr. Wallace's steward."

This time, Dani had no trouble placing the accent, and a glance at his name tag indicated Tommy Asnee was from Thailand.

She faced him, placed her palms together at chest level, and inclined her head a fraction. "Sawatdee kha."

He beamed at her and did likewise, but bowed until his nose touched his fingertips. "Sawatdee khrap."

She had been to Thailand on several occasions and spoke just enough Thai to get herself in trouble. And to know that men and women used different suffixes when exchanging greetings.

Tommy used a passkey to open the door and ushered them in, explaining that the maids had not been allowed in to clean, so everything inside was preserved as Dr. Wallace had left it.

Wu surveyed the room and nodded appreciatively. "This cabin is huge."

Skála smiled. "This is one of our deluxe loft suites. The bedroom is upstairs."

Wu gazed up at the vaulted ceiling. "I'm sure this room costs a buck or two."

"We normally charge fifteen thousand for this stateroom, but Dr. Wallace is a member of our Seafarer Reward Club, and he's earned a lot of points. I checked. He got it for half price."

Even at half price Dani thought it was steep. Then again, she'd never been on a pleasure cruise before, so perhaps it was worth the expense.

She and Wu began a methodical examination of the cabin, slowly working their way through the lower level.

"Is this complimentary with the room?" Wu asked.

She turned to see him pointing at a fruit basket wrapped in clear plastic and resting on the coffee table in front of the sofa.

Skála turned to Tommy with a raised brow.

"It was a gift," Tommy said quickly, taking the cue. "From a lady passenger."

Dani and Wu exchanged glances.

"Who was she?" Wu asked. "And when did this happen?"

"I found her in the hallway in front of his room last night around twenty-one hundred hours," Tommy said. "I remember her name was Belinda. She told me she met him in the casino and liked him. She asked me to leave it in the room for him."

Skála's jaw tightened. "So you put it inside?"

Tommy's smile faltered under the captain's withering glare. "I know the basket came from our gift shop. It was sealed in plastic. Why would I think anything was wrong?"

Dani walked over to the fruit basket. "The wrapping hasn't been opened, and all the fruit is perfectly arranged. Wallace didn't eat any of it."

"So no poisoned apple," Wu said dryly.

Her boss must have harbored the same suspicions she did about Wallace's bizarre behavior before he jumped. He hadn't consumed enough alcohol to be heavily intoxicated. And his demeanor seemed more erratic than drunk.

Dani circled the coffee table to examine the fruit from all sides. "There's an envelope lying on the table behind the basket. Wallace's name is written on the back."

She had been reaching for the small cream-colored envelope when a sharp command from Wu stayed her hand.

"Don't touch it!" He took a step closer, ready to intervene. "If that basket turns out to be relevant, the envelope could have prints on it."

Embarrassed by her blunder, Dani retrieved a small baggie from her pocket. As the others looked on, she opened it and pulled out a pair of latex gloves. The gloves and the inside of the bag were sterile, making it the perfect evidence-collection kit.

She picked up the envelope by its corner and dropped it into the baggie before doing the same with the card. Then she read the neatly printed message.

ENJOYED OUR TIME IN THE CASINO.
HOW ABOUT DINNER TOMORROW NIGHT?
—BELINDA

"I want to talk to this Belinda," Wu said to Skála. "Can you track her down?"

Skála nodded. "She had to use her room card to buy the fruit basket at the gift shop. Plus, we will have her on video and can follow her all the way up to Dr. Wallace's stateroom."

Perfect. It might not lead to anything other than a lonely lady trying to meet a man, but they needed to interview Belinda, who had come in contact with Wallace shortly before he died.

They continued searching the room while Skála contacted security to review footage of all gift shop transactions involving a fruit basket.

They went upstairs to check out the loft bedroom, where a search of Wallace's closets revealed he was neat and organized. A man like that would keep notes and records of his work. The thought reminded her of Flint and Patel, and she wondered if they were making any progress.

"I have information about the woman buying the fruit basket," Skála called up to them from the main floor.

Dani and Wu hurried down the loft stairs to find the captain frowning.

"What's wrong?" she asked him.

"Her name is not Belinda. She is Ursula Cole in cabin 11506." His frown deepened into a scowl. "Where she is staying with Paul Cole. Her husband."

CHAPTER 26

Wu tried to wrap his mind around the new development. The woman who sent a fruit basket to Dr. Wallace used a fake name. And she was married—and sailing with her husband.

He was not inclined to judge others for their personal decisions, but his discomfort had nothing to do with morality. Did Ursula Cole, a.k.a. Belinda, lie about her name to step out on her husband, or was the whole thing an elaborate plot? He wasn't the type to jump to conclusions, but this case was more complex than any he'd encountered . . . since the last time he'd come out from behind his desk to work with Vega.

She seemed to attract danger. And a certain cruise ship captain. A recollection of Skála's arm pulling her body tight against his flashed through Wu's mind. The Czech had to be six and a half feet tall and looked like a leading man playing the role of a sea captain in his starched white uniform.

Wu banished the thought before it gained traction. Whatever Vega chose to do with her personal life was none of his business. Her next comment provided a welcome distraction.

"So Ursula Cole was lying to her husband, or Wallace, or both," she said. "To get to the bottom of it, we need to talk to her."

"And her husband too," he added.

During their conversation, Skála had been busy on his shipboard radio.

"The security director tells me Mr. and Mrs. Cole are having cocktails in a bar on the promenade deck right now. He will keep them under video observation and notify me if they leave."

Wu had an idea. "Do you have any plainclothes security personnel?"

Skála hesitated a beat, then shrugged. "We don't want passengers to know, but yes, we do."

"I don't want to spook the Coles. Could you get a plainclothes detail in the bar to keep an eye on them until we get there?"

Skála tapped the transmitter in his ear and conveyed the order as he headed for the door.

Wu had been on the local FBI SWAT team out of the Atlanta field office years ago and knew tactics and weapons. But he was more analytical, preferring to devise a plan of attack that included several backup options in case things went sideways.

In this case, however, the one he now considered a person of interest was trapped on a cruise ship and under surveillance. There was no reason to delay what could prove to be a critical interview.

He paused to instruct the steward to secure the cabin again before hurrying after Skála and Vega. In less than ten minutes, they had made it to deck 5, the promenade deck. They were headed to the bar when Skála tapped his ear again.

"The couple left the bar," he said, quickening his pace. "The plainclothes officers aren't there yet. The security director was monitoring them on the camera system, but he lost sight of them in a blind spot."

Wu and Vega trotted to keep up with the captain's ground-eating strides as he led them toward the other end of the massive vessel.

Suddenly, Skála uttered a harsh guttural word Wu assumed was an obscenity in Czech and broke into a run. "A passenger just reported a man and woman getting ready to jump overboard from deck 5."

CHAPTER 27

If someone had told Dani this morning that she would be on the bridge of an ocean liner in the Caribbean by the end of the day, she wouldn't have believed it.

But thirty minutes after sprinting along the promenade deck, she was standing between Wu and Skála, looking at an array of monitors.

She, Wu, and Skála had gotten to the railing seconds after Ursula and Paul Cole plunged down. Dani had scanned the frothing waves by the ship's hull at the waterline but hadn't seen them. Crew members rushed from their posts to assist, flinging life rings attached to ropes into the sea from the starboard and aft sides of the ship.

With nothing left to do on deck, Skála had escorted Dani and Wu to the bridge and introduced them to his second-in-command, Staff Captain Christos Marinakos, who had begun implementing the proper protocols upon hearing the "code Oscar" alert—code name for a passenger overboard.

Marinakos had already alerted the US Coast Guard and sent a call out to all watercraft in the area to aid in the search for the passengers. Upon Skála's arrival, he relinquished the conn to the captain and moved to face the enormous picture windows that provided a view of the water over the bow, where he began scouring the seas with an expensive set of binoculars.

"Continue bringing her about," Skála told the helmsman, who sat at a control panel covered in switches and buttons that resembled an airplane cockpit.

Marinakos had ordered the ship to stop and turn around, a maneuver that involved a vast amount of space in the water. Dani had been expecting a spinning wheel of some sort and had been surprised to see the helmsman piloting the massive vessel with a small joystick.

Dani glanced up at Skála and hesitated before bringing up the two-hundred-ton blue whale in the room. "At what point do you consider them lost at sea?"

"There is no rule about that. All I can say is I am not ready to do it yet."

She grasped his predicament. She had never heard of any luxury cruise where three passengers had jumped overboard—unless the ship was sinking. It was by no means Skála's fault, but the cruise line would probably sanction him anyway. He might even lose his command. This, of course, would be in addition to the emotional toll such a loss would inevitably take.

"I know this is difficult," Wu said to him. "I can offer you the full support of the FBI. I've already arranged for our helicopter to join the search. The Black Hawk has FLIR and other technology that could prove helpful in spotting anyone at the surface of the water."

When the captain gave him a knowing look, Dani was sure he understood what Wu hadn't said. Namely, that anyone who had sunk beneath the waves would be undetectable from the air.

"How soon will your helicopter be here?"

Wu glanced at his watch. "Less than fifteen minutes." He tipped his head toward Dani. "When the pilot is finished searching the area, he has orders to pick us up from the helipad on the ship."

Wu hadn't shared that detail with her. She had assumed they'd disembark in Puerto Rico tomorrow morning. On the other hand, this solved the problem of where to sleep.

"But what about the stateroom?" she asked him. "We still need to go through it."

"Taken care of," Wu said. "Our helicopter is bringing two technicians from the Evidence Response Team. We'll switch places."

She marveled at Wu's simple but brilliant efficiency. Tonight's helicopter flight, expensive as it was, would serve many purposes.

"So you will be leaving us soon?" Skála said to her.

She turned to him, tilting her head back to meet his gaze. "There's no time to waste."

Was she imagining things, or had the light in his gray eyes dimmed a fraction?

"Of course." He reached out to her, seemed to think better of it, and dropped his hand back to his side. "I understand."

She had never been to the Czech Republic but had heard Prague was beautiful. It might make a good vacation destination. If she ever had any time off.

CHAPTER 28

Dani and Wu were once again flying at two-thirds of Mach speed in the Gulfstream. Fortunately, their pilot seemed to take it as a challenge to see how fast she could get them from point A to point B.

While they waited for Patel to patch the team together from their three respective locations, Dani had time to reflect on the disturbing events aboard the ship.

After the Black Hawk had completed a fruitless search of the surrounding sea, the same pilot who had brought them to the ship set it down on the helipad again. She and Wu had taken the two evidence techs to Wallace's stateroom, where Dani handed over the baggie containing the envelope and card she'd collected from the table with the fruit basket.

Between Wallace's stateroom, the Coles' cabin, and the two places where they had jumped ship, the ERT would be busy until the vessel sailed into the Port of San Juan tomorrow.

After answering all their questions, Dani and Wu took their seats for the flight back to the mainland. As the bird lifted off, Dani spotted Captain Skála on the deck, dressed in his impeccable white uniform, standing apart from the rest of the crew, a solitary figure watching her departure.

When the helicopter touched down at Miami International, their pilot already had the jet fueled up and ready to go back to New York. The whole experience had been a whirlwind that reminded her of some of the ops she'd been on in the past, where they had gone from one hot spot to another with little downtime in between.

"Patel's ready," Wu said, glancing at his phone. "I'll call out the numbers."

Dani leaned forward to access the panel beneath the screen mounted to the plane's interior. As Wu read out the access code Patel had sent him, she tapped in the digits for the secure video link patching them together.

The screen split in two, with Patel on the right and Flint on the left. She had no idea how Patel managed to set up a video call between Denver, New York, and a jet in midair—with all three feeds on a rotating encryption to prevent hacking. Someone with his skills could wreak havoc on the dark web. She was glad he was on their side.

Wu opened the virtual meeting by posing a question to Flint. "Have you confirmed the explosion was rigged?"

"Affirmative," Flint said. "With all the technical expertise on the scene, it didn't take long to find trace evidence of additional wiring connected to the front doorbell. They believe it sent a signal to a device beside the gas line in the basement."

Dani couldn't imagine what had gone through the scientist's mind as he realized what was happening. "Any idea how he got himself into this fix?" she said. "Was it just because he might know Tina Castillo's whereabouts, or was he involved with something else?"

"I spoke to his current boss at JVF Research Laboratory," Flint said. "He couldn't shed any light on the situation. Neither could Easton's ex-wife or his adult daughter, who both live in Texas. There's no sign that his current position would make him a target, and he didn't have any habits like gambling that might have caused problems."

"What's his field of expertise?" Wu asked.

"He's a mechanical engineer. Got his PhD from Stanford, then was hired by Exmyth out of a postdoctoral research program twenty years ago. He worked there until he was recruited to come to New York."

Wu turned to Patel. "What did you find at Exmyth?"

"I started working with the CFO as soon as I got here," he said. "He was helpful at first, then developed a case of amnesia. There's definitely some bullshit going on with the books." He grinned. "He thought I couldn't get through the firewalls, but I ventilated them in about twenty minutes."

So the person in charge of finances was hiding something. Interesting.

"What's Dr. Wallace's specialty?" she asked him.

"He's a chemical engineer," Patel said.

She combined the new facts with what they knew about Dr. Castillo. "Two types of engineering and quantum physics. What were those three up to?"

"All the data surrounding their work was deleted, so I couldn't tell. But the fact that someone did a surgical removal of those files—along with their personnel files—means I know where to look first."

Dani considered the ramifications. Information about the research and the scientists who conducted it had been systematically removed. Someone was hiding something and leaving a trail of bodies in their wake.

"Can you recover the deleted files?" Wu asked.

Looking aggrieved, Patel put a hand to his chest. "I'm genuinely hurt."

"I'll change the question," Wu said. "How long will it take you to recover the files?"

"Sterling did a decent job of purging the stuff from the system. He took the extra step of digitally shredding the computer files and physically shredding the physical documents."

"You say Sterling did it personally?"

"It's up for debate, but he came in early this morning before everyone else got here. His card was used to get in, and the files were accessed using a fingerprint and retina scanner that matched his." He raised a brow. "And before you ask, his body still had all his digits and both of his eyeballs."

"Why is it up for debate?"

"Because all the video cameras were shut down remotely just before his arrival."

Dani made the assumption that Sterling wasn't alone, which led her to the next question. "There hasn't been time for an autopsy, but do the detectives think whoever was with Sterling also killed him?"

"A couple of them think Sterling deliberately overdosed on his heart medication, but the general consensus is that it was a murder staged to look like suicide."

They would get more information after a forensic analysis.

"What about the search of his home?"

"Everyone's still there. They haven't found anything of interest yet, but they're mirroring his PC for me. I'm also mirroring the system here so I can keep investigating remotely if you need me to come back to New York."

Wu nodded. "I'll need you back at 26 Fed. Right now, your top priority is to find out whatever you can about Tina Castillo and figure out what her team of scientists was working on. Someone is going to a lot of trouble to cover their tracks."

Dani phrased it another way. "Someone is cleaning house."

CHAPTER 29

Dani had just switched off the live feed to end the three-way video call when Wu's phone chimed with a text. He pulled it out and glanced down at the message and groaned.

Had someone else died? "Bad news?"

"Hargrave." He stood and walked down the aisle toward the rear of the plane. "I'll be back." He made his way through a partition separating a small private office and closed the door behind him.

She wasn't surprised Wu wanted to talk to the assistant director alone. During the only personal interaction she'd had with Hargrave, his suspicious attitude toward her had bordered on hostile.

She decided to make use of the time alone to come up with ideas about how to locate Tina Castillo. A nagging voice in the back of her mind warned her the scientist might already be dead. In fact, she might have died anytime in the past several months after Toro made the video.

The thought of Toro's video gave her an idea. She could spend the remaining hour of the flight reviewing his statements. There hadn't been a lot of time for careful analysis given their hectic pursuit of the scientists. Maybe she'd missed something.

With luck, Patel might still be available through his laptop if she entered the passcode to reestablish the comm link. Worth a try. She reached out and switched the system on.

The FBI seal took up the entire screen as Wu's voice came through the small speaker. "If you'd give me a chance to explain, I could—"

Assistant Director Scott Hargrave's distinctive voice cut him off. "I don't want to hear any excuses. You've made headlines around the world. That little stunt of yours with the helicopter landing on the cruise ship? Most people don't even know the FBI has Black Hawks . . . and we intended to keep it that way."

What the hell? She had assumed Wu was speaking to Hargrave over the phone, but they had opted for a video call. The plane's comm system had two linked terminals, but she was getting only the audio.

She shouldn't be hearing this. Her boss clearly wanted privacy. She stretched out her hand to turn off her terminal.

"I should never have approved Agent Vega for this case," Hargrave's disembodied voice continued through the speaker.

She froze. Why was the assistant director in charge of the New York field office talking about her? And why had he been warning her boss about her? She felt horrible for doing it, but she stayed put and made no move to tell Wu she could hear the entire conversation.

Hargrave plowed on. "Every case she's involved in ends up with a news conference and a body count. She's trouble. And you have zero objectivity when it comes to her."

"Vega's one of my best," Wu said. "She's unconventional, but she gets results, and—"

"And she's young, single, and good looking," Hargrave finished for him. "Come on, Steve. I have eyes."

She felt her jaw slacken. The assistant director had just implied her boss was attracted to her. Was it possible? He was a consummate professional, and she was within his chain of command and therefore off-limits. Even if that weren't the case, he was handsome, sophisticated, and articulate. She was rough around the edges with a bit of a potty mouth. How could he find her remotely appealing? No, Hargrave had it wrong. Or was he trying to jam Wu up somehow?

Wu's voice took on an edge she'd never heard before. "Agent Vega is on this case because of her prior relationship with Gustavo Toro, nothing more."

"Speaking of which," Hargrave said, switching gears, "Toro was involved in things that are only now beginning to come to light. You've started a chain reaction that's gone all the way to the director."

If Dani were a better person, she would turn it off. But she wasn't. So she kept listening.

"What are you talking about?" Wu asked, his tone shifting from defensive to wary.

"The husband and wife who jumped ship," Hargrave said. "We can't find any trace of them in any database. You know what that means?"

"Their identities are fake. And they have a powerful organization behind them to backstop the aliases well enough that we can't penetrate them."

"Precisely. And who springs to mind?"

If Hargrave had posed the question to Dani, her response would have been simple. A highly sophisticated rogue organization.

Wu had reached a similar conclusion. "Foreign or domestic," he said simply. "Either way, we're dealing with a serious threat."

"I can't risk saying more, even on an encrypted comm link," Hargrave said. "Just get your ass to DC tonight. Director Franklin wants to see you in his office to answer for this clusterfuck personally."

"We're headed to LaGuardia. We'll be landing at nine and—"

"Tell the pilot to put in a request for a stop at Reagan National before resuming the original flight plan to LaGuardia. Agent Vega can continue on to New York," Hargrave said. "Use my name if you get any pushback from air traffic control."

"Yes, sir."

"I took the train to DC earlier today, so I'll be in Director Franklin's office too. We'll both be waiting for you, and we expect answers."

Dani heard a stream of obscenities coming from Wu and assumed Hargrave had disconnected the link. She quickly turned off the comm system. Ten seconds later, when the door to the rear office opened, she was busying herself and pretending she hadn't overheard the ass chewing.

"Change of plans," Wu said to her. "We're stopping in DC so I can brief the director. You'll continue to LaGuardia in the jet. I'll advise the pilot."

Dani studied her boss, who had his professional mask firmly in place. Had she not overheard the brief conversation, she would have had no idea that Wu had been taken to task, mostly due to her, and was about to be so again.

She wasn't interested in climbing the ranks, but she understood that the stakes for Wu were as high as possible. He was risking his reputation, and quite likely the trajectory of his career, on this case. And she played a large role in its success or failure.

"Director Franklin has questions," Wu continued. "And I need to answer them in person. I'll find a way back to New York as soon as possible. Meanwhile, you all can make headway on this investigation." He paused, then added, "Before we get shut down."

She realized her boss was using himself as a kind of human shield, protecting the team from incoming attacks while they went about their business.

Her estimation of Steve Wu continued to rise. He was the type of leader that often went unappreciated. She'd seen it in the military as well. Those with courage and vision were sometimes shunted to the side by others who lacked those qualities. Those who viewed them as threats. She could only hope Director Franklin would see the truth, no matter how Assistant Director Hargrave tried to shade it.

She could say none of this, of course. Not without giving away the fact that she'd listened in on his private conversation.

Wu dragged a hand through his thick, dark hair. "This is now a race to find Tina Castillo." His dark eyes found hers. "And you'd damned well better get there first."

CHAPTER 30

Undisclosed location

Foley opened his laptop to check on the situation. Alarmed, he scrolled backward through various time stamps to see what was going on.

Vega and Wu had been on a flight from Miami to New York. So why had the plane stopped at Reagan National Airport in DC for twenty minutes before continuing to its original destination?

His instincts told him this was about to get ugly. He hated loose ends, and now he had two more.

Not only had the operatives burned their identities as Paul and Ursula Cole, but they might have left enough DNA to reveal their true names if there was a problem with the full-spectrum decontamination spray.

One of their subsidiary chemical companies was developing an oxygenated liquid formula that could be easily atomized to disperse over a wide area, destroying all DNA. They had used it in their cabin before making their way to the promenade deck. Fortunately, they had remembered to take it with them over the railing so it wouldn't be recovered by CSI types later.

But he couldn't be certain it had worked, and if he didn't deal with the situation swiftly, their real identities might ultimately expose the corporation.

He brought his fist down on the desk, succeeding only in hurting his hand. But the momentary pain focused his mind on the current problem.

Damage control.

He could not change the past, but he could damn well change the future. To accomplish this, he would operate in the realm of worst-case scenarios. If he prepared for that, anything less would be easy. So what was the worst case for this mission?

The Feds were going to test the card that had come with the fruit basket for fingerprints. They wouldn't find any, of course, but they might spot the tiny listening device that had been slipped inside the wrapped basket. The operative who posed as Ursula was one of his best, and she had a knack for opening letters, packages, and parcels without leaving any sign of a disturbance.

The bug had allowed him to hear everything Captain Skála, Daniela Vega, and Steve Wu said when they were in Wallace's stateroom. Ursula and Paul had also been listening and had already sprayed their cabin and prepped their gear when he ordered them to enact the backup plan.

He could mop up the situation with his operatives, but he could not control what the FBI did with the evidence they had recovered from the scene. Right now, Agent Vega was in possession of material that could blow their whole operation. And she didn't even understand the real significance of the card she had collected.

Perhaps she should have an accident before she or her boss realized what they had.

Considering this, he reflected on Ursula and Paul. He doubted if anyone knew about the technology they had used to make their escape.

When no one spotted them bobbing in the waves, everyone would assume the pair had been dragged under in the ship's wake and drowned. To further confuse rescuers, Ursula and Paul had instructions to swim east, farther out to sea, rather than head for the shore.

Foley had deployed their own retrieval craft, designed to appear like a deep-sea fishing boat. The skipper would use an underwater transponder to send out a beacon to guide the two operatives directly to him. When the coast was clear, he'd pull them aboard and provide them with disguises and new IDs before discreetly ferrying them to a private marina.

That had been the original plan anyway, but the FBI plane's unexpected stop in Washington had prompted him to reevaluate the situation. Ursula and Paul had drawn attention to themselves—and therefore to the organization. The boss paid his contractors top dollar. In exchange, he demanded complete silence and absolute discretion. Ursula and Paul had failed in both categories, so their usefulness had come to an end.

Time to trim more loose ends.

He picked up the phone and tapped in a number.

"Yes, sir."

"Your mission parameters have changed," he said to the skipper. "From search and rescue to catch and kill."

CHAPTER 31

Wu was well aware Director Franklin did not suffer fools gladly. And Assistant Director Hargrave was going out of his way to make Wu appear as foolish as possible.

The three men sat at a round table in the far corner of the director's office in the J. Edgar Hoover Building in Washington. The meeting had barely gotten underway, and it was already going badly.

Hargrave opened his laptop. "I'd like you to see something." He rotated it so the screen faced Wu. "This was posted on YouTube. It's gone viral."

A YouTube video of the Black Hawk landing on the ship filled the screen. He scanned the title at the top of the screen.

AGENTS CHASE COUPLE TO THEIR DEATHS

WARNING: VIEWER DISCRETION ADVISED

Wu braced himself for the worst as the YouTuber, who sounded like a frat guy on spring break, narrated in the background.

"Guys, check this out. Looks like one of those black-ops helicopters you see in movies, right? Wait. People are getting out. Oh man, those two gotta be secret agents or something. What the hell are they doing here? Maybe there's a spy on the ship or something . . . or . . . oh shit, maybe this is about that dude who went overboard last night."

The video cut to Ursula and Paul Cole climbing onto the railing on the promenade deck. The footage was shot from an upper deck, affording a bird's-eye view of the scenario.

"This day just keeps getting weirder. Now it looks like those two might jump. Hold on, they're strapping something onto their faces. If anyone knows what that is, put it in the comments and I'll pin it to the top of the feed."

Despite the severity of his situation, Wu's curiosity was piqued. He also couldn't identify what Ursula and Paul were securing over their mouths. They reached down toward their feet, and Wu assumed they were going to pull off their shoes to help them swim better when the angle of the shot shifted. Now Wu, Vega, and the captain could be seen running along the opposite end of the promenade deck toward the couple.

The narrator's voice grew excited. "It's those agents from the helicopter." The video panned back to the couple, just in time to see them launch themselves into the air and drop out of sight. Then the railing was empty. "What the actual fuck?" Frat Guy said. "They must've done some serious shit to jump ship."

Hargrave tapped the screen to stop the video and raised an expectant brow at Wu.

"We didn't chase them to their deaths," Wu said, not troubling to hide his frustration. "The title was clickbait. It's not what happened."

"The truth is that no one knows what really happened," Hargrave said. "Because their bodies haven't been found."

"Not for lack of trying. The captain did everything by the book. The Coast Guard was there in twenty minutes, and the helicopter wasn't far behind."

"There's reason to believe they made it to safety," Hargrave said. "Did you see what they were doing before they jumped?"

"Putting something over their mouths."

This time, the director filled him in. "It's a new kind of underwater breathing apparatus. A completely tankless rebreather that filters oxygen directly from the water. In fact, it's so cutting edge that it's classified. As of now, SEAL Team Six is testing it. No one else has any knowledge of its existence. At least, they didn't before now."

Hargrave scowled. "I'm sure our adversaries will get to work either stealing or reverse engineering the equipment—and they'll have a good idea how to do it."

Exactly how this was his fault Wu didn't know, but it seemed Hargrave was determined to lay the exposure of highly classified technology at his feet. "You're saying they never resurfaced because they could swim underwater indefinitely."

Franklin nodded. "Eventually, fatigue would set in, but yes, they could get far away from where the ship was, especially with those retractable fins."

"Fins?"

"Video forensics isolated the frames when the pair jumped," Franklin said. "Flippers had extended from the fronts of their shoes. That's another black project under development by a military contractor."

"They came into this situation well funded and well prepared with contingency plans," Hargrave said. "They had to get all that equipment past security."

Wu shared what he'd learned from ship's security. "Screening personnel mainly check for weapons, drugs, and alcohol during embarkation.

Not stuff that probably looked like fancy diving equipment. We can't find either of their names on any flight manifests arriving in Miami before the cruise. They could have used aliases to travel, but we also haven't found anyone who bought a round-trip ticket and didn't make the outgoing flight. It's possible they're based in Florida and drove to the Port of Miami."

"What about face rec?"

Wu had already directed Patel to check. "Another problem. Their faces aren't in any database anywhere. No driver's licenses, no social media, no criminal records. They're ghosts."

"Or they've been scrubbed," Franklin said. "What about their names?"

"Same thing. It's as if they never existed."

Very few organizations had the ability to expunge data so thoroughly that even the FBI couldn't find any trace of them.

Wu looked for any advantage he could find. "If the tech was so tightly controlled, we should be able to contact the developer and work our way down a list of everyone who had access to it. That should yield their names."

"We're already doing that," Franklin said. "But we have to work through the DIA, so it's taking longer than I'd like."

The Defense Intelligence Agency was the military equivalent to the CIA and would have direct access to all classified military contractors, subcontractors, and records involving any branch that was currently testing equipment. Wu could imagine the bureaucracy involved with pulling that information from classified files.

Franklin went on, "In fact, I'm having to push back on the DIA right now. The other two scientists had worked on projects with military applications in the past. They're highly concerned that this is a concerted effort to undermine our security and military response capability."

"Do they have an idea who's behind it?" Wu asked. "Are they accusing anyone?"

"Foreign actors, domestic terrorists, rogue nations." Franklin waved vaguely. "The usual suspects. Nothing specific, but they want a full briefing on our investigation up to this point."

"There's more you don't know," Hargrave said, showing every sign of relishing Wu's discomfort. "I personally contacted the lab in Miami to get the results of their testing. They didn't find any latent prints on the card collected from Dr. Wallace's stateroom, but they ran it through more processing and found something else."

The fact that Hargrave had gone to extraordinary lengths to be the first with pertinent information—and that he'd chosen this moment to bring it up—meant whatever he'd learned would cause trouble. At this point, any comment or question might sound like weakness or fear, so Wu made no response.

Franklin turned to Hargrave. "You need to read SAC Wu in."

They'd already informed him about the diving gear, so what else were they about to share?

"There was a toxin on the card," Hargrave said, no longer playing out the suspense. "It's called Z-94E, and it causes hallucinations, paranoia, and delusions."

Wu searched his memory and came up blank. "Never heard of it."

"That's because it wasn't supposed to leave the facility where it was developed," Hargrave said. "In fact, it's a by-product of chem-bio research being done by a private contractor. They were researching toxins our soldiers were exposed to overseas. They wanted to reverse engineer it to find an antidote to be used in the field. Instead, they inadvertently created this substrate. It's proven to be far worse. They tested it on some volunteers and had to restrain them to prevent them from killing themselves until the drug wore off. The most challenging thing was that it was slow to act and slow to leave the system, requiring about eight hours total."

Wu thought he knew where this was going. "If this wasn't supposed to leave the lab, only a limited number of people would have been able to deploy it."

"Exactly," Hargrave said. "And that's the problem. The lab is located in New Jersey. We have a team there now going through their records. All samples were supposed to be destroyed, but some were smuggled out."

The sheer brilliance of the operation sank in. "Wallace jumped into the ocean. There can't be an autopsy that would link his death to the toxin. He's on camera voluntarily jumping, so it looks like a suicide. The toxin was only on the card that was sealed inside the envelope, and even if the steward did take it out to put it on the table, they always wear gloves. So does the staff that cleans the rooms, so they wouldn't be affected when they cleaned up the stateroom after Wallace's death. Everything would go into the incinerator."

He had learned that the ship incinerated garbage so it would take up less space before disposing of it after returning to port.

Franklin said, "The entire incident would have been written off, and no one would have ever known."

"Except now we do," Wu said. "And judging by everything else that has happened, we have to assume they know that we know."

"Which still puts them a step ahead," Hargrave was quick to add. "They have time to do damage control . . . maybe."

Franklin sighed. "Someone working at the lab in Jersey might be about to have an unfortunate accident."

"This is sounding more cloak-and-dagger every minute," Wu said. "Who would risk so much to get to the stash of evidence Gustavo Toro's hiding?"

"The treasure he keeps talking about." Franklin gave his head a small shake. "Whoever's after it is spending a fortune to find it, which means they're implicated. But we're just speculating. We need facts."

"I plan to get those facts, sir."

"I'd like you back with the team to do that," Franklin said. "This investigation is highly sensitive, and the implications are far reaching. I need a high-ranking executive there, and your work in counterterrorism makes you the best fit. But you have another assignment before you leave Washington."

"Sir?"

He regarded Wu a long moment before continuing. "As of now, the team coordinating the investigation in New York consists of Agent Vega, Detective Flint, and Analyst Patel, correct?" When Wu nodded, he continued, "That puts Vega—a junior agent—in charge by default, and I'm not comfortable with that."

Hargrave hurried to agree, and Wu ignored him, keeping his attention on Franklin.

"Sir, I can catch the next flight to New York after I'm finished with whatever I need to do here," he offered. "Until then, Agent Vega has my full confidence. She's proven herself to be capable, resourceful, and—"

"It's like I was telling you," Hargrave said to Franklin. "He's lost all perspective when it comes to Vega."

Franklin eyed Wu with a calculating expression, as if weighing the merits of the implied accusation.

Wu had heard enough. If he didn't shut the assistant director down hard, he would continue to undermine Wu at every chance he got—and he would have plenty of opportunities.

He slowly turned his coldest glare on Hargrave. "If you have something to report about my conduct, do it now. If not, then stop with the innuendos . . . sir."

Hargrave appeared startled for a moment before he recovered. "I didn't mean to imply—"

"You damn well did. And I won't put up with it."

"Gentlemen," Franklin said. "We're all professionals here." He turned to Wu. "When I mentioned the military wanting a briefing on our investigation earlier, I was referring to a meeting scheduled at the

Pentagon tomorrow morning. All three of us will be there, but you'll be taking their questions. I suggest you get a good night's sleep and come up with as many answers as you can."

Hargrave said, "That means Agent Vega will be on point even longer."

"It's not ideal, but she'll have to manage," Franklin said, then regarded Wu thoughtfully. "We'll probably be at the Pentagon for two or three hours, then I'm flying out to Los Angeles for an afternoon meeting as soon as we're finished." One silvery brow lifted. "I can ask the pilot to make a quick stop at LaGuardia on the way."

Suddenly, his fatigue evaporated. "Thank you, sir." He'd be back in New York a lot faster.

Franklin shifted his gaze to Hargrave. "For the duration of this assignment, SAC Wu will report directly to me."

Hargrave started to object, checked himself, and snapped his mouth shut. Not only had his campaign to torpedo Wu failed, but it had backfired, making him appear petty and vindictive.

Wu didn't know the director well, but he was getting the impression that Franklin was an excellent judge of character.

CHAPTER 32

9:00 p.m.
Bellevue Hospital, Manhattan, New York

Dani thanked Dr. Maffuccio again. It was thirty minutes past visiting hours, but her mother's treating psychiatrist had allowed her to bring her brother and sister for a family visit.

Wu was in Washington dealing with whatever the assistant director had in store for him. Flint and Patel had already gone home for the night, informing her they would all meet early the following day. This might be her last chance to see her mother until this bizarre case was resolved.

She hated being away from her family when her mother was in such a delicate state. Camila was showing signs of improvement but still needed constant care. Convinced her presence would speed her mother's recovery, Dani had called the hospital shortly before she landed to beg for permission to come.

The main reason Dr. Maffuccio had accommodated the request was because Camila had been lucid for the past hour and was asking to see her children. This was a major step, and everyone wanted to support the patient's progress.

Dani felt sure the other reason was Erica. Her younger sister could charm anyone. Warm and loving, she had connected with the staff at Bellevue during her visits over the years.

No one would ever describe Dani as charming. Or warm. Or loving. She was a warrior by training and by nature. Like her Army Ranger dad.

And then there was Camila Vega. Dani had never fully understood how her mother's mind worked, even before her mental break. Now that Dani had reconnected with her, she was able to perceive things they had in common. Growing up, she'd seen her mother working on all kinds of puzzles. She was also the one who always watched mystery and detective shows on TV with Dani. They raced each other to see who could figure out whodunit faster.

"What are you smiling about?" her sister asked.

She gestured to Camila. "I was thinking of all the times Mom let me stay up late to watch *Columbo* reruns."

Camila's face lit up. "I remember. Old shows, but good shows."

She grinned. "*Columbo*'s timeless."

Erica shook her head. "I seem to recall a few arguments. You and Mom wanted to watch a crime show, I wanted a rom-com, and Axel wanted sci-fi."

This time, Camila actually laughed at the mention of the bickering over the only television they owned. Dani hadn't heard her mother laugh in the decade since her father died. It was a sweet, melodious sound she hadn't realized how much she'd missed.

At the sound of a sniffle, she turned to see Erica's eyes brimming with tears and Axel smiling. They, too, had been deprived of that particular joy for much of their young lives.

Their father's death, combined with their mother's institutionalization, had left a gaping hole in their family structure that could never be fully repaired. Dani's heart ached most for Erica and Axel, whose childhoods had ended far too soon.

A part of her longed to reclaim the past. They had all been effectively orphaned, and Dani wished she could have the chance to go back in time and be there for them more than she had. Of course, she was no longer a seventeen-year-old girl. Now she was an adult with a career and her own place, but she had missed her chance to nurture them as they grew.

They were both legally adults charting their own course. Any guidance, support, or comfort she could provide was no longer needed.

Despite the joy of the moment, she suddenly felt an emptiness inside. An ache she couldn't quite define.

A small birdlike hand took hers, and she looked into her mother's soulful eyes.

Damn. She didn't think Camila was still able to read her anymore. She had always been able to sense others' pain, a trait Erica shared.

"Problem?" Camila asked.

Dani gave her mother's hand a gentle squeeze. "Something at the office," she said. "It's nothing."

Camila raised a skeptical brow, and Dani was reminded that she'd never been able to lie to her mother and get away with it.

Camila dropped her hand, and Dani was worried she'd offended her mother. She had started to say something when Camila grabbed her hand again and pressed something into her palm.

Dani glanced down at the folded scrap of art paper her mother had given her. "What's this?"

Receiving no answer, she unfolded the paper to see a beautiful multicolored design.

"That's beautiful," Erica said, crowding in close.

"That's geometry," Axel said from her other side.

They were both right. And she could appreciate the pattern carefully rendered in the image. "Thank you," she said, refolding and tucking it behind her creds. She didn't want to stuff it in her pocket and forget it was there until it was destroyed in the wash.

Camila's eyes glazed over as she retreated into the dark recesses of her mind. "Let us not be weary in well doing, for in due season we shall reap, if we faint not."

Dani sighed. Their brief visit had come to an end. She only wished she could understand whatever her mother had been trying to communicate.

CHAPTER 33

Dani didn't know humans could type that fast. Patel had to be doing over 120 words per minute, and a lot of it was code. How could he keep it all straight in his head?

She had met Flint and Patel, who had taken a red-eye from Denver to New York, in the private conference room connected to the SAC's office only minutes ago. After a fortifying round of coffee, they had immediately gotten to work. Wu was counting on them to make progress while he was in Washington in the hot seat, and she was determined to do her part.

"I found this yesterday morning," Patel said. "The boss asked me to review Toro's videos and the rental contract he signed for the security box at the Toltec."

An image of the contract appeared on the wall screen opposite them.

Patel continued as he navigated on his connected laptop. "After the morning was literally blown to shit, I never had a chance to tell you all about it. I mean, it's a small thing, but I've learned not to take anything for granted on this case."

Flint studied the wall screen. "What did you find?"

In response, Patel zoomed in until the driver's license Toro had used with the name Geraldo Trujillo took up the whole screen.

"Looks legit," Flint said. "He must have paid a high price for this kind of quality fake."

Dani asked, "Did you find out if the listed address is real, or if he has any connection with it?"

"It's a real address, but I think he chose it at random after checking a Google map of neighborhoods in Des Moines. I did a complete rundown on the elderly widow who lives there. She's into quilting, canasta, and church bake-offs. No way is she colluding with an international hit man."

"Or it's the perfect cover," Flint said, deadpan. "Maybe Granny's smuggling weapons in the quilts or drugs in the apple pies."

They shared a chuckle before Patel zoomed in tighter on the bottom of the license. "This was where I ran across a problem."

Capital letters DD were followed by a string of letters and numbers.

"What does DD stand for?" Flint asked.

"I had to look it up. It's an abbreviation for Document Discriminator, a security code some states have started putting on driver's licenses to indicate when and where they were produced." He glanced up at them. "I checked the database, and this number is bogus."

"It's a fake ID," Flint said. "Of course it would be a fake number."

Patel shook his head. "No. Everything else on the license is formatted precisely to look like the real thing. This isn't even in the ballpark, but the print is so tiny and it's all the way down at the bottom, plus most people don't even know what it is, so it wouldn't draw attention."

Dani had stopped listening. She was totally focused on the wall screen as she studied the row of characters.

DD X455214Y3702855

Flint followed her gaze. "Toro could've just put in a string of random—"

"I don't think he did," Dani said, then turned to Patel. "You found the hidden hacker-speak code Toro put on the contract. Now I think you've found the hidden code he put on the driver's license he used."

She could feel the intensity of their stares. "I'm not one hundred percent sure I'm right, but you can help me find out."

"Must be nice to have all that codebreaker training from the military," Flint said. "I don't see squat in that line of letters and numbers."

She smiled. "If I'm right, it has nothing to do with my cryptanalysis skills. But it has everything to do with having been in the Army." She pointed at the screen. "To me, those look like coordinates."

"Latitude and longitude?" Patel frowned. "Where are the degrees and minutes, and the compass directions? That's not the right format."

"Apparently, you ignore the DD, since that part belongs on the driver's license, and focus on the part that doesn't. See the X and Y mixed in?" When they nodded, she went on. "Think of that as the X and Y axis, but X is called 'easting' and Y is called 'northing.'" She pointed the letters out on the screen.

DD X455214Y3702855

"So you plot it like a graph?" Patel asked.

"The system was developed during World War II by the US Army Corps of Engineers. It's called Universal Transverse Mercator, or UTM, and the Army eventually adopted the system after a few tweaks."

"So that's why you saw it," Flint said. "But would Toro know about it?"

"It's not a secret or anything. There's no reason he wouldn't. No special skills involved." She shrugged. "He probably wanted a series of numbers that wouldn't obviously look like coordinates."

"I found a UTM mapping site online." Patel's fingers were flashing over the keys. "Entering in the X and Y now."

As he typed, the map shifted to the right and began to zoom in on North America. Dani had the sensation of parachuting out of a plane as she seemed to be falling to the ground with dizzying speed.

When the image finally came to a halt, she had a bird's-eye view of a swath of Arizona desert. They all waited a few seconds before Patel split the screen. On the left was the Google Earth image. On the right was a professional photograph of a saguaro cactus with brown-beige mountains in the background. Printed bold letters lined the bottom.

LOST DUTCHMAN STATE PARK

"That can't be right," Flint said. "Tina Castillo can't live in a public park—at least not legally and not for five years. And Toro wouldn't hide his treasure there either. Anyone could stumble across it."

"I know," Patel said. "But this is where the coordinates took us."

She wasn't ready to give up on her theory yet. "Lost Dutchman is a strange name for a park. What's the history?"

Patel was already on it before she finished the question. While he sorted through various sites, she contemplated the possibilities. One was that she was simply wrong. It wouldn't be the first time. But what if she'd been correct? What did it mean?

Patel sat back in his chair. "Un-fucking believable." He looked up at her. "You were right. Lost Dutchman State Park is in the Sonoran Desert at the base of the Superstition Mountains, which are in Pinal County, Arizona, east of Phoenix."

"Superstition," Dani repeated. She recalled hearing Toro use the word in one of the videos she reviewed on the flight yesterday. "What's the connection?"

The wall screen flickered, and the image of a flat-topped mountain appeared. It was like nothing Dani had ever seen. The mountain itself was cast in hues of purple, with white snow dusting the top. The sides looked like they'd been gouged, and the base of the mountain was in a dusty beige desert dotted with brush.

"These are the Superstition Mountains," Patel said.

"And?" Flint prompted.

They waited while Patel scrolled down his screen.

"Okay, this is where it starts to get weird," he said after speed-reading another minute. "The search connected a bunch of words, but it gets into the area of folklore rather than fact."

Flint waved off his concerns. "Let's hear it anyway."

"There's the legend of the Lost Dutchman's Mine," Patel said. "Back in the eighteen hundreds, a prospector named Jacob Waltz claimed he found a gold mine in the mountains." He frowned. "But it didn't end well for him . . . or anyone else who went looking for the mine, which is now said to be cursed."

Dani had no patience with superstition, curses, or creepy stories, but one part of the tale intrigued her. "Toro referred to his stash of evidence as a treasure. That must be related to this somehow."

Patel nodded. "According to legend, Waltz located a gold vein with the purest ore ever found in Arizona."

"Who's the Dutchman?" Flint asked. "Was Waltz from the Netherlands?"

Patel chuckled. "He emigrated from Germany, but the locals misunderstood when he said he was from Deutschland. With his accent, they thought he was saying he was a Dutchman."

"I take it no one knows where the mine is anymore?" Dani said. "So it's lost?"

Patel nodded. "And plenty of people have died trying to find it."

"Shouldn't it be called the Dutchman's Lost Mine?" Flint said. "The Lost Dutchman's Mine makes it sound like the prospector went missing." He shrugged. "I'm just saying."

"But Toro gave us the coordinates for the park, presumably because no one knows where the mine is. So what are we looking for?"

"Jacob Waltz died in 1891, so it's not him," Flint said. "We're supposed to find Tina Castillo."

"Maybe she's a descendant?" Patel asked. "There must be more to the location."

Flint said, "It's a clue all right, but we're not seeing the answer."

She agreed. "Maybe because we need to go to Lost Dutchman Park to see it."

CHAPTER 34

Wu was inside one of the largest office buildings in the world, standing among some of the most powerful people on the planet.

It should have been a heady experience, but instead he was wary. Among the military and law enforcement upper echelon were a couple of civilians in business suits. Their visitor passes marked them as government contractors with top-secret clearances, but what were they doing here?

A sergeant emerged from behind a closed door and snapped a salute before making an announcement to the small crowd. "The SCIF will open in five minutes at oh-eight-thirty hours. Your seats have your names on them."

This morning's meeting had been deemed confidential enough to warrant a sensitive compartmented information facility, a SCIF, where they could discuss highly classified subjects in a completely secure area.

The sergeant stood at attention beside the door, which had closed again, presumably prepared to open it at the correct time and not one second sooner.

"Ready with your answers?" Director Franklin asked him.

The director's driver had stopped at their hotel to pick up Wu and Hargrave, allowing them an opportunity to discuss the likely questions they would field and strategize responses on the way from DC to the Pentagon.

"Yes, sir." He shifted his gaze to Hargrave, who was having an animated conversation with a businessman with perfectly barbered hair wearing a custom-tailored Italian suit. "Can I assume the contractors are here because they designed the classified tech?"

Franklin nodded. "They're best qualified to track down where the couple on the cruise ship got it."

Wu was about to pose another question when his cell phone buzzed in his pocket. "I have to take this," he said, glancing at the screen. "It's Agent Vega."

"Let's hope she's made some headway," Franklin said, stepping away to give him privacy.

Wu turned his back to the milling group and held the phone to his ear. "SAC Wu."

"We've had a break."

"Talk to me."

He listened closely as Vega outlined a bizarre series of discoveries that led to a state park in the Arizona Sonoran Desert. She was in full flow about a Gold Rush–era prospector and a cursed mine lost to history when he interrupted her.

"I'm about to go into a SCIF."

He didn't need to say more. Vega would understand that no cell phones, tablets, laptops, or smart glasses and watches were permitted inside. In fact, the sergeant posted at the door had started to beckon meeting attendees over to an electronics deposit area where they had to secure their devices before the meeting.

"I'll make it quick," Vega said. "We need to fly out to Arizona as soon as possible."

"You're asking for the jet." He made it a statement.

"Toro gave us those coordinates for a reason. This part of Arizona is a four-and-a-half-hour drive from Las Vegas. Toro could have easily made it there and back in the same day. Anyone who knew he was at the Toltec wouldn't realize he was gone at all."

"I need more to go on to authorize that kind of expense."

"We'll use the travel time to keep working," she pursued. "Patel is just as effective at thirty thousand feet as he is on the ground."

True enough, but Wu wasn't satisfied. "We still have two main objectives. We find Tina Castillo and protect her, and we locate the stash of evidence Toro concealed. You already admitted it won't likely be in a public park on state-owned land."

"I understand, sir."

She sounded somewhat deflated, but he had to bring her around to the realities of their situation. They did not have an unlimited budget or resources. Franklin wanted the bulk of the investigation to be restricted to a small group, so they couldn't chase every hint of a lead.

"Give me something solid," he said to her, "and I'll get you whatever you need."

"But your meeting, it—"

"Call me anyway. If I don't answer, leave a message. I'll check my phone on every break and when the meeting's over." He glanced at the sergeant, who was giving him a pointed look. "I have to go."

He disconnected and had started toward the sergeant when a heavy hand landed on his shoulder. He turned to see Hargrave.

"The director made it clear he wasn't comfortable with Agent Vega leading the team," Hargrave said. "And you're ready to authorize an expensive flight across the country if she comes up with an excuse to make the trip."

Hargrave had stopped talking to the contractor and sidled his way behind Wu to eavesdrop on his half of the phone conversation. He felt his blood pressure rising but forced his features to show no sign of irritation.

"I'm not sure if you were able to hear Agent Vega's side of the discussion, but they've had a breakthrough that needs further investigation."

Hargrave reddened slightly. "I mostly heard what you said, but it was enough to know that—once again—you're allowing her far too much leeway for a junior agent."

"She may be new to the Bureau, but she's seen combat and made plenty of life-and-death decisions."

Hargrave had the look of a hunter who had caught a wolf in his trap. "Exactly. It's her background in combat that makes her a liability to us. We are not a military operation, and yet she's too quick to revert to her military training. She has a foot in each world, and you can't see it . . . or you won't see it."

The implication, once again, hung in the air between them. Having learned his lesson, this time Hargrave didn't speak his accusation out loud. But he didn't have to.

Wu would have challenged him further, but they were out of time, so he played his trump card. "Director Franklin asked me to report directly to him going forward. I don't need to discuss this with you."

Hargrave bristled. "The jet assigned to the New York field office is still under my purview, and I'll be the one to decide how it's used." He signaled the sergeant, who had seen to the collection of everyone else's electronics. "Take SAC Wu's cell phone."

The sergeant blinked. "Sir?"

"SAC Wu is expecting time-sensitive information critical to our meeting. If he gets a text or a phone call from Agent Daniela Vega from the FBI, interrupt our meeting and let him know. He will take the call or the message immediately."

"You want me to interrupt the meeting?"

Apparently, this was not standard operating procedure.

Wu said, "It's okay, Sergeant, I'll—"

"It's not okay," Hargrave said, voice rising. "This is urgent, and we need the information without delay." With an almost imperceptible flick of a glance between their visitor identification badges, the sergeant discerned that an assistant director in charge outranked a special agent in charge. Steeped in military protocol, he made his decision in less than a second.

"Yes, sir," he said to Hargrave and held his hand out to Wu.

With Director Franklin already inside, he admitted a temporary defeat and laid his cell phone on the sergeant's open palm.

Hargrave's show of concern didn't fool Wu for a second. Ordinarily, supervisors were briefed on all developments, but Hargrave had been cut out of the investigation and was licking his wounds. His remarks demonstrated that he intended to make Wu's life difficult. Would he also ensure Wu failed so he could be called in to take over?

This skirmish went to Hargrave, who had outmaneuvered him, but he would not yield the battle . . . much less the war.

As he walked into the SCIF, he couldn't help but wonder what on earth Gustavo Toro had been doing in the Arizona desert and why he would lead them there with his well-hidden clue.

Knowing Toro, whatever it was couldn't be good.

CHAPTER 35

Six and a half months earlier, Saturday, March 23
Sonoran Desert, Arizona

Toro was a consummate professional. He was ruthlessly efficient, never expending more time and effort than necessary to accomplish his objective.

But not this time.

He was deliberately drawing out the man's suffering, delivering blow after blow despite the doomed man's pleas for mercy.

He looked down at the form quivering on the dusty ground. "Get up."

His command was met with sobs.

"Get your ass up. I'm not going to tell you again."

"K-kill me."

Oh no, that would be too easy. If he merely wanted the man dead, he would have snapped his neck and been done with it. This person, however, demanded special treatment. After knocking him unconscious and tossing him in the trunk of his car, Toro had bound and gagged him before hauling him far out into the desert.

The man had been surprised when Toro hoisted him out and untied him. Then Toro laid out his terms. "We fight to the death. No weapons.

Hand to hand only. The winner drives the car back to civilization, and the loser's carcass rots out here until the buzzards find him."

"You're shitting me."

"No, but you're probably going to shit yourself before this is over."

The man had bolted, but Toro easily caught up and tackled him to the ground. After that, the fight was on. As Toro had suspected, the asshole was no match for him.

The man was roughly Toro's height and weight, but he clearly wasn't used to brawling. To use an old expression, he had a glass jaw. A fact Toro discovered when he smashed his fist into his face. Blood had poured freely from both nostrils and his lower lip. That was when the begging had begun in earnest.

Now the fight had gone out of his opponent, who lay tucked into a fetal position, sobbing. Toro regarded him in silence. He had taken no pleasure in what he'd done, but he did get some satisfaction. And that was probably all he would get.

He leaned down and dropped his voice. "Yes."

Two bloodshot eyes rolled up toward him. "What?"

"Yes, I'll kill you now."

Toro waited for the man to panic and try to run or fight, but he just sobbed louder. Frankly, he was tired of the noise. It would be a relief just to get some peace and quiet. Well, quiet at least. Toro never had peace.

He moved around to position himself above the man's head. With practiced efficiency, he reached down and gripped his chin with one hand and the side of his head with the other. A heartbeat later, he jerked both hands in unison, snapping the man's neck with a loud pop.

He had chosen this location due to the nearby abandoned copper mine. The Southwest was dotted with hundreds of deep shafts, and it had been simple enough to pry the boards over the entrance loose before shoving the man's body down into the darkness.

He nailed the boards back in place and mopped his brow with the back of his hand. His work here was done.

As he turned to walk back to the waiting car, he considered how this kill had been different from the others. There was no client. There had been no contract. There would be no payment. But the reason behind his actions today changed everything. His dangerous lifestyle would eventually catch up to him. He decided then and there to set things in motion to do what he no longer could when that day came.

For a man who had never known peace, the sense of purpose he now felt was as close as he was likely to get.

CHAPTER 36

Present day, Thursday, October 10, 8:30 a.m.
26 Federal Plaza, Lower Manhattan, New York

Dani didn't believe in curses, but if a place were ever to have that distinction, it would be the Lost Dutchman's Mine.

She and Flint had been listening as Patel recounted a disturbing history that included plenty of people who'd tried to locate the fabled mother lode, only to end up dead.

"It's hard to separate fact from fiction." Flint was in homicide detective mode, conducting an investigation into a very cold case. "Sounds like a lot of people went up into the Superstition Mountains and never came back down, but was it the heat, wild animals, accidents, or foul play?"

"Or an attack," Patel said, staring at his screen. "I found another legend. This one claims the Dutchman wasn't the first to locate the mine. It was discovered a century earlier, when Arizona was still part of Mexico, by three brothers. They were members of the Peralta family, who were descendants of Spanish conquistadors."

Patel scrolled down, continuing his recitation. "According to this account, the three Peralta brothers set up a huge operation with over two hundred miners on the mountain. They got plenty of gold out before all of them were killed by Apache warriors who were angry that they were disturbing tribal land."

"Go on," Flint said when Patel stopped. "We've gone down every other rabbit hole, may as well try this one."

The account sounded like a mix of folklore, legend, and cautionary tale. Dani agreed with Flint, however, there could be valuable information contained in the narrative. She listened intently as Patel went on.

"The story goes that the three brothers were warned about the attack ahead of time. They destroyed all entrances to the mine and made a map so they could return sometime in the future. But they were killed before they could leave."

"I'm sure the map's long gone," Flint said. "It's been more than a hundred and fifty years."

"Nope." Patel clicked his mouse, changing the display on the wall screen. "It was carved into a set of stones."

Dani studied the new picture featuring four stones with carvings etched into them. Her heart began to pound as recognition dawned. "Wait, do you have a transcript of Toro's videos?"

Laying a hand on his chest, Patel pretended to be hurt that she had called his abilities into question. "I'm not a total amateur, Vega." He split the screen and began navigating to different files. "Which one do you want?"

If it weren't considered completely unprofessional, she might have thrown her arms around him in a bear hug. "Whatever they're paying you, it's not enough."

He grinned. "I know, right?"

"I need the transcript from the video in the Toltec Hotel security box," she said.

Moments later, a script resembling those she'd seen produced by court stenographers appeared on one-half of the screen. She followed the printed version of Toro's words as Patel scrolled through them.

"Stop." She pointed at a phrase. "Right there."

PEOPLE WHO BELIEVE IN SUPERSTITION THINK
I HAVE A HEART OF STONE. THAT I'M LOST. BUT
THE ANSWER IS REALLY JUST PERSONAL TASTE.

"That phrase was always odd to me," she began. "Way too poetic for Toro. He was always more the eliminate-problems-and-ask-questions-later kind of guy. This sounds like he's either becoming philosophical, or . . ."

She waited to hear their impressions. Curious to know if they'd arrive at the same conclusions she had.

Flint's sandy-blond brows furrowed. "Or he's speaking in code. Trying to communicate something."

"I was thinking the same thing," Patel said. "As a gamer, I've had to deal with my share of exposition NPCs."

Flint shot him a look. "I don't speak Gamer-ese."

Fortunately, Dani had enough experience with her brother Axel to pick up gamer jargon along with hacker-speak. "An NPC is a non-player character," she said to him. "One that gives you information you need to solve clues or navigate the world of the game."

Flint looked at each of them in turn. "You're saying Toro's message is coded, and you recognize this part of it." He waited for her nod of agreement, then faced the screen. "The word 'superstition' stands out. It's got to have something to do with the Superstition Mountains."

Flint had never witnessed the videos that had started the investigation. This was his first exposure to the kinds of clues Toro used, and she wanted to hear his analysis. The photograph showed four red sandstone tablets containing carvings of a horse, a cross, a heart, and a very crude map.

"That one has a heart carved into it." Flint jabbed a finger at the screen. "A heart of stone."

"When Toro mentioned that phrase, that's what I thought of too," Dani said, then turned to Patel. "Where are these carved tablets?"

"They're called the Peralta Stones," Patel said, frowning. "The ones in the picture are reproductions. I can't find any sign of where the originals are located now." He sighed. "Unfortunately, most conventional scientists and historians believe the Peralta Stones are fake, and so is the map carved into them."

"Makes sense," Flint said. "Otherwise, there would be a working gold mine in the mountain right now."

Patel nodded. "So why would Toro want us to waste our time on a map that could be fake?"

"He wouldn't," Dani said. "There's something else we're supposed to figure out." She returned her gaze to the screen. "It'll be somewhere else in that weirdly phrased message he left. Or in Lost Dutchman State Park."

"He'd still have to give us more clues," Flint said. "That park is enormous."

Patel clicked back to the original screen so they could study his cryptic message.

While Patel and Flint discussed options, Dani sat back in her seat, letting her mind wander. Toro had provided coordinates that referred to the Lost Dutchman's Mine story for a reason. She read the words over and over.

PEOPLE WHO BELIEVE IN SUPERSTITION THINK I HAVE A HEART OF STONE. THAT I'M LOST. BUT THE ANSWER IS REALLY JUST PERSONAL TASTE.

The first sentence referred to the mountain range and one of the carved Peralta Stones. The second was another reference to the legend of the missing gold mine. But what did the last sentence mean? It didn't refer to anything she could think of, except that they needed an answer.

And then it hit her. *"The answer is really just personal taste,"* she muttered.

"What's that?" Flint asked.

She turned to face him. "Look at the last sentence. It tells us what the answer really is."

"It's just personal taste," Patel read from the screen.

"In specific terms, it's *just* personal taste. Nothing else. Only that."

Flint shrugged. "I can tell you're headed somewhere, but I'm not following."

"Taste is subjective," Patel said. "Toro can't expect us to arrive at an objective meaning that way."

"Then we have to look at that phrase objectively." She began to pace. "How can a figure of speech be objective?"

No one answered. They all studied the words in silence. She looked for patterns, found none, then looked at the individual words, found nothing, then finally broke it down to the individual letters.

And then she got it.

She gestured to Patel's laptop. "Can you bring up an online anagram creator and enter the words 'Peralta' and 'stone'?"

Patel did as she asked, then hit Enter.

Flint cursed. "How the hell did you know?"

In a list of possibilities, one of the phrases formed by scrambling "Peralta Stones" was "personal taste."

"This is it," Patel said. "This is where we need to be."

She was itching to call Wu and make another request for the jet but remembered his last comment to her. "The boss needs something solid to authorize the jet," she said.

They both seemed to understand. They were on the right path, tantalizingly close, but not yet there.

CHAPTER 37

Wu had spent the first twenty minutes inside the SCIF fielding questions—getting grilled would be more accurate—about what had happened in Denver, in New York, and on the cruise ship.

Director Franklin had let him handle it, only intervening once when the conversation had veered a bit too close to the subject of Gustavo Toro. Wu had skirted around any mention of Las Vegas, which couldn't be explained without disclosing information about the video that had sent them to the Toltec.

Wu, Hargrave, and Franklin had all agreed during the drive to the Pentagon that they wanted to keep his name and involvement out of the discussion if at all possible. Yes, everyone in attendance had security clearances, but that information was on a need-to-know basis, and Franklin didn't believe anyone else needed to know.

He was pleased the director saw things his way, which made it a lot easier to push back against generals, admirals, and CEOs of contractors who weren't used to being refused.

"I'd like more details about the couple on the cruise ship," one of the contractors said when Wu finished giving his overview. "What have you found out about them?"

The name placard in front of him indicated he was Karl Vaden, CEO of Vaden-Quest Enterprises. Wu thought this was rich coming from the person who was supposed to be digging up information for his team.

He began tactfully. "Mr. Vaden, I understand one of your subsidiary companies is developing the underwater breathing technology?" At his nod, Wu continued. "I believe you'd be better equipped to answer that question than I am."

Vaden reddened. "NCIS has been scouring our records, and I was wondering if the FBI could provide more to go on."

Wu wasn't surprised the Navy's investigative arm had dispatched a team to find out how two classified prototypes had gone missing from a secure development facility. Judging by his demeanor, the CEO didn't appreciate having one of his subsidiaries under the microscope. If they found wrongdoing, or even sloppy security protocols, Vaden-Quest could be in huge trouble.

A woman in a crisp Navy dress uniform, whose placard read Captain Hickman, spoke up. "We're still reviewing lots of files. It's going to take time. But we haven't found any obvious breaches in security yet. All the prototypes have been accounted for."

"So the gear used by the couple on the ship wasn't stolen?" Vaden asked in a thinly veiled attempt to emphasize the last point.

"That's correct, sir," the captain said. "We believe the underwater breather and retractable fins were produced by personnel who accessed the manufacturing equipment during off-hours, or they obtained classified schematics and materials to create them in their own facility."

Interesting news. Captain Hickman's preliminary report implicated the subcontractor under the Vaden-Quest umbrella. Whoever ran that subsidiary company was either crooked or incompetent. Sensing Vaden was about to launch into defensive mode, Wu had no trouble deciphering what his statements really meant.

Vaden said, "We're assisting the investigation completely."

Meaning they were actively trying to cover their asses at every turn.

"We believe in complete transparency."

Meaning they'll hide any evidence of wrongdoing if they can get their hands on it.

"I was merely trying to get a better handle on what will be helpful."

Meaning he wanted to find out how much they had already discovered and pass the intel along to his team of corporate lawyers.

Hargrave found his voice for the first time since the meeting began. "Your corporation's commitment to our national security is well established," he said to Vaden. "We are simply checking up on the subsidiary company tasked with developing this equipment."

Wu could read between the lines of Hargrave's comments as easily as Vaden's. The assistant director didn't suspect Vaden of any wrongdoing.

Which was something Wu would never have done. Because no one was above suspicion.

Vaden visibly relaxed before turning back to Wu. "Regarding the scientist on the ship, Dr. Wallace, did he voluntarily jump overboard?"

This was another area where Wu had been deliberately vague. He was about to respond that the security footage from the ship showed Dr. Wallace completely alone at the time of the incident, so he wasn't pushed, but he had nothing else definitive to add at this point in the investigation.

Before he could say any of this, Hargrave rushed to answer.

"Dr. Wallace jumped, but there may be more to it. Our lab conducted an analysis of material from his stateroom and found a toxin. We're still trying to source it, but—"

"We'll let you know if we develop any information that has a bearing on your interests," Director Franklin cut in, effectively stopping Hargrave from revealing more.

Wu noticed the tightening of Franklin's jaw and the slight narrowing of his eyes as he glanced at Hargrave. The director had evidently realized the same thing Wu did.

Hargrave would age out and be forced to retire soon. There had been rumors that he was looking for a cushy retirement job where he could capitalize on his access, his clearances, and his insider information to snag a high-paying executive position.

And Hargrave had just revealed which company's executive board he wanted to join.

CHAPTER 38

Dani continued to pace as she focused on the screen, willing herself to see another hidden clue. Or a connection she had missed.

If only she were smarter, faster, better, she could figure out what Toro was trying to communicate. Her frustration mounted as the answer continued to elude her.

"Any ideas for other names we can try?"

Flint's question interrupted her thoughts. She stopped and turned to see him looking at her expectantly. Patel wore a similar expression with his fingers poised over his keyboard. Her colleagues had obviously been working on the problem without realizing she was doing the same thing—but independently.

Patel seemed to catch on and brought her up to speed. "Remember how we were wondering if she got married?"

She nodded, recalling their discussion about how many women took their husband's surnames, even these days.

"I'm searching through Arizona public records to find women Castillo's age with a last name related to any keywords we've come across. We've tried Waltz, Peralta, Dutch, Heart, Miner, Stone, and

Gold." He blew out a sigh. "There were quite a few. We need to narrow the pool. I don't want to waste time doing a deep dive on each one."

"Maybe we need a different approach," she said, resuming her steady strides back and forth across the room. "We know something happened to Tina Castillo, and we suspect foul play, right?"

"For all intents and purposes she ceased to exist," Flint said. "People don't erase themselves for shits and giggles. It's damned hard to start over with a whole new identity, which is why most people who disappear are eventually presumed dead."

She halted and turned to Flint. "You're right. It's hard to even get a job. She was a quantum physicist. Would she try to get a job in her field, or would she choose another line of work to avoid drawing attention?"

"She couldn't become a science teacher without a background check," Patel said. "But somehow, I don't picture her waiting tables or selling insurance either."

Dani agreed. "Can you pull up all the results you found for each name?"

Their idea was better than anything she'd come up with so far, so she studied a list of potential candidates, which totaled dozens. "How did you narrow down the pool?"

"We searched for females born in the same year," Flint said. "In case she changed her date of birth."

A reasonable precaution if Castillo had gone into hiding. "Can you expand it to include the year before and after?"

More names appeared, expanding the list. They were going in the wrong direction, but she didn't want to exclude anyone too soon.

"How about NCIC?" she asked. "Can you check the database for anyone on the list who was listed as a suspect, victim, or witness to any crimes?"

This time, several names dropped off.

Dani played a hunch. "Cross-reference the names with Geraldo Trujillo and Gustavo Toro."

After another search, Patel glanced up at her. "Nada."

She tried another angle. "Toro said the answer was just personal taste. Peralta Stones. He emphasized those with his final words. Let's focus on Peralta."

Patel deleted everyone else from the list, leaving only a pool with the surname Peralta. Dani studied the screen.

"Pull that one up."

Patel expanded the details of a missing person report. The owner of an accounting firm called the Apache Junction police when one of his employees, thirty-five-year-old Alan Hooper, didn't show up for work two days in a row. Angela Peralta's name appeared in the witness section as the last person known to have seen Hooper.

Flint grew interested as well. "You catch the date on that report?"

"March, six and a half months ago." She met the detective's gaze. "Less than two months before Toro made the videos."

They all read on in silence. Angela Peralta had been dating Hooper for several weeks. The police wouldn't do an extensive investigation for a missing adult with no signs of foul play or any reason to believe he was at risk, but they stopped by to get a statement from Angela after his boss told them about the relationship.

Angela had last seen him three days earlier. The officer became concerned when he spotted what appeared to be a fading bruise on both of her upper arms, as if someone had gripped her hard. He also noted a hint of discoloration under a layer of makeup on her cheek.

Dani was impressed by the officer's observational skill and his attempts to get Angela to tell him if Hooper had assaulted her. She seemed fearful, refusing to implicate her former boyfriend, but did not have an explanation for her injuries.

The officer went so far as to check her five-year-old son, Tace Peralta, to be sure he didn't have any sign of injuries. He described the boy as happy and healthy.

"Was Hooper ever found?" she asked Patel.

"There's no follow-up on the police report," he said. "I'll see what I can find."

Flint turned to her. "Do you think Angela Peralta is Tina Castillo?"

She gave it some thought. "Not sure yet. We need more info."

"Already on it," Patel said before she could ask him to do a background check.

Someone could change their identity fairly effectively, but it wouldn't usually stand up to the kind of resources the FBI had to scour through even a carefully constructed backstory. It was one of the things that bothered her about Paul and Ursula Cole, the mystery couple from the cruise ship. What kinds of resources did they have at their disposal?

Patel's words interrupted her thoughts. "First, Hooper. I couldn't find any death certificate or anything further from law enforcement. He had an ex-wife in California, though. After his disappearance, she hired a lawyer to help her get access to his bank accounts and the proceeds from the sale of his house. He owed her back payments on alimony because—get this—she wasn't able to work after he beat her badly enough to put her in the hospital. That's when she filed for a divorce, which was finalized before he moved to Arizona."

"Asshole," Flint muttered. "I guess we know what caused Angela Peralta's bruises."

"What about her?" Dani asked. "Anything in Angela's background that could connect her?"

"Absolutely nothing." Patel pushed back from his computer. "Which is why I'm convinced your hunch was right."

She blinked. "Come again?"

"Angela Peralta's data goes back all the way to her birth in Flagstaff, Arizona, but every time I wade in, the water only goes up to my ankles."

Another Patel-ism. "You're saying her background is shallow."

He nodded. "Anything older than a couple of years gets sketchy."

The implication was clear. Angela suddenly popped into existence at the same time Tina Castillo dropped off the radar. They were one and the same person.

Flint stared at her. "How the hell did you know?"

She rested a hand on her hip. "I used the SWAG technique."

"SWAG?"

"Sophisticated wild-ass guess," she said. "Rangers use it going into dangerous situations with plenty of unknowns."

Which was exactly what she intended to ask Wu to let her do now.

CHAPTER 39

Twenty minutes earlier
The Pentagon, Arlington County, Virginia

Karl Vaden wondered how long it would take the FBI to put the pieces together. And how quickly he could find someone to take the fall.

Judging by Scott Hargrave, he wouldn't need to concern himself. But Steve Wu gave him pause. Anyone who held the position of special agent in charge of the New York JTTF wielded a great deal of power and influence, and Wu seemed particularly sharp.

"Mr. Vaden," Wu said, leveling him with a hard stare, "I'd like to hear about Vaden-Quest's safety protocols involving their subcontractors and their classified research."

Yes, Wu might prove to be a problem. He was young for someone in such a high position, and clearly had a long and promising career ahead of him. Unless Vaden found a way to do something about it.

For now, he decided to switch tactics to deploy his key advantage. Unlike the FBI, which was hampered by the law, the Constitution, and bureaucratic procedures, Vaden-Quest could reconfigure their operations within minutes.

"I'll make all our company's databases available," he said smoothly. "Always happy to cooperate with a federal investigation."

Those databases would be sanitized first, of course. Leaving behind only what he wanted the Feds to see. He studied Director Franklin to see how his response had landed and caught an approving look directed toward Wu.

Vaden made it his business to understand interpersonal dynamics, and it was clear to him that Franklin thought more highly of Wu than he did of Hargrave.

A pity, because Hargrave was what had been termed in the back rooms of DC politics "a useful idiot." He knew the assistant director coveted an executive slot at Vaden-Quest. The only question was whether he would do what it took to earn a spot that could pay him well over a million dollars a year when bonuses and incentives were included.

He'd met Hargrave a year earlier and quickly sized him up. The man wanted the trappings of wealth and prestige. His high-ranking position in the Bureau afforded him power, but not the money that Vaden enjoyed. He had set about luring Hargrave, and it hadn't been difficult.

The trick with bureaucratic law enforcement officials was overcoming their natural suspicion. Most had gotten into the profession based on a patriotic or community-minded desire to serve their country or help others.

It hadn't taken long to crack the algorithm to access Hargrave's subroutines. He was a frustrated bureaucrat who saw some of those he arrested living a lifestyle of luxury he could never hope to attain. And when he'd arrested them, most used their power and influence to dodge the consequences for their misdeeds. Sometimes, for outright felonies.

After a few lavish lunches and visits to Vaden's posh business properties, Hargrave had begun seeing himself wearing bespoke suits, flying on private jets, and purchasing a summer home in the Hamptons.

Of course, Vaden knew that would never happen for one such as Hargrave, but he gave him enough hope to make him . . . a useful idiot. Hargrave was not overtly corrupt. He was not the type to be bribed or coerced. Instead, he was the kind of public official who needed cultivating. He had to be convinced that he was acting in his country's best interest, all the while concluding he could line his pockets while doing so.

The bottom line was that no government official, no matter how high ranking, ever owned a private jet, a yacht, or a sports team. And yet, they all dreamed. He played on those dreams.

What made Hargrave particularly useful during this meeting was his eagerness to please. Vaden had posed a question about whether Morton Wallace had actually jumped ship. Hargrave's response had been most revealing.

The FBI had recovered a gift card sent with the fruit basket, and they were running tests. Vaden knew full well the results would indicate an unknown chemical compound. The question was, How long would it take them to track that compound down to a formula being developed by one of his subsidiary R&D tech companies?

Okay, so one subcontractor would be credible, but two would raise enough eyebrows to bring the FBI to his company's door with search warrants.

He was considering his options when the doors to their briefing room opened. Everyone watched in silence as the sergeant posted outside entered and made his way to SAC Wu.

Intrigued, Vaden watched as the sergeant bent to whisper in Wu's ear. Interestingly, Hargrave stood and followed Wu out the door. He smiled. Hargrave wanted to remain in the loop. He'd be sure to pump him for information later.

While the two FBI executives were absent, Director Franklin kept his seat in the briefing. If Vaden were in his place, he would have done the same, keeping tabs on what went on among the power brokers.

For his part, Vaden began to formulate a plan. He needed a scapegoat if the crime lab connected all the recent incidents. He hated to give up his most devoted lieutenant, a man he had molded like clay to conduct his most important business.

Of course, Vaden had been disappointed before. Years ago, he'd believed Gustavo Toro could have filled that role, but Toro had turned out to be a liability rather than an asset. Since then, Vaden had further diversified his operation, but he'd used Foley to carry out his most sensitive missions.

Foley had let him down at least once, however, leading to his current predicament. He would have to order more executions, but that was the way of things in his line of work.

In life, there were winners and there were losers. He was a winner. Those whose deaths he ordered were losers. It had always been that way since time immemorial, though the so-called civilized world pretended otherwise.

He'd been listening to the NCIS captain recap her fruitless investigation when the door opened again. He watched Wu walk in, his face a tight but expressionless mask. Close on his heels was Hargrave, features pinched and skin ruddy, blatantly upset about whatever had taken place in the hallway outside.

The two had barely sat down when Hargrave took center stage with an announcement. "We've had a break in the case. A team of agents from my field office is on their way to Arizona."

Vaden noted a covert glance between Wu and Franklin, accompanied by an almost imperceptible frown from Wu, who plainly didn't appreciate Hargrave divulging information about their investigation.

Franklin cleared his throat. "Thank you, Assistant Director Hargrave. We'll keep everyone apprised of developments going forward." This was delivered with a note of finality that firmly closed the subject.

Vaden considered the implications. Hargrave probably thought it would make him sound important to mention a break coming from his field office, and it wouldn't compromise the investigation since those at the meeting believed it only involved missing classified technology.

But unlike the others, Vaden knew the FBI was desperately searching for Dr. Castillo.

There was only one logical conclusion. The team was already busy looking into deaths on the cruise ship, in New York, and in Denver. The only thing that would send them to the other side of the country was Castillo, their primary objective. Somehow, they'd tracked her down.

He realized he couldn't wait for the briefing to end before taking action. He'd just learned everything he needed to know and had to set his plans in motion. The meeting would likely go on for another hour at least. It was an hour he couldn't afford. Not when federal agents were already ahead of him. His mind raced, scrambling for a pretext to leave the SCIF.

"Excuse me." He pushed back his chair and stood. "Bathroom break." To sell the ploy, he directed a wry grin at some of the younger men present. "When you're my age, you'll understand."

As intended, the remark drew chuckles and sympathetic nods from the older men, half of whom probably had enlarged prostates. He made his way out into the hallway. Fortunately, he'd planned for this and didn't need to access his cell phone to communicate. He didn't want the sergeant to tell Franklin that Vaden had requested his phone back to make a call.

Vaden went to the men's room and entered one of the stalls. He fished out a small device the size of a quarter from his pocket and powered it on. When it vibrated, he tapped the surface twice and dictated a brief message that would be transmitted to Foley as a text.

CASTILLO IS IN AZ. GET ON A PLANE. UPDATE TO FOLLOW. FIND HER 1ST.

CHAPTER 40

Foley stared down at the incoming text and cursed. He could tell by the formatting of the message that the boss had used the stealth device to transmit it. There was no way to send a response to the tiny disk, so he'd have to shoot a text to his cell phone. Vaden wouldn't be able to read it until he was out of the SCIF, but he would know his instructions had been received and were being carried out.

FOLEY: UNDERSTOOD. EN ROUTE TO AIRPORT.

His next order of business was arranging transportation.

FOLEY: BOSS WANTS ME IN AZ ASAP.

PILOT: 10-4. WHICH AIRPORT?

FOLEY: PHOENIX. WILL CHANGE IF NEEDED. ETA?

PILOT: PREP TIME + FLIGHT TIME = 2 HRS TO PHX IF I PUSH IT.

FOLEY: PUSH IT.

PILOT: 10-4.

Phoenix was only an hour away, but the pilot had regs to follow that would tack on extra time. He could probably still get there ahead of the FBI, but it would be close. Meanwhile, he would set up his contingency plan.

Vaden had made it clear that failure was not an option. Foley had to prepare for all-out war if the Feds arrived first. He scrolled through his contacts to find the person he needed.

FOLEY: UR TEAM AVAILABLE FOR A JOB? NEED U ON STANDBY.

BRAVO: GIVE ME DEETS.

FOLEY: ADULT FEMALE.

BRAVO: DISPOSAL?

FOLEY: CATCH AND HOLD. MAY NEED EXTRACTION FROM FEDS.

BRAVO: GONNA COST U.

FOLEY: 2X USUAL FEE.

BRAVO: 3X. AND I'LL NEED ALL THE TOYS AND ALL THE BOYS.

FOLEY: DONE.

BRAVO: STANDING BY FOR UR CALL.

Next, he had to get a bead on his target.

FOLEY: NEW SEARCH PARAMETERS FOR CASTILLO.

TECH SUPPORT: READY.

FOLEY: ARIZONA.

TECH SUPPORT: CITY?

FOLEY: IDK

TECH SUPPORT: ON IT.

FOLEY: ALSO NEED REAL TIME TRACKING ON VEGA.

TECH SUPPORT: IS THE SYSTEM IN PLACE?

FOLEY: YES.

TECH SUPPORT: SEND TRACE CODE. WILL MONITOR AND ADVISE OF ALL MOVEMENTS.

An hour later, he was seated in the private jet while the pilot waited for air traffic control to clear him for takeoff when his cell phone buzzed with an incoming message from the boss.

VADEN: ANGELA PERALTA. APACHE JUNCTION AZ.

FOLEY: GOOD SOURCE?

VADEN: INSIDER.

FOLEY: BACKUP ON STANDBY. WILL UPDATE W/ INSTRUCTIONS.

VADEN: U IN THE AIR?

FOLEY: WHEELS UP IN 5.

Now he finally had usable info. Time to move in.

FOLEY: HAVE NAME. NEED ADDRESS & BACKGROUND.

TECH SUPPORT: SHOOT.

FOLEY: ANGELA PERALTA. APACHE JUNCTION AZ.

TECH SUPPORT: HOW DEEP?

FOLEY: LOCATION 1ST. THEN DIG.

TECH SUPPORT: ON IT.

He checked the map. Apache Junction was east of Sky Harbor International in Phoenix. There was a municipal airport close by, but he didn't want to draw attention by parking a multimillion-dollar jet out there. Better to blend in at a busy international airport that was also a travel hub.

As the plane took off, he received another text with Angela Peralta's address, which he immediately forwarded to Bravo. Then another message came through.

TECH SUPPORT: UPDATE - PERALTA HAS A 5 YR OLD KID.

FOLEY: IN SCHOOL?

TECH SUPPORT: KINDERGARTEN. NO PAYMENTS TO AFTER SCHOOL CARE IN HER FINANCIALS. KID WILL BE W/ HER.

FOLEY: OK. STATUS ON VEGA?

TECH SUPPORT: STILL FLYING TO AZ. ETA 1 HR.

He was finally ahead of the Feds. He considered the new information and decided Angela Peralta would be far more cooperative if he took her child as well. He had started to put the phone away when it vibrated once more.

VADEN: CALL WHEN U HAVE HER. MAKE HER TALK.

FOLEY: WILL DO.

VADEN: NO SCREW UPS. GET TORO'S STASH OR U WILL JOIN HIM.

CHAPTER 41

Forty-eight thousand feet, somewhere between Washington, DC, and Arizona

Wu had never been inside the FBI director's jet. The pilot had climbed well above the standard cruising altitude for commercial airliners to avoid other planes. With a clear flight path, the Gulfstream G550's twin Rolls-Royce engines sped them through the air at 670 mph, which was 90 percent of the way to Mach 1.

As Vega would have put it, they were hauling ass.

"What are you smiling about?" Director Franklin asked him.

Wu snatched up a ceramic mug with the FBI seal on it. "Enjoying my coffee." He took a sip, hoping he'd covered the awkward moment. This was not a pleasure trip. There would be no reason to smile.

At last night's meeting in his office, the director had offered to drop him off at LaGuardia on his way to LAX for a meeting in Los Angeles. After this morning's revelations, Franklin had asked the pilot to make a stop in Arizona instead.

The meeting at the Pentagon had dragged on for another hour after he'd come back from taking Vega's call. Then the director received an unexpected call from the President, postponing their departure by an hour. With all the delays, the director's jet had only just attained maximum cruising speed, but Vega, Patel, and Flint would be landing soon.

Franklin said, "I'll confess to an ulterior motive for giving you a ride. This entire investigation began because Gustavo Toro sent a message to me personally. Whatever else he may have felt about the Bureau, he obviously trusted us to do the right thing."

"He trusted *you*, sir."

Franklin inclined his head in acknowledgment. "And that's why I bear responsibility for this case. I never got a chance to ask you for a detailed briefing on the status of your investigation, and frankly, I felt like Assistant Director Hargrave was holding back."

Wu was in a predicament. Franklin had practically invited him to criticize Hargrave. He could easily insert a few well-placed barbs while he provided an overview of their progress to date. Based on his comments in the director's office yesterday, Hargrave had already done as much to him, but he would not sink to the same level.

"I'm sure the assistant director was dealing with many sensitive issues that demanded his attention."

Franklin gave him a speculative look but made no further comment about Hargrave. Wu had the distinct impression he had just passed some sort of test. He was saved from another question when his cell phone buzzed in his pocket.

Ordinarily, he wouldn't take a call or even look at his phone while briefing the director, but these weren't ordinary times. He glanced at the screen. "It's Agent Vega."

Franklin made a motion indicating he wanted to hear.

Wu tapped the screen. "You're on speaker. I'm with Director Franklin."

There was a long pause, and Wu imagined Vega sucking in air before she responded.

"Good afternoon, sirs."

Her voice sounded uncharacteristically formal, and he remembered she'd never spoken to Franklin before. Beyond that, her military background would have made her highly conscious of rank and authority.

He tried to put her at ease. "What's your status?"

"We're starting our descent to Falcon Field."

"Where's that?"

"It's a municipal airport in the city of Mesa. It's east of Phoenix and a lot closer to Apache Junction. We can be at the Peralta property in under fifteen minutes after landing."

Franklin's silvery brows drew together. "Toro said she held the key to locating his cache of information but never explained how or why. Have you been able to reach her?"

Wu already knew the answer but waited to see if Vega had made any progress.

"Negative, sir," Vega said in a voice so crisp it sounded as if she were standing at attention. "She doesn't have a landline, and her cell goes straight to voicemail."

Wu got a cold feeling in the pit of his stomach.

Franklin's expression indicated the lack of response concerned him as well. "What else have you learned about her?"

"Analyst Patel has been checking into her finances, sir," she said. "He learned she receives regular payments from a trust fund established a year ago."

This sounded promising. "Who set it up?" Wu asked.

"It's called the HiPear Trust, and it's anonymous. We hit a wall with the Phoenix law firm that drew up the legal documents. We called their office, but the head partner refused to divulge any information." She sighed. "Attorney-client privilege."

A dead end. "Did Patel go through her bank transactions?"

"She withdrew five thousand in cash two days ago," Vega said. "No credit card charges since then."

"Cell service provider info?"

"We're working on a subpoena for her call and text history," she said. "In the meantime, we pinged her phone and got nothing. Tried a wireless sniffer. Still couldn't find a signal for her device. We think she either stuck her phone in a shielded container or tossed it in a bucket of water."

Wu recalled Vega mentioning that Angela was a single mother of a small child. The idea quickened his pulse. He got to the point. "Angela Peralta and her son are unreachable."

"That's right, sir."

"I know we're trying to restrict this part of the investigation to a tight circle, but I don't like the sound of it." He glanced at the director, who had ordered them to keep it low-key. At Franklin's nod, he continued. "I'm going to contact my counterpart at the Phoenix field office and advise him to send an agent to meet you at the airport."

Rather than contradict him, Franklin lent his support. "Coordinate with the PFO," he said to Vega. "But until SAC Wu arrives, you're in charge."

Wu disconnected to find Franklin leveling a hard stare at him. "I appreciate the diplomatic response when I asked you about Assistant Director Hargrave," he said. "Especially since you must be aware he hasn't extended the same courtesy to you."

Of all the directions this conversation could have taken, he hadn't expected this.

Franklin continued, "But he exercised poor judgment at the Pentagon meeting when he mentioned Arizona. I noticed him talking with Karl Vaden after the briefing ended, so I confronted him about it. He confessed to divulging additional details about Angela Peralta."

Wu's grip tightened around the mug's handle. "What did he say?"

"He gave up her new name."

Although the director didn't use obscenities, he didn't seem offended when Wu responded with colorful language. "He got that information from me, sir."

Wu went on to explain that when he left the SCIF to take Vega's call, Hargrave had followed him out to hear her report—which had included Dr. Castillo's name change.

Franklin didn't get heated. He got ice cold. "Hargrave's on admin leave until further notice."

Wu didn't take any joy in Hargrave's situation, but he appreciated having an obstacle removed from the investigation. He switched to damage assessment. "What are your thoughts on Karl Vaden, sir?"

Franklin paused to consider. "I've known him for decades, but we were never friends. In fact, I opened an investigation on VQE fifteen years ago when I worked financial crimes, but he and his lawyers covered their tracks too well."

Franklin was one of only two directors who had come up through the Bureau as field agents. Wu had never heard any mention of an inquiry into Vaden-Quest Enterprises, which meant it must have been shut down fast.

"Do you think he's a risk?"

"I can't point to anything specific or illegal, but I've always been suspicious." He steepled his fingers. "He beat me once, but I'd love a rematch."

CHAPTER 42

Dani adjusted the binoculars to get a better view of the Peralta house. The strange stillness in the air was broken by a comment from Agent George Sanford of the FBI's Phoenix field office.

"Maybe they're already dead and that's why it's so quiet inside. Have you thought of that?"

Dani had thought of little else since they were unable to reach Dr. Castillo—now Angela Peralta—on the phone.

She lowered her binoculars and turned to Agent Sanford. "I'm not willing to take chances."

Sanford had met them at Falcon Field municipal airport twenty minutes earlier.

And they had been butting heads ever since.

He had a lot more seniority in the Bureau, but she had years of tactical training—and actual combat experience—that he did not. To her way of thinking, this situation called for a combination of tactics and investigative knowledge, so she wished he would get on board with her, but she couldn't use Director Franklin's name to make that happen.

That part of the investigation was still restricted, and there was no way she could convince her Phoenix colleague without divulging a lot of sensitive information. Sanford would have been told only that SAC Steve Wu of the New York JTTF had called, but nothing more specific.

Sanford was stuck on policies and procedures, but this situation wasn't in any manual. She had been trained to adapt her approach to a potentially dangerous situation on the fly. Anyone who couldn't do so washed out of Ranger School.

"Then there's something we agree on," he said, surprising her before adding, "I'm not willing to take chances either. Our SWAT team is gearing up. They'll pull an ops plan together and can be here in less than two hours."

It was an improvement, but Sanford still wasn't getting it.

"Since the beginning of this investigation, we've arrived too late for every single target," she told him. "Three people are dead because we couldn't get there fast enough. This time, it's a mother and her child. I'll take whatever consequences come my way later, but right now, I'm on recon."

Flint stepped into the fray. "I've seen what Vega can do," he said to Sanford. "She's good at recon, and she can provide fresh intel when SWAT gets here."

"I should at least go with her," Sanford said.

Flint gave him a wry smile. "You'd only slow her down."

That settled the matter. She was pleased that Wu had authorized not only the jet but also Patel and Flint to join her. Flint's status with the federal task force gave him law enforcement authority equivalent to hers. Patel was a civilian but would be far more effective on the scene than back at the JTTF if they found any tech to analyze.

Accepting defeat, Sanford handed her a wireless transmitter. "It's programmed on a dedicated secure channel limited to SWAT," he told her. "They'll be able to listen in, but no one else can. The encryption code changes every three seconds."

He'd obviously taken her warning about security seriously. It was the reason he'd finally agreed that they couldn't swear out a search warrant ahead of time. He had grudgingly concurred they were within the law to check on Angela Peralta's welfare. If, however, they encountered any criminal activity when they arrived, they could hold the scene and get whatever warrants they needed.

"I'll make my approach from that direction." She pointed to the west side of the property. "There's a slight rise where I can get a better view."

She worked her way around the edge, using clusters of juniper, mesquite, and palo verde trees for cover. It wasn't much, but she figured it was better than the barrel cactus and saguaro that dotted other sides of the property.

She picked her way through the chaparral, keeping an eye out for scorpions and rattlesnakes, then dropped to the ground and low-crawled to the top of the small hill. From this angle, she could see the front and the east side of the house. She raised her binoculars and rested on her elbows as she surveyed first the terrain, then the home on the property.

What she saw made her uneasy.

Every blind was closed, and every curtain drawn. No light glowed from inside, nor did any shadows cross behind the covered windows. The place had an abandoned air. She twisted the dial, zooming in on the side of the house where two large trash cans sat side by side. One of them bore a recycling symbol, and its lid was pushed up a fraction by bulky cardboard boxes.

Dani tapped the transmitter in her ear and whispered, "Which day of the week is recycling collected?"

A minute later, Sanford relayed the response from Patel. "Yesterday."

"The bin is crammed full," Dani said. "Angela never took it out to the curb."

The lot was large, but the house was situated near the front edge of it. She only had to wheel the recycling out to the end of the driveway.

She had seen enough. "I'm going to knock on the door."

"Wait for—"

"They could be lying inside hurt, or worse." She got to her feet. "Or someone could have snatched them. No matter what happened, every second counts."

She tuned out Sanford's increasingly insistent demands for her to return to the perimeter with the others and wait for SWAT. Instead, she made her way to the front door, focusing on the windows, watching for any sudden movement.

But there was none. Everything remained as still and silent as the grave.

By the time she was knocking on the door minutes later, she knew there would be no answer. She went through the motions anyway, then touched her comm.

"There's no response," she said. "We have enough for a welfare check."

"It'll be cleaner if we get paper first," Sanford said.

She overheard Flint talking to Sanford in the background but couldn't make out the words. The detective was probably recounting how many times he'd personally broken into someone's residence to check on their welfare when he had reason to believe they might be in danger. It was an exception that allowed for a warrantless search of the premises—at least of any parts where a person might be. Going into drawers, computers, or cabinets would require a signed warrant.

At issue was whether this could wait, and Dani concluded it could not. If Angela Peralta and her son turned out to be dead or missing, they needed the freshest trail possible to follow.

Having arrived at her decision, Dani began to pry open a window. By the time she climbed inside, Sanford and Flint were right behind her. Patel, an unarmed civilian, waited outside for the all-clear.

Ten minutes later, they had searched the premises and Patel was with them in the living room. The Peralta family was gone, but at least there was no sign of a struggle.

The question was, Did they flee or were they taken?

Over an hour had passed since their arrival, and the answer to that question still eluded the team. Nothing had seemed out of place until they got to the kitchen, where a photo album lay open on the counter. Two photos had been slipped out of their plastic sheath and placed beside the album.

She leaned forward to scrutinize both pictures and froze. "The Peralta Stones."

One was of the sandstone tablet with the heart shape in sunken relief. Lying beside it was a rock made of red quartzite that had been cut and sized perfectly to fit into the heart-shaped opening. The second picture featured the Peralta Stone with a cross chiseled into it.

"This has to mean something," Flint said, then pointed at the album. "There are more pictures of the stones, but someone pulled these two out and put them here."

Patel took several close-ups. "Maybe it's about her name change, but why just these two stones?"

Once again, Dani had the impression of a clue drifting nearby, but too far away to grasp. At the moment, however, a more pressing issue demanded her attention.

They had to either put out an APB and enlist every law enforcement agency's help to find them, or hunt for them quietly below the radar. Since Wu had left her in charge, Dani would make the call, and the decision could have deadly consequences if she chose the wrong course of action. She needed more information.

She turned to Flint, who had called the Apache Junction Police Department. He'd managed to connect with a supervisor willing to provide information to a fellow cop without asking too many questions. "Interaction with local PD?"

"No police contact besides the missing person report we found earlier."

"License plate reader hits?"

"AJPD is small. They don't have that tech, so I reached out to the state police. In Arizona, that's the Department of Public Safety. Angela's vehicle and tags haven't shown up on any major freeways in the past week."

She turned to Patel. "Relatives, friends, associates?"

"Couldn't find anything on social media. Her background, which is obviously fake, has all her relatives in Mexico."

"Health concerns?"

"Can't be sure without getting a subpoena for medical records."

She glanced from Flint to Patel and back again. "What am I forgetting?"

"Best-case scenario, Angela took her son and went into hiding," Flint said. "But if she did, we can't put out an APB. Any cop who ran across her would plug in her info and get an instant alert. If whoever's behind this has a way to monitor the system, they would know right away."

Patel added his thoughts. "And we wouldn't want to freeze her assets. The cash she withdrew will run out. We don't want to limit her ability to hide." He grimaced. "If that's what she's doing."

"It'll be suspicious if we don't conduct some kind of search, though," Flint said. "But we could sort of half-ass it."

"What about scenario number two?" Dani said. "Angela and her son were abducted." She did not mention scenario number three, in which they were dead, preferring to focus on a rescue operation rather than a murder investigation.

"If that's the case, then we do the opposite," Flint said. "We assume the boy is being used to control the mother, so we turn up the heat."

Dani said, "A public appeal and a full-court press with law enforcement carries its own risks. The Peraltas could become a liability fast."

She swept a stray tendril of hair from her face. "Not to mention how so much media scrutiny will make it impossible for us to work quietly. And whoever is behind this will have the ability to check up on our investigation."

She had as much data as she was going to get, but it still wasn't enough. Whatever she did now would be judged by others with the benefit of twenty-twenty hindsight. Some people believed good leaders were those who made the best decisions.

Experience had taught her otherwise.

Good leaders made the best decision they could with the least amount of information. Given 90 percent of the facts, most people could choose the correct course of action. But with only 10 percent of the facts . . . well, that required a different calculus.

She straightened. "Hold off on the APB."

Silently, she prayed the Peraltas were safely in hiding, and that they could hold out long enough for her to find them before anyone else did.

CHAPTER 43

8:00 p.m. local time
Kokopelli Suites Hotel, Mesa, Arizona

Dani realized she was coming to rely on Wu, not only for his expertise and knowledge, but for his calm, capable presence. Which made it awkward to realize he was hiding something.

Wu had arrived over an hour earlier and met them at the Peralta property. She had been sweaty, coated with a thin layer of desert dust, and scratched by cactus spines thanks to her recon adventure.

Wu looked freshly shaved, his suit was immaculate, and he smelled of soap with a hint of cedar and sandalwood.

Figured.

When she apprised him of the situation, he immediately affirmed her decision to delay putting out a BOLO for the Peraltas. The fact that a child was involved made things exponentially more challenging. Wu ended by saying he would change the order if they didn't locate them by the end of the day tomorrow.

They had spent another hour at the scene. Agent Sanford of the Phoenix field office had requested an Evidence Response Team to process the house and collect DNA samples.

They all knew the techs had done it in case DNA was needed to identify bodies, but no one spoke of death. Those kinds of worst-case scenarios always lurked in the wings. No need to give them energy by voicing them.

Dani had followed behind the techs, studying each part of the residence after they finished. She was looking for any breadcrumbs Angela Peralta might have left for them to follow. After hours of searching, she'd found nothing. Patel had been equally frustrated to learn that Angela had left no electronic devices of any kind for him to crack into.

When the scene finally shut down, Sanford agreed to post someone on the property in case Angela returned. Darkness had fallen by the time he dropped the team off at a hotel in nearby Mesa, coordinating with another agent to leave an SUV for their use while they were in town.

Once again, the group was gathered around a table, trying to make headway, with Flint a welcome addition to the mix.

Now that she was seated directly across from her boss, Dani had a chance to study him. A student of body language himself, Wu was good at concealing his emotions. All the time they'd spent in close proximity had given her the ability to detect the tension in the set of his jaw and the reluctance to meet anyone's eyes.

Yep, definitely hiding something.

She met the situation head-on. "You never filled us in about what happened at the Pentagon this morning. Or what you and the director discussed during the flight here."

She was totally overstepping by asking him for such information. Normally, executive-level conversations were considered private. If the special agent in charge chose to share the particulars, he would. It was not her place to ask. Then again, this situation was far from normal.

Wu gave her a hard look, offering no response.

She returned his gaze, refusing to back down. His dark eyes bore an intense, unreadable expression. He had the authority to order her off the case and onto the next commercial flight to New York. Hell, he could order her to sit at home until further notice.

Flint and Patel glanced back and forth at each of them.

Wu seemed to come to a decision. "Director Franklin and I had a lengthy discussion about the investigation. I've been debating about how much—and when—to share."

Everyone on the team held a top-secret clearance, so that wasn't the issue. This must be something involving high-level workings of the Bureau way above her pay grade. Whatever the situation, they needed to know what they were up against.

"The director wants me to put together a separate task force to investigate a new lead, and I've decided all of you will need to be on it. May as well start briefing you now."

He spent the next half hour recounting what had happened before, during, and after the meeting in the SCIF that morning.

She was appalled to hear that Assistant Director Hargrave had divulged Angela Peralta's name to a defense contractor, regardless of his security clearance. When Wu went on to describe the director's concerns about Vaden-Quest Enterprises, she was positively alarmed.

"If Vaden notified a team to go after Angela as soon as he left, they might have gotten to her first," Dani said. "Especially if they were closer than we were."

"We all agreed there was no sign of a struggle," Wu reminded her. "She's eluded them for five years and she's smart. I still think she ran as soon as she heard about her former colleagues."

Flint had another concern. "I'm assuming the expanded task force will be crawling all over VQE?"

Wu nodded. "It's going to take a dedicated team. Vaden has an entire contingent of attorneys on retainer. He can throw as many resources at thwarting our investigation as we can conducting it."

"The investigation could drag on for years," Dani said.

"Not if I can help it," Patel said. "Remember how I've been trying to reconstruct all the purged and deleted files at Exmyth Technologies in Denver?" He looked around the table. "Well, I finally started getting results." He had an air of barely contained excitement. "I found out what the three scientists were working on."

That got their attention, but Patel wasn't done yet.

"And I have a theory about why Dr. Castillo became Angela Peralta."

Patel sometimes had a flair for the dramatic, but Dani realized that, unlike the special agents he worked with, he never got to tackle a fleeing felon and put them in cuffs. For him, a cyber chase was pure adrenaline.

"Remember how Sterling told us he assigned her to a team that was researching advanced propulsion systems?" Patel looked at each of them expectantly.

She recalled the discussion but didn't grasp its significance. "How does this lead to Dr. Castillo's disappearance?"

"This wasn't ordinary rocket science," Patel said. "Or how to make cars go faster. They were literally trying to figure out warp drive."

Flint frowned. "Like *Star Trek*?"

Patel nodded. "Sort of, until . . ." He trailed off, then opened his laptop and started mousing through various files. "Let me show you what I mean."

He turned the screen to face them.

Dani studied rows of equations and formulas. "Unlike you and my brother, I don't have a degree in mathematics."

Patel smiled. "It's supposed to look like that. Because it's total bullshit."

Wu looked intrigued. "Are you saying they falsified the data?"

"That's exactly what I'm saying. They were committing fraud."

Flint said, "Maybe you should just lay it out for us."

"The only way I was able to reconstruct this data was because Exmyth had a government contract, and I could backtrack from that. NASA wanted new tech to send rockets, satellites, and shuttles into space. Their own scientists were working on it, of course, but they outsourced some of the research to get it done faster."

Made sense. A shotgun approach would assure that private industry would recruit the best talent they could find.

"After nearly four years, Exmyth provided their results to government inspectors, who decided they hadn't made much progress and cut the funding, terminating the contract."

"I'm not seeing a fraud," Wu said.

Patel grinned, deliberately stringing them all along. "That's because you haven't heard the rest. Shortly after they lost the government contract, Exmyth was bought out by a large multinational conglomerate."

Wu sat up straight. "Vaden-Quest Enterprises."

Patel nodded. "Dr. Castillo was separated from the other scientists and given her own lab," he said. "She was tasked with working on antigravity." He gave his head a small shake. "I know it sounds ridiculous, but I found a paper trail. In fact, it looks like the kind of paper trail you'd leave if you wanted someone to find it."

Dani got that strange tingling sensation on the back of her neck that meant things were coming together. "So Angela Peralta—Dr. Castillo at the time—deliberately left a record of what she was doing before she disappeared."

Patel pointed at her in silent acknowledgment before going on. "I believe she left a hidden code in her files that didn't allow them to be completely corrupted. Otherwise, they could've been totally obliterated."

"What was she hiding?" Flint asked.

"From what I can gather, the timing was too perfect between losing the government contract and getting bought out." He gave them a significant look. "For a butt-ton of money. More than what they were worth on paper."

"On paper?" Wu said. "That means they had other value?"

"I think so," Patel said. "And so did Vaden-Quest, because they went all in on Exmyth."

Dani figured the only reason a huge company would overpay to buy out a small one that had just lost their biggest contract was because they saw hidden value. "Vaden-Quest had the inside scoop on something Exmyth had in development."

"That's what I thought too," Patel said. "So I focused on Dr. Castillo's work in her new assignment. That's when I found it." He paused, adding a bit of drama. "She was working on antigravity . . . and making progress."

Wu tilted his head in thought. "The timing looks like Castillo realized her work in propulsion might have an application for antigrav."

Dani was no physicist, but she'd heard enough about antigravity to know that scientists had been working on it for decades, thinking it was the path to the future.

Flint voiced his confusion. "Propulsion pushes you forward. Gravity pulls you toward the ground. What does one have to do with the other?" He crossed his arms. "In other words, why would her propulsion research lead her into another field entirely?"

"On the outer edges of science, there's a relationship," Patel said. "It hasn't been proven yet, but some theoretical physicists believe that altering gravity could propel an object a hell of a lot faster. Maybe faster than light."

Dani summed it up. "That would be the Holy Grail of travel."

"That would be quantum travel," Patel corrected. "And that's why some physicists say it's impossible." He lifted a shoulder. "Personally, I think those physicists don't have enough imagination. I mean, Einstein said nothing traveled faster than the speed of light, but then quantum physics kind of pissed him off."

Dani recalled learning of Einstein's frustration with entangled subatomic particles reacting with no apparent regard to established laws of space and time. "He called it 'spooky action at a distance.'"

Wu had his own take. "Theoretically, if humans didn't have to contend with gravity, we could travel a lot faster—without turning our bodies into mush from g-forces."

"Tina Castillo had just gotten a PhD in quantum physics," Patel said. "I think that's why Richard Sterling recruited her for Exmyth Technologies. He was getting ready to bid on a government contract in her field of study."

As a small firm, Exmyth couldn't have paid for Nobel Prize candidates. Sterling would have sought out young scientists toiling in obscurity who were looking for a break . . . or at least a way to pay the bills. A newly minted PhD, Tina Castillo wouldn't have been at the top of anyone's list in the world of elite science and academia.

"Sterling took a gamble on relatively unknown scientists," she said. "Hoping it would pay off if one of them made a big discovery."

"I see where you're going," Wu said. "Easton was a mechanical engineer and Wallace was a chemical engineer. Castillo was the quantum physicist. She would theorize and they would realize."

As usual, Wu had gotten to the heart of the matter. And it seemed as if Castillo's thinking had veered into a related field that could prove lucrative.

Flint characterized it in his own way. "I suppose you could say she was hired to mine for copper and struck gold instead."

"Exactly," Wu said. "I recall a case where a government contractor created a textile that reflected light so that it made anything behind it virtually invisible. The CEO saw the potential to make a hefty profit, but the problem was that Uncle Sam had paid for the lab, the scientists, and years of salary for everyone involved in the development."

Flint's brows went up. "I'm guessing he told the government he hadn't gotten any results, then tried to sell the new tech?"

Wu's expression darkened. "Worse. He tried to sell it to our adversaries."

Dani imagined being out in the battlefield only to have invisible troops or weapons begin taking out swaths of American soldiers. The advantage would make even the tiniest terrorist cell nearly invincible. "Tell me you shut him down before he sold all the secrets."

Wu nodded. "One of the scientists got wind of it and came to us. We secured FISA warrants that allowed us to catch him before he completed any transactions."

Under the Foreign Intelligence Surveillance Act, federal agencies could seek court approval for surveillance on those suspected of espionage or terrorism. In this case, classified technology had been prevented from falling into the wrong hands.

"Do you think that's what Sterling was up to?" Flint asked him.

"At this point, it's the only thing that makes sense," Wu said. "Especially if Castillo found out he wanted to sell her work to the highest bidder and she wanted to blow the whistle."

That put everything in a whole new light. "He'd want to silence her, but not before he got all her notes and research."

"Couldn't Easton provide that?" Flint asked. "He was the lead scientist on her team. Or Wallace?"

Patel had an answer. "From what I pieced together, it looks like she shared her part of their joint project, but when she started working on theories in a related field, she kept them to herself until she could tell if they were worth sharing."

They all paused to consider the implications.

Dani tried to connect the dots. "Toro sent us after Castillo, but he made us work to figure out her name is now Peralta. Did he want us to find her because he knows she was on a path to figure out new tech that could be worth billions?" She blew out a sigh. "I'm not buying it."

"In the video, he told us she had the last piece of the puzzle," Patel said. "It sounded like he was referring to the evidence he's hidden. His so-called treasure."

"And we still haven't found her," Dani said. "I'm worried we're too late."

"Let's see if we can brainstorm an answer," Wu said.

That strategy worked for most people, who bounced ideas off each other in a group setting. Dani's mind, however, worked differently. She preferred to work alone and in silence, using free association. She realized her process was more like her mother's than she would have believed in the past. But the Rangers had turned her into a team player, so she gave her supervisor's method a try.

Two hours later, they had come up with more questions than answers.

"We're going around in circles," Patel said. "I don't know about you guys, but my brain is extra crispy."

Dani had started the day at 26 Fed, then hopped a jet to Arizona. Perhaps jet lag was setting in for all of them.

Wu glanced at his watch. "Damn. It's nearly ten o'clock."

"Tell that to my body," Patel said. "There's a three-hour time difference, so it feels like one in the morning."

Wu dragged a hand through his thick black hair. "The pilot's in a room across the hall."

Flint looked around. "There's plenty of room for us all to crash here. I say we get some rest and reconvene in the morning."

"Agreed," Wu said, then gave Patel an apologetic look. "Can you set up a secure direct video link to Director Franklin? He wants regular updates."

Patel opened his laptop. "I'll set it up now."

Dani went through the door to the adjoining suite and dropped her go-bag on an upholstered chair in the corner. After a quick shower, she brushed her teeth and rummaged through her black reinforced nylon duffel. Her grasping fingers found the men's extra-large T-shirt she'd kept for years. She pulled it over her head, making sure the 75th Ranger Regiment shield was in front. She made a beeline for her bed, snuggled into the cool sheets, and ordered her subconscious mind to work on the problem as she slept, a technique that had served her in the past.

Tired but wired.

Something she'd experienced on many occasions over the years. There were times when, despite how drained she was, sleep did not come easily.

Tonight, she tossed and turned, replaying the day's events in her mind. She finally began to drift off as images from their search of the Peralta home morphed into images from another search years earlier.

When she was on a classified mission with the Rangers.

CHAPTER 44

Gunfire echoed through the building all around her.

"Corporal Vega, you're up."

Dani shouldered her rifle and rushed through the smoke-filled corridor toward the squad leader's voice.

"Where do you need me?"

Staff Sergeant Rutger jerked his chin toward a door to his right. "We found a symbol vault in this room when we cleared it. The documents have gotta be inside."

Before their deployment, they had been briefed on a new system being used by the terrorists. After their electronic transmissions were regularly intercepted, they resorted to using paper documents transported by hand to deliver instructions throughout their network of cells. This created another challenge.

How would they keep others from confiscating their plans?

Sources had explained that they created special vaults carved into the stone walls of the compounds. Crude wooden levers were lined up in a row underneath the vault. If the correct lever was lifted, the heavy stone door would slide open. Raising any other lever would break open a glass vial inside the chamber, dumping acid onto any papers, photos, maps, or other valuable intel inside. The Americans called the hiding places "symbol vaults" because a series of symbols carved above the small recessed chamber indicated which lever should be lifted.

The system was low tech, requiring no electrical components, and highly effective. Two previous missions had resulted in a failure to recover any usable material.

Which was the reason she was here.

Three Ranger squads had been deployed to secure a compound that intelligence had determined to be the base of operations for one of the most notorious and deadly terrorist organizations in the world. The staff sergeant in charge of her squad had placed her in the middle of the formation, a relatively protected position during a high-risk operation.

"This might take a minute," Sergeant Rutger said in his characteristic understatement. "I'll designate someone to watch your back while you work it out."

A voice she recognized spoke up from behind her. "I'll do it."

Jason Holt stood guard in the doorway as she headed straight for the vault, which looked exactly like the drawings they had seen. She faced the stone wall and focused all her attention on the task at hand, placing total trust in Holt to keep her safe.

There were five levers, which meant only a 20 percent chance of getting it right by sheer guessing. She inspected each lever for signs that one of them had been handled more than the others. Wood held oil from human skin. No such luck. The end of each was wrapped in identical strips of cloth. All were clean, and she had no doubt they were changed frequently.

She glanced up at the six symbols carved into the stone above the vault. They were simple, ancient shapes. A circle, a square, a star, a triangle, and a rectangle, in that order. Which one was the correct choice? She considered what she knew about each shape and the symbolism behind it. The problem was that geometric shapes held many meanings going back centuries, often differing by culture and tradition.

Gunfire broke out in another part of the compound, reverberating through the corridors. Her pulse kicked up. She needed to figure this out quickly. Shouts sounded in two languages. Hostiles had been hiding on the premises, and her squad was flushing them out.

"Hurry up, Vega," Holt said. "Sarge is holding the rooms in front of us, but he can't go forward yet."

Of course, he wanted to join the squad in the firefight. She refocused on the carvings. Even though they must have been done in the past year, the fact that they'd been etched in stone made them seem timeless.

Her current situation wasn't timeless. A battle raged all around them. She realized that her squad would not retreat until she got the documents. They would know that if they fell back, the enemy would retrieve and destroy them. They were waiting for her. If she didn't hurry, they would die.

If she was in this position, that meant whoever created the vault would have anticipated that their own people might be caught in the same situation. The answer had to be simple, straightforward, and easy to remember. She looked at the symbols again.

Which one was correct? She turned the question over in her mind. The correct one. The one. One was correct. That meant one was different. She studied the shapes again. They were all different, but four of the five had something in common.

The answer came to her at the exact moment a spate of automatic gunfire ripped through the room. She hit the deck instinctively, pulling the rifle from her shoulder as she went down. More blasts, these she recognized from Holt's weapon. She rolled to the side, seeking cover behind a stone pillar near the side of the room.

A bullet tore into her left upper arm.

She shouldered her rifle as a pair of terrorists entered the room, their weapons at the ready. They were not firing, and she didn't stop to think why. She simply opened up on them. They hadn't known she was inside, and it cost them their lives.

Silence filled the space. When the smoke cleared, she saw Holt lying motionless on the ground, a pool of blood widening on the dusty ground beneath him.

"No!"

She rushed to his side, careful to keep her weapon trained on the door. The terrorists' ammo had pierced Holt's body armor. She slapped her hands on the oozing wounds.

"Stay with me, Holt."

No response.

"Holt, don't you dare die on me."

Still nothing.

"Please, Holt, don't leave me. Not now." She choked back a sob and finally whispered the words she'd been holding back. "I love you."

CHAPTER 45

The following morning, Friday, October 11, 8:00 a.m.
Kokopelli Suites Hotel, Mesa, Arizona

"Holt!" Dani sat bolt upright in the strange bed. Had she yelled the name loud enough to wake the others?

The men's extra-large 75th Ranger Regiment T-shirt she'd slipped on last night clung to her sweat-damp body. It was the only thing belonging to Holt she'd managed to keep when his effects were shipped back to his grieving parents. She'd never met them and didn't feel it was her place to tell them she loved their son. Not when she had never even admitted it to him.

Until the moment he died. Until it was too late.

Shortly after joining the unit, she would catch Holt watching her. It had taken months for her to realize his expression held none of the resentment she had seen in some of the others who didn't think women should be Rangers.

She found herself returning his covert glances, but her flirting skills were virtually nonexistent. Finally, she took matters into her own hands. At the end of their next mission, she waited until he was alone and, with zero finesse or subtlety, walked up to him and asked him out.

He responded in kind, also with zero finesse or subtlety, by pulling her into his arms and kissing her. Hard.

They had not been able to spend much time together but made the most of stolen moments. She had decided to share her growing feelings when the mission at the compound was over, but he had given his life to guard her.

Something she would never allow anyone else to do.

She'd never gotten over Holt's death, or her role in it. He was the reason she slept alone every night—except when he joined her in her dreams.

He might still be alive if she'd cracked the code faster. They wouldn't have been in that room for the sneak attack. That was when she became obsessed with improving her skills. Never again would her failure bring harm to someone else.

Four Rangers had died in that operation. They had secured the compound after all enemy combatants were taken prisoner or killed. After a field dressing from one of the medics, Dani went back in to pull the lever. She had been right. It was the one beneath the circle, the only geometric symbol that contained no angles.

The incident was part of the reason she'd left the Army after ten years of service rather than staying for a full military retirement. She was often asked the question, and always found a way to dodge it.

There was no dodging her nightmares, however, and she suspected they would haunt her for the rest of her life. But why, when her body needed rest and recovery, had her mind sabotaged her with ghosts from the past?

The answer to the clue back then had been so simple, yet maddeningly out of reach, as bullets flew and bombs detonated while her team put their lives on the line for her.

She'd never felt the weight of another person's sacrifice since. Or had she?

What about Toro?

She recalled a moment during the undercover mission when they'd been compromised and trapped together. Only one of them could survive, and Toro had chosen her life over his.

So maybe there was a third man who had taken a piece of her heart.

The thought of Toro brought her back to the situation at hand. As much as she didn't want to dwell on how the overseas mission had ended, she forced herself to consider why that particular memory had bubbled up to the surface.

In her dream, everything had been vivid. The carvings in stone practically glowed, as if calling her attention to them.

Shapes.

She'd picked out the correct shape among the others. What was the connection?

She sat on the bed and released her mind to freely roam among the possibilities. She closed her eyes to help her visualize patterns that began to take form, discarding one possibility after the other until . . .

Her eyes flew open as the answer snapped into focus. As before, she cursed herself for not seeing it sooner. Was she too late?

CHAPTER 46

8:10 a.m.

Wu absently gazed at the image of Kokopelli etched into the ceramic mug and reflected on the morning's developments.

He'd set his alarm to wake up early to brief Director Franklin, who agreed with their assessment that the whole case had its roots in what happened in Denver five years ago. Franklin also supported Wu's decision not to alert law enforcement, pointing out that any bulletin they disseminated would have to include that Tina Castillo's alias was Angela Peralta, potentially exposing her if she had taken her son with her and gone into hiding somewhere. Wu assured him the BOLO would go out if they didn't find any sign of her by the end of the day.

"That java taste as good as it smells?" Flint had wandered into the kitchenette in search of caffeine.

"They left out a basket filled with Starbucks pods for the machine," he said. "That should make Vega happy."

Flint took one of the mugs from a tray on the counter and shoved it under the dispenser before loading a pod of dark roast.

Wu was about to take another sip when the door to the adjoining suite unlatched, and Vega raced into the living room area.

"I figured it out," she said, breathless.

She glanced from him to Flint, then back to him again.

He and Flint stood beside each other, mute. He wasn't sure if Flint was stunned into silence by Vega's announcement or by the unexpected display of her smooth bronze skin. The oversize T-shirt covering her upper body skimmed the tops of her thighs and did nothing to conceal her long, toned, very bare legs.

Wu kept his eyes on her face. "I'll pour you a cup of coffee while you get dressed."

Vega glanced down, apparently just realizing she'd rushed from her room without stopping to put on pants.

She turned and spoke over her shoulder. "Be right back."

He glanced at Flint. "Can you wake up Patel? He should hear this."

Flint nodded and left the living room area.

Less than five minutes later, they were all sitting at the same table where they'd been last night, each with a mug of coffee. With tousled hair and a rumpled shirt, Patel looked like he'd just rolled out of bed. Vega, now wearing black BDUs with her T-shirt, was brimming with excitement. Flint had recovered his composure after Vega's unexpected appearance in the living room and now had his cop face firmly in place.

Everyone looked at Vega expectantly.

"Can you pull up the photos of the house you took yesterday?" she asked Patel. "I need a close-up of the pictures Angela left on the kitchen counter."

Wu recalled the photographs. They had discussed possible meanings, but Vega had obviously come up with a new idea. She waited until Patel turned the screen to face them before pointing at the photos.

"Remember how we thought these pictures were about her name changing to Peralta?"

"I couldn't get my head around it," Flint said. "But it sounds like you've come up with a reason."

"If I'm right, it's the best possible news," she said. "Because it means Angela and her son weren't kidnapped. They're in hiding."

Whatever her theory was, Wu hoped it was correct. It would mean he'd made the right call about not putting out a BOLO. He'd stayed up several hours last night second-guessing his decision. If they were being held captive, or worse, it would be on his head. He could withstand whatever sanctions the Bureau dished out, but he would have a hard time living with his conscience.

"When I get stuck and need a fresh perspective, I put myself in the other person's place," Vega went on. "I'm Angela Peralta. I've been in hiding since before my only child was born. Everything's been quiet, but then I learn that my two former colleagues and my former boss are all dead in the space of forty-eight hours. I can't take the chance that my cover will hold. At a bare minimum, I should lay low for a while until I know the coast is clear, so I go into hiding."

So far that tracked.

"I've gone online to search for news stories about the investigations into the deaths of Easton, Wallace, and Sterling. I see that the FBI is looking into all three cases, but I'm afraid to go to them for help, but I do decide to leave a clue behind as kind of a backup plan. If anyone figures out who I really am, they'll come to my house looking for me, so that's where I'll leave it. It's got to be something only the FBI would understand."

She pointed at the screen. "Angela left out an album with over twenty photos of the day she took her son to the museum. Each of the Peralta Stones was featured in a separate picture, but these are the only two she pulled out. Why?"

She glanced at them eagerly, her eyes lingering on his as if she expected him to grasp her meaning. He hated to disappoint, but he was nowhere closer to understanding than he had been yesterday.

"I had a dream last night," she said when no one responded. "A nightmare, really. It was about one of the times when I was deployed overseas with my unit. We were in a terrorist stronghold, and I had to decode something." She dismissed the rest of the story with a wave of her hand. "I won't bore you with the details. Bottom line is, there was a pattern involving shapes."

Wu was certain the details weren't boring in the least. Like others he'd met who had served in special forces, Vega was humble about her elite training and the harrowing missions she'd been part of. He respected her privacy and didn't press for more, but if he ever had the chance, he might try to get behind the wall she'd built around herself.

"I woke up thinking about shapes, and that's when I realized we'd been looking at the photos the wrong way. We were focused on the name Peralta, and the museum itself, and figuring out where the real stones were located, but we should have paid more attention to the shapes carved into the stones."

"A heart and a cross," Patel said. "Where does that get us?"

"Angela may have only had moments to rush out the door. If everything went to shit, she'd want us to find her. The clue had to lead to her bolt-hole, but there would have to be a way for her to be certain only the good guys would find her. So she'd need a buffer."

"What kind of buffer?" Flint asked.

"A person. Someone who could ask the right questions and make sure. Someone she trusted with not only her own life, but the life of her child."

"Her background didn't reveal any close friends or family," Patel said. "I checked into every corner of her life. If she even had so much as a poker buddy, I'd have known about it."

Patel seemed to take the idea that he could have overlooked someone so intimately connected with the subject as a slight on his professional skills. Wu recalled reviewing Patel's background before requesting him for an assignment to the Counterterrorism Division. Patel had graduated near the top of his class at MIT. He could have made a fortune working in private industry, as his parents had expected. Like Wu, however, Patel forged his own path, choosing a career fighting crime as a civilian analyst despite his family's objections. And like Wu, he was meticulous in his work.

Vega raised a placating hand. "This isn't someone who would've shown up. I only thought about it because of something about my own family. Do you remember seeing a crucifix on the wall?"

"There were two," Wu said. "One was hanging in the foyer and the other was in the main bedroom."

"We had them in our apartment when I was growing up," Vega said. "My mother is very religious. Seeing them in Angela's home made me conclude she is a practicing Catholic."

Wu suddenly got it. "She would trust her priest."

Vega beamed at him, then turned to Patel. "Can you do a search for Catholic churches in Apache Junction?"

His fingers flashed over the keys. Apache Junction was a small city. Only two responses appeared.

St. George Roman Catholic Parish

Our Lady of the Sacred Heart Catholic Church

"A cross is sacred," Flint muttered. "And, well, the heart is obvious." He looked at Vega. "Even after you explained it, I don't know how you did it, but this feels right."

"Did you already call the church?" Wu asked her.

"I checked the schedule. Morning Mass started at eight." She checked her watch. "It's almost half past. It should be over in thirty minutes or so."

Wu got to his feet. "That gives us just enough time to get cleaned up and get over there. We won't be able to call ahead, but maybe it's better if we see the priest in person anyway."

As the others followed suit, he wondered when he would stop being surprised by how Vega's mind worked. He knew a few things about her family, so perhaps unconventional thinking was an inherited trait, but she had obviously spent years honing her skills.

She had breathed new life into an investigation that had gone cold. They had a solid lead, and, for the first time, it felt like they might be one step ahead of their nameless adversary.

CHAPTER 47

9:15 a.m.
Our Lady of the Sacred Heart Catholic Church
Apache Junction, Arizona

Dani recalled the last time she'd gone to confession.

In stark contrast to the ornate cathedral she attended in New York, this quaint Arizona church was constructed in the old Spanish Mission style, complete with a huge brass bell, adobe walls, and a terra-cotta tile roof. Aside from the services held inside, the two buildings seemed to have nothing in common.

Until she met Father Ramirez.

His kind brown eyes and warm handshake restored a sense of connection she hadn't realized she'd been missing lately. Her line of work made it difficult for her to feel comfortable entering a holy place, even if only to ask for guidance.

"Everyone's gone now," he said. "We can go back to my office."

They followed him down a corridor to a small cluster of offices at the rear of the building. His office door, blending with the motif, was darkly stained heavy wood with a wrought iron cage over a square cut into the center. When they entered, Father Ramirez gestured toward a grouping of furniture that gave her pause.

The priest noted her reaction and chuckled. "A parishioner willed this collection to the parish."

The chairs, sofa, and love seat were constructed of roughly hewn logs—bark still attached—and the dense seat cushions were covered in cowhide—fur still attached.

Flint appeared to be equally shocked. "Can't imagine what his house looked like."

"No," Father Ramirez said amicably. "You can't. And I wouldn't try to describe it. We're all simply grateful to have the furniture."

Once they all settled themselves, Wu wasted no further time on chitchat. "Father, we need to discuss one of your parishioners. It's time sensitive."

They had arrived just as morning Mass had ended. Wu had discreetly shown his credentials to the priest, who told them he would help them as soon as he saw everyone out the door. Naturally, that had involved promises of praying for a couple of sick relatives, planning a christening, and explaining to an elderly gentleman how to make arrangements for his bedridden wife to get Communion at home from one of the lay priests.

Dani had seen a vein in Wu's temple begin to throb moments before Father Ramirez finally returned to them.

"Before I can offer any assistance," he said to Wu, "I'll need to have a closer look at your identification."

They spent the next agonizing few minutes showing their respective IDs to the priest in a scene that forcibly reminded Dani of Toltec manager Maddie Pimentel inspecting their creds before providing information. She began to wonder if Toro had been involved in this arrangement or if Angela had learned this extra level of precaution from him. It was, after all, the extra buffer she'd anticipated, but with yet another layer.

Once Father Ramirez was satisfied, Wu started again. "Father, we believe one of your parishioners, Angela Peralta, is in danger. We need to find her to safeguard her."

"Angela," the priest murmured. "I have been praying for her and her son."

They exchanged excited glances. On the drive over, they had discussed what to do if the priest had taken information in confidence and felt he couldn't reveal it. The fact that he'd confirmed not only that Angela attended his church but that he knew she was in need of prayer indicated he might be able to say more.

"When did you last see her?" Dani asked.

He turned to her. "Two days ago. We prayed together. She confided that some bad people were after her and that she needed a place to hide." He studied each of them in turn and sighed. "She did not tell me any of this in confession. In fact, she told me to share it with any federal agents who came looking for her . . . if I checked to be sure they weren't impostors."

"Do you know where she and her son are?" Wu asked.

He regarded them a long moment before answering. "I do."

Silence filled the office. Father Ramirez made no further comment. He seemed to be waiting for something, but she couldn't figure out what. Surely, he knew they wanted the answer. Why not just provide it?

She took a chance. "Where are they, Father?"

The priest was silent so long she became concerned he wouldn't answer. Then, "She asked if I knew of a place where no one would find her. A place she and her son could stay in hiding for weeks if necessary." He gave them an imploring look. "What is she mixed up in?"

Dani felt torn between two worlds. Raised by a devoutly religious mother who believed confession was good for the soul, she felt drawn to confide in Father Ramirez. On the other hand, she had taken an oath to serve her country and had also passed a rigorous background check giving her access to classified materials. She was never allowed to divulge sensitive information, even to a man of the cloth.

She was about to say as much when Wu spoke up. "I'm sure you understand confidentiality. You can't break yours, and we can't break ours."

Again, her boss had put it all succinctly. He'd shown respect while drawing a bright line they would not cross. Now it came down to Father Ramirez. Would he accept the limitations and help them anyway, or had Angela given him other instructions?

He gave Wu a knowing look. "Then we understand each other."

Did that mean he couldn't say any more? Was this a dismissal? Had they failed some sort of test?

Patel, apparently thinking along the same lines, added a plea. "We think someone might try to harm her. Maybe her child too. Please help us so we can protect them."

Father Ramirez nodded thoughtfully. "She warned me this might happen. And she told me what to do." His brow furrowed. "Let me show you something." He stood and retrieved a brochure from his desk before returning. "We have many programs here at our parish."

Dani watched as he unfolded the glossy pamphlet that detailed all sorts of outreach and community services. Sensing Wu's growing impatience, she tried to steer the priest toward the objective.

"Is Angela involved in one of these programs, Father?"

He flipped another page and pointed at a map. "This is our church retreat. It's a hundred-acre parcel of land that was donated to the parish nearly eighty years ago. We've set it up as a wilderness retreat for our youth, the vestry, marriage counseling, and our latest mission, internet addiction."

The map showed what looked like a campground out in the desert. Dani could see how anyone addicted to the internet would be forced to go through withdrawal when they had no hope of Wi-Fi for miles around and a risky trek through the desert to reconnect.

"Is that where she is?" Wu asked.

"All I can say for sure is that's where I sent her and her son two days ago," Father Ramirez said. "But I can't imagine her going anywhere else. The camp is all set up with electricity, water, indoor plumbing, and air-conditioning. She took plenty of food for both of them, and I'm supposed to bring more supplies and check on them every two days—which I was going to do this afternoon. It's about an hour's drive from here."

"Is there a group out there now?" Flint asked.

"The next group isn't scheduled to be there for over a month, which is why I told her to use it."

Patel said, "With no Wi-Fi or internet, I'm guessing you can't call her."

"Correct."

They were in a bind. Even if Patel jumped through the hoops to reposition a satellite to get calling capabilities, it would do no good if Angela's phone wasn't connected to receive.

"We can't wait around for backup. We have to get to her now," Dani said. "There's no choice."

Wu shot her a look. "There's always a choice. I just need to make the right one."

With those words, he was taking the blame for whatever happened next onto himself and absolving them of all responsibility. It was his decision.

"Has anyone else come looking for Angela?" Wu asked him.

"You're the first."

One look at her colleagues told her they were all thinking the same thing. How long until someone else showed up?

Wu appeared to come to a decision. "I'm taking Agent Vega and Detective Flint," he said to Father Ramirez. "Mr. Patel is a civilian analyst. He'll stay here and provide information to the FBI Phoenix field office's SWAT team when they arrive."

The priest registered shock at the mention of a tactical team, but quickly regained his composure. "What can I do to help?"

Wu had deftly communicated how dire the situation was without divulging any classified information. Father Ramirez, for his part, had expressed his willingness to put himself and his church at their disposal.

Well played all around.

Now all they had to do was get to Angela, but were they already too late?

CHAPTER 48

One hour later
Sacred Heart Wilderness Retreat
Sonoran Desert, Arizona

It had been a while since Dani used her orienteering skills. No longer going on far-flung missions, her usual environment was now New York City, where a quick glance at a street sign told you where you were.

The map in the brochure had been little more than a thick black line meandering through triangular shapes that represented scattered peaks. A set of wavy squiggles near the site of the retreat indicated a stream fed by the Salt River, but Father Ramirez had warned them it often ran dry a few months after monsoon season.

Fortunately, the skill came back to her quickly and she guided Wu, who was at the wheel of the SUV. Flint was in the back, trying to get a signal on his phone and having no luck.

"That's it," she said as they crested another hill.

About a hundred yards ahead, two railroad ties had been planted upright on either side of the dirt road. A third beam was balanced between them at the top, forming a large archway. A rustic sign made of a weathered plank dangled from a pair of horseshoes nailed to the overhead tie. The words SACRED HEART WILDERNESS RETREAT were branded into the wood.

"Kind of funny to have an entry gate when there's no fence," Flint said. "It's all just wide-open land."

Dani surveyed the area. "I can make out ten cabins, a larger building for gatherings, and what looks like a mess hall."

Wu drove through the entrance. "There are tire tracks in the dust, but I don't see any vehicle."

"Or any sign of Angela and her son," she said. "My guess is she hid her car somewhere nearby and is holed up in one of the cabins."

"Makes sense," Flint said. "It's dead quiet out here. She probably heard us coming and hunkered down."

Wu pulled over, bringing the SUV to a stop. "She has no idea who we are. She's got to be terrified." He buzzed down his window and called out, "Ms. Peralta, this is the FBI. We need to talk to you."

When they received no response, Dani opened her door and put one booted foot on the ground. "We want to help you and your son."

Nothing.

"She might have taken off again," Flint said. "Should we search the place?"

"May as well," Wu said. "We came all this way."

They got out and began methodically looking inside each cabin. They were approaching the third one when a female voice called out to them.

"Stop, or I'll shoot!"

They halted, each reflexively drawing a weapon.

"We're with the FBI," Wu repeated. "We need to—"

"What you need to do is leave. I have a gun pointed straight at you."

Dani looked at the open window of the third cabin but couldn't see anyone. She assumed Angela was keeping out of sight. Or someone else was forcing her to stay hidden while getting them to leave.

"Are you and Tace alone?" Dani asked, deliberately using her son's first name to show her they knew what was at stake.

"Go. Away. Now."

Dani detected a note of fear and tried to reassure her. "We don't want to hurt you, Angela. We want to protect both of you."

By silent consensus, the men were letting Dani take the lead, no doubt hoping another woman might seem less threatening. She took a step closer.

And Angela pulled the trigger.

CHAPTER 49

Our Lady of the Sacred Heart Catholic Church
Apache Junction, Arizona

He was the forsaken one.

Foley recalled the day he'd been refused Holy Communion. Since then, he hadn't given a second thought to harming a priest. But for some reason, it didn't sit well today.

So he merely supervised and left the wet work to the team he'd called in from LA.

Foley looked away when their leader, a mountain of a man code-named Bravo, slugged Father Ramirez in the stomach for the second time.

The priest released a loud grunt and slumped against the ropes binding him to the chair.

Bravo gave the one called Sanjeev Patel a considering look. "What about you, pretty boy? Ready to talk?"

Foley knew Patel was a computer specialist, but the asshole refused to tell them where his laptop was.

Bravo's second-in-command, code-named Charlie, adopted a conversational tone. "I suppose he is kind of pretty, isn't he? But maybe not so much with a broken nose and some missing teeth."

The computer wasn't as important as finding Vega, who would lead them to Angela Peralta, who would lead them to Toro's stash of evidence.

They had been able to track Vega as far as the church, but the signal dropped about a mile down the road. Foley's tech-support specialist had performed a partial reboot of the company's private satellite, but that didn't solve the problem. He was now rebooting each subsection of the software, which would take half an hour. And there were still no guarantees.

Foley had decided to get the information they needed the old-fashioned way. Fortunately for him, everyone had left the church, but some parishioners would return soon. They were on borrowed time in the rectory, where the priest lived on church grounds.

Foxtrot, another member of the team, offered his opinion. "I hate to mess up his face," he said. "I'm thinking another part of his body is more important to him."

"Damn," Charlie said. "You don't fool around."

Foxtrot scowled. "I'm talking about his hands." He gestured to Patel's bound wrists. "That's how he makes a living. How he programs codes that interfere with our work."

Bravo left the unconscious priest to stand beside his men. "I've got a hacksaw in my tool kit."

Foley had heard enough. "He'll bleed out. Besides, I don't want us covered in blood if we get pulled over driving to wherever the hell Vega is."

"We can't drive anywhere until they tell us where to go." Bravo turned back to Foxtrot. "Give me a ball-peen hammer. I'll pulverize every single one of his fingers into hamburger meat. He won't even be able to feed himself when I'm done."

The gleam in Bravo's eyes bordered on indecent as Foxtrot went to fetch his bag.

"While we're waiting," Foley said to Patel, "I'll make you an offer. Bravo will only destroy one hand if you give us the ETA on your backup."

He had assumed they would notify the local FBI field office in Phoenix, but he wasn't sure they had requested backup. He didn't know what the protocol was for interviewing a priest about a missing woman and child, but it probably wasn't considered a high-risk undertaking that required extra personnel. Still, better to know for sure.

Patel's dark eyes found his, but he said nothing.

"Fine. Have it your way."

Foxtrot returned with the hammer and was just handing it over to Bravo when Foley's phone buzzed with an incoming text.

"Stand by," he said, glancing at the screen. "It's tech support." He quickly scanned the message.

SIGNAL REGAINED. TARGET IS APPROX ONE HOUR EAST. COORDINATES BELOW.

Foley clicked on the link and saw a geo-mapped series of waypoints leading out into the desert.

He addressed the team. "We've got a lock on her location. Let's move."

Bravo pointed the hammer at the two prisoners. "What about them?"

Charlie offered his opinion. "I say we kill them. Dead men tell no tales."

Foley looked from the analyst to the priest, who had regained consciousness and was following the discussion.

Ramirez closed his eyes and inclined his head in prayer. "Forgive them, Father, for they know not what they do."

CHAPTER 50

Sacred Heart Wilderness Retreat

"One step closer and the next bullet goes into your chest!"

Dani registered the panic in Angela Peralta's voice. Never good when the person shouting has a gun pointed at you.

The good news was that the first round had gone wide deliberately, which implied Angela could handle her weapon. The bad news was that she felt threatened and would protect her child.

What if they'd raced all over the country to find Angela before ruthless killers did, only to have her shoot them?

Dani wasn't sure if it would make the situation better or worse, but they were at a stalemate now, so she took a gamble. "Gustavo Toro sent us to find you."

Her words were met with silence. She wasn't sure what Angela's relationship with Toro had been, but she had her suspicions.

"Toro's dead," Angela finally called out. "And you will be too if you don't leave."

Not the reception she'd been hoping for. "He wanted us to find and protect you."

"Yeah, right." Angela sounded scornful. "You think I'm going to fall for fake FBI agents?"

"What can I do to convince you?"

A long pause, then, "Tell me something about Toro that only some-one he trusted would know. Something personal. A secret."

Dani thought back to her undercover assignment with the former hit man. There was one thing he'd shared with her that she would never have believed, and yet it was true. She opted to share this partic-ular piece of information because she now felt confident her suspicions about Angela and Toro were correct.

"He had a code. He would never harm a child."

The door to the cabin slowly creaked open, and a woman matching Angela's photo on her Arizona driver's license stepped out. Her right hand hung by her side, gripping a pistol with its muzzle pointed at the ground.

Dani, Wu, and Flint all lowered their weapons in unison.

When Angela spoke, she was no longer shouting threats. "I hated everything about what he did, but the fact that he wouldn't cross that line is the only reason I'm alive today."

"You mean because you have a child?" Wu asked.

She shifted her gaze to him. "Gustavo Toro was sent to kill me. When he showed up, I told him I was three months pregnant. At first, he didn't believe me, so I showed him the sonogram. That's when he decided to go against his orders." She let out a humorless laugh. "A killer with a conscience . . . who knew?"

In his videos, Toro had described Angela as the target of a nefarious organization . . . never as someone he'd been contracted to murder. Dani tried to fit this new information into the template she had already constructed about what had happened between Toro and Angela. She had assumed they had been romantically involved. She'd even specu-lated that he might have fathered her child, but Angela was already pregnant when they met, so that wasn't possible.

"We're glad Toro's clues led us to you," Wu said. "But we need to get you to a safe location right away." He hesitated before adding, "If we found you, others can too."

Angela's grip tightened on her gun. She seemed to be considering raising it again. "I'm not going anywhere with you until I see some ID." She narrowed her eyes. "I know how to tell fakes from the real thing."

She stepped closer to inspect Dani's creds first. "Give it here."

Dani placed the folded leather case into Angela's outstretched hand. Angela took it and angled it different ways in the bright sunlight, probably looking for a hologram. A scrap of paper fluttered to the ground.

Angela stooped to pick it up. "What's this?"

"My mother's artwork," Dani said. "It's a—"

"Geometric design," Angela finished. "And I recognize the pattern." She met Dani's eyes. "Your mother did this?"

How could she explain? "She has a special gift with colors, shapes, and sounds."

Angela looked back down at the paper, transfixed. "Calling it a gift is an understatement."

Dani couldn't help but wonder if this had something to do with what her mother's treating psychiatrist, Dr. Maffuccio, had been talking about. Was her mother's drawing a manifestation of her brain's unusual connectivity?

"I'd like to study this," Angela continued. "There could be applications for—"

"We can discuss that later," Wu said, redirecting everyone's attention. "Right now, we need to get going. Where's your son?"

Angela's head snapped up at the mention of her child. She handed the paper back to Dani and didn't bother inspecting anyone else's ID. "I told him to hide. I'll get him."

Without another word, she turned and hurried back inside the third cabin.

Dani turned to Wu. "There's only one road in and out of here. We'll have to keep a lookout for any vehicles heading our way as we go."

He pulled out his phone and shook his head. "I'd love to call Patel and ask if our SWAT team showed up at the church, but I haven't had a signal since we were about half an hour out from the church."

They were truly isolated. Cut off from all communication. If her boss wanted to use the sat phone, he'd have to request repositioning. Not a quick or easy process working through the channels of a government bureaucracy when several other agencies shared the same satellite.

Flint said, "We should be okay as long as we get out of here quickly. If we see anyone coming, we can—"

His words were cut off by a shrill scream from inside the cabin. They all rushed in to find Angela holding the lid to a large whiskey barrel.

She pointed inside. "He's gone!"

Dani rushed over and peered down into the huge empty barrel. "Was he in there?"

Angela nodded. "I told him to hide inside. Why did he run off?"

Dani noticed movement in the bottom of the barrel and figured out the answer. She bent down for a closer look. "There's a scorpion in there."

While they were outside talking, Angela's son had realized he wasn't the only one hiding in the dark, confined space.

Flint looked around. "Where the hell did he go?"

Dani had a sinking feeling. They were in the Sonoran Desert, where rattlesnakes, mountain lions, javelina, coyotes, and Mexican wolves roamed. The only question was whether the killers pursuing them or a dangerous animal would get to the five-year-old boy first.

CHAPTER 51

Tía Manuela's Castle Hill apartment
Bronx, New York

Axel thought his computer was glitching when the comm light for a program that was still in beta mode began flashing.

When he listened to the audio link, he quickly discovered there was no glitch.

And someone might have just murdered Sanjeev Patel.

Axel had been secretly working with Patel, who frankly was way too cool to be a Fed, on custom software. The whole thing had been Axel's idea, and he didn't want anyone to know—especially his big sister or her boss—until they knew if it would work.

He and Patel were developing algorithms to identify similarities in crimes around the world and back in time. Dani had explained how the FBI and other agencies accessed massive databases to link crimes and develop suspects, but Axel wanted to apply machine learning for predictive analysis too. The new software could take behavioral profiling to the next level.

Patel had linked their computers, walling off sections so that Axel would have limited access.

A few minutes ago, Patel had sent a one-way thirty-second transmission burst to their shared software. Axel had heard enough to understand that he needed to send help, but he had zero clue where Patel was. Was Dani with him? She'd only told Axel she was on a top-secret case straight from the FBI director. They could be in Timbuktu for all he knew.

He cursed under his breath as panic began to set in. He took a breath. What would Dani do? He took another breath. She damn sure wouldn't panic and fall apart.

Dani would take him through a mathematical progression to calm his nerves when he was a kid. He took a second to do that now, and felt a sense of order begin to form from the chaos.

You've got this, Axel.

He would find a way to break down the firewalls and access all of Patel's computer, then maybe he could communicate. If it wasn't too late.

Forcing the thought away, he worked his keyboard. Patel was good. The barriers were solid, but he used their shared software to access another comm link. He glanced at the name beneath it and cursed again.

DIRECTOR FRANKLIN

The person who, according to Dani, had sent them on this mission. He blew out a sigh and clicked on the secure link.

CHAPTER 52

Sacred Heart Wilderness Retreat

Wu had planned to scoop up Angela and her son and whisk them off to a safe house as quickly as possible. An unforeseen crisis had changed everything.

He'd investigated missing child cases earlier in his career and knew what to do. Pushing back memories of previous searches that had ended in tragedy, he took command, assigning everyone a task.

As always, the biggest problem was keeping distraught parents from dissolving into hysterics. He could see the signs in Angela's increasingly frantic behavior.

He kept Angela with him to answer questions after sending Vega and Flint out to scour opposite sides of the campsite. If Tace was hiding nearby, he'd be more likely to come out if he saw his mother rather than strangers.

While they hunted, he questioned Angela. "Who's after you, and why?"

He was curious to see if her answers matched their research.

She continued moving from one area to another, checking every tight space that might hold a small child. Wu could tell she was considering how much to say before responding.

"You're the FBI," she finally said. "You know that three of my former colleagues are dead."

"Richard Sterling, head of Exmyth, and your fellow scientists, David Easton and Morton Wallace."

"I thought they were safe as long as I stayed hidden." She stopped searching to glance at him. "What suddenly happened after all this time? Why did he have them killed?"

Now they were getting somewhere. He ignored the first question and focused on what he wanted to know. "Who had them killed?"

She turned away again. "Karl Vaden."

It was the answer he expected, but there was still a certain amount of surprise in hearing her say the name. "How do you know it was Vaden?"

"I was getting close to a breakthrough in antigrav technology . . . or so everyone thought. Sterling told me Vaden-Quest Enterprises was going to buy Exmyth. Vaden wanted me to stop working with my team. I would get my own private lab and report directly to him. I couldn't even discuss my theories with anyone else."

"He wanted the tech all to himself, then."

She nodded. "I refused. Told Sterling I wouldn't transfer to VQE. There are plenty of rumors about their tactics in the scientific community, and I wanted no part of it."

"Did Sterling agree?"

"Of course not. The only reason he was getting so much money—and still keeping his position as CEO of what later became a wholly owned subsidiary—was because of my research. Things got ugly after that."

He didn't expect to get the answer he wanted but asked anyway. "Did Karl Vaden threaten you directly?"

She gave him a look. "Not his style. He's the type who hires people like Toro to do his dirty work."

Something didn't add up. "You said he sent Toro to kill you, but you were far more valuable alive than dead."

She glanced away again, and he could see the wheels turning. She was being evasive. He was about to press her further when he noticed Vega and Flint standing in the doorway to the main building. Their puzzled expressions told him they'd been listening.

He decided to put off delving into Angela's secrets until later. The first order of business was to find her son and get them both to safety. He motioned to Vega and Flint. "Any sign of Tace?"

At the sound of her son's name, Angela looked to them for a response. When they shook their heads, she swiped a tear from her eye.

Vega approached Angela. "Have you ever played hide-and-seek with Tace?"

"Yes," Angela said, her voice strained. "But it was more than a game. We knew this might happen someday, so we ran drills."

"By 'we,' you mean Toro," Vega said.

This time Angela let the tear slide down her cheek. "Toro taught him how to find cover and conceal himself. How to stay quiet, and not to be scared. He told Tace that if there was nowhere to hide, he should run as far and as fast as he could." She wrung her hands. "And if I got into trouble, he should do both."

"Both?"

"First, run far, then hide somewhere. Tace thought it was all a game."

Wu took in the new information and switched tactics. He addressed Flint. "Stay here with Ms. Peralta. Vega and I will continue the search into the surrounding area."

He wouldn't order someone from another agency into danger if he could help it, and the desert wilderness around them posed very real threats.

Flint crossed the room to stand beside Angela, then checked his cell. "Still no signal. Patel should have made contact with the Phoenix field office by now. With any luck, a helicopter's headed our way."

Wu didn't point out that a helicopter's FLIR system might not detect body heat if Tace had crawled into a cave, which would also keep him well hidden from eyes in the sky. No sense upsetting Angela any more than she already was.

Instead, he gave the detective a quick nod. "Backup should be here soon."

Vega cocked her head. "Or maybe now."

She pointed to the sky just as Wu made out the distant thumping of massive rotor blades slicing the air. Relief flooded through him. Once the copter landed, he could explain their situation and get help searching for Tace.

And maybe a flight to the nearest hospital for the boy if it proved necessary.

He forced the thought back as the Black Hawk's distinctive shape came into view, then dropped into a low approach. The pilot had spotted them and was choosing the best place to land.

He watched as the bird came in lower.

"Hit the deck!" Vega shouted, rushing past him.

Then the sky thundered as the ground in front of him erupted into two rows of dirt clouds exploding in parallel lines aiming directly toward them. He instinctively dived toward Angela, only to find that Vega had already launched herself onto the woman they had come to protect.

As Vega tackled Angela to the ground, he sprawled on top of them. A torrent of incoming fire from twin guns mounted on the helicopter ripped through the sandy earth where they had been standing moments ago.

Out of the corner of his eye, he saw that Flint had thrown himself face down.

The helicopter zipped past them, then swung around in a tight circle with its nose pointed in their direction, preparing to strafe them a second time.

CHAPTER 53

Dani was crushed under Wu's solid weight.

It had been his instinct to cover both her and Angela with his body, but she had instincts of her own, and they did not involve allowing someone else to take a bullet for her.

Not when she was already protecting the target of the attack with her own body.

When Angela groaned, Dani angled her head to the side to yell at her boss. "We've got to get our asses back inside."

They both stood, each hooking a hand under one of Angela's armpits to yank her to her feet and hurry her toward the main building while Flint followed close on their heels. As they ran, Dani performed several mental calculations in the space of a second. She had seen the kind of devastation a Black Hawk could cause. The guns on this one appeared to be fixed, so running sideways would buy them a few seconds to get inside.

The wooden structure offered no real protection against .50-caliber rounds, but at least the gunner couldn't see through the roof to get a bead on their precise location. The attackers would, of course, continue to blast the building until they reduced it to splinters, but Dani recalled that the Communion altar inside was topped with a thick stone slab. She could think of no other options.

"Under the altar," she ordered as they ran through the entrance. She made sure everyone was tucked beneath the makeshift cover, giving Flint an approving nod when he wrapped a comforting arm around Angela's narrow shoulders.

They waited, but nothing happened. Only the sound of the whirring rotors overhead broke the silence.

She glanced from Flint to Wu, who seemed equally baffled. What was going on?

And then an idea occurred to her. If her guess was correct, this was about to become a shit show. She crawled out from under the altar.

Wu reached out to grasp her arm. "What are you up to?"

"Recon," she said simply. "It's what I do."

"Not this time."

"We need intel. I can get it."

"No."

They both stared at each other. Wu had not released his grip.

Flint finally interrupted the standoff. "I don't like it any more than you do," he said to Wu. "But Vega's right. You're the one in charge, but in this situation, we should defer to her."

Wu turned from Flint, his dark eyes narrowing on her. He started to say something, but seemed to think better of it.

The moment he let go, Dani darted toward the wall, putting her back against it, and edged sideways toward the nearest window. What she saw kicked her pulse into overdrive.

Four ropes were dangling from the helicopter's open side doors. Men in black tactical gear were getting into position at the top of each, preparing to descend to the ground. She could make out another four ready to follow the first team down.

She'd been right. This was about to become a shit show.

CHAPTER 54

Dani made several key observations at once. The extra bulk around their torsos indicated the men were wearing body armor. Their helmets would have similar protection, meaning she could not shoot center mass to stop them. She would have to aim for their thighs, which were the largest parts of the human body not covered by a ballistic vest. Hitting any part of the leg would be disabling, but tearing open a femoral artery would be lethal.

She pulled her Glock from the holster on her webbed belt and took careful aim. She'd have to time her shots perfectly.

"What are you doing?" Wu called out from under the altar.

"Evening the odds." She gave him the bare essentials. "At least eight tac operators about to come down on fast ropes. I'll take out as many as I can."

Because she'd rappelled from a helicopter countless times, Dani knew the men would be at their most vulnerable in the seconds it would take them to position themselves and slide down the rope. Once their boots hit the ground, they would shoulder their weapons, get into attack formation, and storm the building.

She put her index finger on the trigger, tightening it slightly until she met resistance.

Totally focused, she barely heard Wu order Flint to stay under the altar to protect Angela. With her eyes on her front sight, she sensed Wu coming up behind her.

She bent her knees slightly, allowing him to take the higher position. "I'll take the two on the left, you take the ones on the right."

She diverted her attention to her vision and dialed down her other senses. The sound of Angela's terrified sobs, the feel of Wu's chest pressed against her upper back, the faint scent of sandalwood clinging to him, all faded into the background.

There was only the figure, now silhouetted against the bright-blue sky as he began his descent. To make the shot, she gauged his downward speed and aimed a fraction lower—not where he was, but where he would be in the next instant.

Breathe out.

A steady squeeze of her index finger.

Bam!

Breathe in during the recoil, then a quick shift of the muzzle to acquire the next target as the first plummeted to the ground.

Breathe out.

Lead the second man by a fraction. Another steady squeeze.

Bam!

She looked for another shot.

Wu had taken out one of his two targets. The last one still clung to the rope as the helicopter began a rapid climb.

The pilot, now aware the men were getting picked off from the fast ropes, was evacuating them from their exposed position. Rounds tore into the walls of the building to their right and left as the remaining men returned fire. The abrupt movement of the helicopter, however, created an unstable platform, making their shots inaccurate.

Wu had hit the deck when they began taking incoming fire. It was the correct thing to do, but she understood that this was merely a tactical retreat. The enemy would regroup and attack again. The fewer of them left to do so the better.

As the helicopter rotated around to fly away, she focused on the man still dangling by the rope. The pilot had stopped climbing and was now flying in a straight line away from her. The distance was increasing, but she was now able to get a clear sight picture with the target just above the front sight, which was evenly spaced between the rear sight notch.

Breathe out. Squeeze.

Bam!

The black-clad figure dropped from the rope as the helicopter disappeared behind the building.

Four down. How many more to go?

CHAPTER 55

Wu scrambled to his feet and pulled Vega back from the open window. "When someone is firing at us is not the time to stand in an open window. You made the perfect target."

She held the gun in her right hand and released the magazine, catching it in her left as it dropped. "First, it was our best chance to thin the herd of attackers, because they're coming back. Second, they couldn't shoot for shit while that helo was changing altitude and whipping around." She opened a pouch attached to her belt and pulled out a fresh magazine, shoving the partially empty one into its place. "It was a calculated risk."

Wu didn't care for her calculations, but he saw her point. "Right now, you're the most valuable member of our team. You've got to prioritize your safety." He appealed to her fiercely protective nature. "If not for yourself, then for Angela Peralta and her son."

Her resigned expression told him his tactic had worked.

"Those assholes will get them over my dead body."

Okay, so maybe it had backfired.

"Let's see if we can avoid that." He seated a new magazine into his Glock. "There should be extra ammo in the SUV."

Flint, who had come out from under the altar, spoke up. "I'll make a run for it."

"No." Vega's tone was sharp. "There's no time. They're regrouping for another attack."

Flint halted. "What do you think they'll do next?"

She faced the entrance. "The front door is twelve o'clock." She pointed to her left and right. "There are windows to our three o'clock and nine o'clock." She jerked a thumb over her shoulder. "The back wall to our six o'clock behind the altar has no window. It's a blind spot for us."

Wu understood. "So they'll approach from our six and make entry through twelve, three, or nine."

She nodded. "They can get to the ground safely if we can't see them. Then they'll be able to surround the building. If they stay below window level, we won't see them. They can pick us off if we try sticking our heads out to spot them."

He pictured the team of mercenaries, out for vengeance for their fallen comrades, dropping to the ground and preparing an all-out assault. "We need to be ready when they come."

He regarded Vega. She had done her time in exactly such perilous circumstances. He was keenly aware of the possible fallout from putting a combat veteran into a situation that resembled the kind of warfare scenarios she'd been involved with. He also knew she had lost team members close to her in an overseas deployment involving a desert compound that probably resembled their current surroundings. He'd garnered a few details from the background investigation in her personnel file to know that asking her to lead them in this situation would place a hardship on her.

He also knew that drawing on her experience was their best chance for survival. Doing so would throw her back into a dark place of death and destruction. He could be kind and understanding, allowing her to assist while he pulled a plan together. But he was humble enough to know their best hope was to be a heartless bastard and demand that she take point. Earlier, Flint said they should defer to her experience. Wu hadn't made it official because he knew the price of leadership. Agents had died under his watch, and he wanted to spare her the self-recrimination and nightmares that came when things ended badly.

He continued to study her. She stood tall and strong. Fierce and loyal. Cunning and brave. He was man enough to admit she was the better tactician for these circumstances, but could he allow her to bear the pain of a tragic outcome?

He made a silent vow to stand by her side through the fallout, whatever it may be. He would protect her from the professional blowback, and comfort her through the psychological effects in the worst-case scenario.

He kept his eyes on Vega, hating himself for putting this on her, but knowing it was the right decision. "We'll follow your lead. What do we need to do?"

He could see her visibly shift from federal agent to special forces soldier. Her eyes hardened, her spine stiffened, and her face took on a look of grim resolve. The metamorphosis took only an instant but was a sight to behold.

She addressed all of them. "I doubt they'll try to gas us because they'd have to wear masks that limit their vision. They'll probably use a flash-bang to make a dynamic entry. We need to be prepared."

Years ago, Wu had been a SWAT operator in the Atlanta field office. He was familiar with flash-bang grenades designed to stun and disorient everyone in the vicinity before the team burst into a confined space. There was no way to properly defend yourself since the loud explosion and bright light were a shock to the central nervous system.

"It's going to take time to recover," Vega went on. "So we need to slow them down after they get inside." She pointed at Angela. "Get back under the altar. Don't come out unless one of us gives you the all-clear." Angela sank out of sight, and Vega turned to Flint. "Help me drag some of these pews in front of the front entrance and both windows." She saved her last order for Wu. "Scatter every other piece of furniture or decoration you can find throughout the space, especially between the door and the altar."

He wasn't Catholic, but still felt sacrilegious as his gaze landed on a crucifix hanging behind the altar.

Only as a last resort.

He spotted a recessed area in a nearby wall, raced to it, and read the inscription.

Our Lady of Guadalupe Prayer Alcove

At least two dozen votive candles in amber glass holders sat in neat rows beneath a wooden carving of a Madonna. He darted a glance at Vega, who was busy moving pews with Flint. Blowing out a sigh, he stooped and began rolling the cylindrical containers in every direction.

Next, he looked across the room and spotted a cabinet. Yanking it open, he pulled out four bells, a shallow silver bowl, two ornate candles, and three glass jars filled with clear, thick liquid. Aware he was desecrating holy objects, he set about strategically tossing them where they were sure to be underfoot. After a moment's hesitation, he opened the jars and poured what turned out to be oil on the floor.

Meanwhile Flint had picked up one end of the last wooden pews. "How many are we up against?"

Vega lifted the other end. "At least four tactical operators. The pilot is their only transportation. They'll have him land out of sight, so he won't be involved in the fight. I'm guessing they'll have someone in command calling the shots, but that person won't show up right away, if at all."

As they moved the furniture, Vega added another thought. "They'll enter in pairs to back each other up. My guess is they'll come in through the front door at twelve o'clock and the three o'clock window so they'll be at right angles and avoid a cross fire."

"Why not the main entrance and the nine o'clock window?" Flint asked.

"That's the one we were shooting from. They'll avoid that." She shrugged. "Doesn't matter either way because we'll be behind the altar. The stone won't completely stop the noise and the flash, but a thick barrier like that will definitely help."

Angela called out, "So we have to wait here while they come and kill us?" Her voice broke. "And what about Tace?"

Wu knew Tace's only hope was for them to survive and find him, but he phrased it differently to Angela. "It's actually a good thing he's hiding right now. They may not know he's here, but even if they do, they won't find him." He tried for an optimistic tone. "We can take him out of here with us when we leave."

Angela looked dubious but ducked back under the altar.

When they finished rearranging every movable object in the place, he could appreciate Vega's plan. The area resembled a mini obstacle course. As she'd said, it wouldn't stop them, but they would have to move more slowly to navigate to the altar. It was clever, but had they bought enough time?

He'd barely finished the thought when the three o'clock window shattered. A metal canister dropped to the floor amid the shards and rolled toward the center of the room.

Vega had been right about the flash-bang grenade.

CHAPTER 56

"Down!" Dani grasped the back of Wu's waistband and yanked him into a squatting position beside her. Angela and Flint were already hunkered below the stone altar. They all barely had time to cover their ears and scrunch their eyes shut before the world exploded around them.

Unlike regular explosive devices, flash-bangs were designed to overwhelm the senses. A blinding strobe of light. A deafening crash of thunder. A bone-jarring shock wave. It was like standing in the room during a lightning strike, and it left anyone in the vicinity stunned and disoriented. Even the inner ear was affected, causing dizziness and confusion.

She'd been exposed to these tactical devices during training, so she knew what to expect, but that didn't mean she could override her body. Fortunately, the stone barrier mitigated some of the effects of the blast, giving her the ability to recover faster than the enemy tac team would have expected.

It was their one advantage, and she made good use of it.

Aware her balance was temporarily compromised, she did not jump to her feet and start firing. Instead, she got into a stable position on all fours and crawled to her right, peeking around the edge of the altar in time to see two men in full SWAT regalia kick open the front door.

The first one inside was saying something, but she could only make out, "Foxtrot, Echo, go."

Two other operators, presumably with the code names Foxtrot and Echo, had smashed the last bits of jagged broken glass from the three o'clock window frame and were climbing in.

A moment later, one of them stumbled over the long, rough-hewn pew Dani and Flint had dragged under the window and tipped on its side. He tried to regain his footing, but slipped in the consecrated oil Wu had splashed around and fell to the wooden-plank floor. As planned, the others slowed their advance, navigating the pews, bells, candles, and other church paraphernalia strewn about like a holy minefield.

While the downed man lurched to his feet, Dani used the time to perform a rapid threat assessment.

Wu, ever the diligent G-man, spared a moment to make the required announcement. "Stop, FBI!"

No one expected a hit squad that had arrived in a helicopter strafing them with high-powered fire to pay the slightest heed to his warning. The announcement served to give them a chance to surrender and to document that those who fired on them were aware they were federal agents and that any assault on them constituted a separate offense.

She also knew the boss was covering their backs, because every bit of force they used was now further justified. All good evidence for the inevitable examination of the Office of Professional Responsibility.

Dani had already shifted into Ranger mode. When faced with a team of trained mercenaries, it was kill or be killed. When they resumed their advance, she raised her pistol and fired twice in rapid succession, aiming for the thighs as she'd done before.

She registered that her initial shot penetrated the first man's upper leg, but the next round went a bit wide. In reality, the fact that she'd hit only one of her targets made no difference. His teammates would have to divide their attention to care for him, slowing them even more.

She had to retreat behind the altar amid a barrage of incoming rounds as they kept her at bay. Behind cover and pinned down by gunfire, Dani couldn't see what they were doing. She did, however, recognize the first man's voice when he shouted at his men.

"Hold your fire!" A brief pause, then, "Foxtrot-India-evac-Echo-white."

He was giving the team new orders. Dani called on her codebreaking skills, listening closely as he continued.

"Bravo-cover-red." Another pause. "Stick to the mission."

The call names and color system were similar enough to what she'd used in the military for her to make a likely interpretation.

Usually, the white side of a structure was the front, or the primary point of entry. From that perspective, green was right, red was left, and black was the rear side of the building.

If she was correct, the two who came in the front door were Bravo and India. Foxtrot and Echo entered through the window, and Echo was the one she'd shot. Bravo had just told Foxtrot and India to evacuate Echo through the front door while he covered them, exiting through the smashed-out red-side window.

There was no time to explain all of this, so she leaned toward the others and spoke in a rapid undertone. "They're doing a tactical retreat."

She resumed her position, straining to hear booted footsteps over the sound of Echo cursing as he was carried outside. Instinctively, she processed her observations and Bravo's coded message to come up with usable intel.

Since India represented the ninth letter in the alphabet, she concluded there were at least nine enemy combatants—four of which were casualties. Bravo had used his own codename to quickly apprise his team where he was and what he was doing. Did that mean he'd replaced Alpha, or did they have a commander calling the shots offsite? If so, that presented more of a challenge.

And what about the directive to "stick to the mission"? That implied they were on the verge of violating strict parameters when Bravo stopped them from blasting the stone altar to rubble. If she could figure out their rules of engagement, she might turn the information to her advantage.

She was familiar with their rifles, which could be switched to fully automatic mode, but they hadn't made the shift. Continuous bursts of fire into the stone altar would eventually reduce it to rubble, so why hadn't they?

Only one reason came to her.

They wanted Angela alive.

Everyone else was expendable, but as they retreated, Bravo was aiming his suppressive fire exclusively on Dani's corner of the altar. So they somehow knew about Dani's background, which made her the primary threat to their mission.

They were targeting her.

Time to test her hypothesis. She cut her eyes to Wu, who would never approve of her plan.

Too bad he wouldn't have a choice.

CHAPTER 57

Five minutes earlier
Black Hawk helicopter, on a ridge 150 yards from the Wilderness Retreat

Foley tapped the comm link. "You have *one job*," he yelled at Bravo. "Neutralize Vega and then get it done!"

His eyes were riveted to the split screen, giving him a real-time view from each operator's helmet cam. So far, it had provided a front-row seat to injury and failure on his team's part.

He'd warned the men about Vega, but they had still underestimated her. And now they were paying the price.

He glanced down at the men lying at his feet on the helicopter's cabin floor. Two were dead—one broke his neck falling to the ground from the fast rope and the other bled out from a gunshot wound to the thigh. The other two had used the med kit to field dress their injuries. Judging by their appearance, they might not make it. Either way, half his team was out of the fight.

While they evacuated their comrades, he had devised a new approach. Unfortunately, Vega was turning out to be every bit as hard to kill as Toro had been five months ago, and just as lethal.

He watched Foxtrot throw a rock through the red-side window and toss a flash-bang inside. After a few seconds, a concussive explosion shook the building.

Foley pictured Vega reeling and stumbling, and his lips tightened in a satisfied smile. She was about to be very dead.

He focused on the split screen to monitor the team's movements from multiple perspectives while listening over the comm system.

Bravo, the team leader, spoke to the others through the comm. "Go, go, go."

Foxtrot used the butt of his gun to smash out the remaining shards of glass jutting up from the windowpane while Bravo and India kicked open the front door. Foxtrot's quadrant of the screen whirled, spinning to the ground. When Bravo swiveled his head to check on his colleague, his helmet cam showed Foxtrot sprawled on the floor after he'd tripped over a pew.

Dumbass.

Foxtrot cursed and struggled to his feet while the others threaded their way around an array of objects strewn across the floor. Foley was certain the makeshift obstacle course had been Vega's doing, and she'd successfully slowed them down, making them easier targets. But fortunately, the flash-bang had rendered her and her crew unable to take proper aim.

Or so he'd thought.

A shot rang out. Echo shouted and went down. The camera briefly showed the ceiling, then refocused on Echo's gloved hands clutching his thigh as blood pooled on the floor beneath him.

Bravo, India, and Foxtrot all opened fire on a stone structure toward the back of the room where the round had come from. It looked like a raised table, but with three closed-in sides. Memory kicked in, and Foley recognized that it was an altar where the priest would prepare the Holy Communion.

Filled with rage, the men were blasting away at the stone slab.

He tapped the comm and shouted at Bravo to get the team under control, then listened as he relayed new orders.

"Hold your fire!" The shooting stopped. "Foxtrot-India-evac-Echo-white. Bravo-cover-red." Another pause. "Stick to the mission."

Foley had instructed them to take out Vega first. After that, the other cops had to be eliminated before snatching Angela and her son—alive and preferably unharmed. For now.

Foley watched India and Foxtrot carry Echo out while Bravo laid down suppressive fire. As soon as they made it outside the building, they stopped to render what first aid they could to their injured comrade.

He took the opportunity to formulate a new plan. "They're trapped in there," he said to Bravo. "And they have limited ammo. Force them to use it up, then go in and finish them."

Bravo's response was terse and angry. "I'm open to suggestions."

Did he have to think of everything? "Trick them. Throw something through the window or the door. They'll assume you're storming the place and shoot at it."

Bravo's helmet cam moved sideways as he scanned the area. "Can't find anything. It's—"

His words were cut off by the crack of a pistol, and Foxtrot went down.

Bravo sank into a tactical stance, swiveling around toward the sound. Squinting at the screen, Foley caught a glimpse of Vega darting out of sight around the back corner of the building. While Bravo's team was distracted, she had gotten outside and gone on the offensive.

Not good. Not good at all.

India was now dividing his time between two fallen comrades while Bravo raced to put his back against the wall. He shouldered his rifle and began a steady advance toward the corner where Vega had just been.

With sickening clarity, Foley realized Vega's ploy. He tapped the comm. "Stop!"

Bravo halted. "I'm after the primary target."

Foley scrunched his eyes shut. These men had zero ability to think creatively, which was something Vega did extremely well.

"It's a setup. Do not engage," he ordered. "She's leading you away from your main objective. Repeat. Do not engage."

"I don't give a fuck what you say. That bitch is going down."

Foley could only watch, certain this scenario would end badly, as Bravo made his way along the outside wall. The tactical team had trained together and formed a bond, resulting in a total loss of objectivity.

Giving up on Bravo, Foley spoke to India. "Bravo's keeping Vega busy. Now's the best time to go inside and take out the other cops."

India's helmet cam panned down to the two men sprawled on the ground, groaning in agony, their belts cinched around oozing thigh wounds. "What about—"

"The best thing you can do for them now is to finish the mission so we can all get the hell out of here."

India glanced up toward the building. "We've lost sight of Vega. She's sniping at us, picking us off one by one."

"It's called asymmetrical warfare," he said. "And she's damned good at it. Forget her and focus on the main objective."

More gunfire erupted, and Foley shifted his gaze to Bravo's quadrant of the screen. He was sprinting toward one of the cabins, firing as he went in an effort to keep Vega in place. The dipshit was so hell-bent on killing her that he didn't realize she'd laid a trap, and he was about to run headlong into it.

Grinding his teeth, Foley grabbed his gun, reflecting on his mantra.

If you wanted something done right . . .

CHAPTER 58

Dani had long ago accepted that both of her chosen professions involved putting her life on the line. In this instance, she also had to trust Wu completely. If he didn't come through, neither would she.

The man code-named Bravo, apparently the team leader, was spraying the cabin where she was hiding with bursts of full-auto fire as he advanced on her position. In less than a minute, he would either arrive or the high-powered rounds would take out enough chunks of the wooden walls to render the cabin useless for cover or concealment.

"C'mon, Wu," she muttered under her breath.

Thoughts of her boss reminded her of the heated exchange they had shared before she left the main building. She'd pointed out that the mercenary team had avoided shots that might injure Angela, which made sense if the goal was to force her to hand over her groundbreaking research.

Wu agreed with her conclusion that they were targeting Dani first, but the part where she intended to draw their fire was a nonstarter. She reminded him that he'd put her in charge of the operational part of the rescue and then proceeded to pull rank.

She outlined his role in the plan and slipped away before he could mount an argument or physically try to stop her.

Desperate times . . .

The tactical team had entered through the front door and the three o'clock window, so she climbed out of the nine o'clock window on the opposite side of the building. Her assumption that they'd remain near the front door where they'd carried Echo outside to treat him had proven correct. With superior firepower, they'd assumed they controlled the battlespace. But they were wrong, and once she was free to operate in the open, she employed guerrilla warfare techniques.

Her first order of business had been to reduce their fighting capability by taking down Foxtrot. That served to separate the last two who were still standing, making them easier to deal with. Of course, that also meant one of them would chase her.

The plan had worked perfectly, but everything now depended on Wu.

She crouched down, unable to pop up to see how close Bravo was getting without the distinct likelihood of catching a bullet in the forehead.

She could hear next to nothing over the sound of incoming rounds tearing the wood around her into splinters. She took three seconds to do a tactical reload, bracing herself for an all-out gun battle against a much better armed and armored attacker.

All at once, the rifle fire stopped.

In the eerie silence that followed, she peered around the corner to see Wu in a shooting stance, with the muzzle of his gun aimed at Bravo's prone black-clad figure about ten yards from her position.

She released a breath. Wu had exited the chapel behind her, then waited for one of the team members to come after her. Once he was out in the open, Wu would have a clear shot.

What Dani hadn't known was how her boss would react. With a law enforcement background, he'd been trained that every single use of force had to be justified. Would he order the man to stop and try to make an arrest?

Whatever had been Wu's original intention, Bravo had lost any opportunity to surrender by spraying a continuous stream of automatic gunfire directly at her. Under these circumstances, she felt confident anyone reviewing their actions would conclude Wu had acted to save the life of his fellow agent.

She was just wondering where the last member of the hit squad was when a scream emanated from inside the main building.

It was Angela Peralta.

CHAPTER 59

Wu faced a life-and-death dilemma.

He'd taken down Bravo with a shot to the thigh and was running toward where he lay on the ground when Angela's shriek halted him in his tracks.

Between the flash-bang and repeated firing without ear protection, his hearing was compromised, but her anguished wail was audible despite the ringing in his ears.

He noticed Vega leaving her cover behind the cabin, no doubt rushing to help Angela. What Vega didn't know was that the downed tactical operator might still be able to shoot her despite his injury.

He had a split second to decide whether his duty to protect his agent or a civilian took precedence. Any hesitation could result in both their deaths.

He chose Vega, reasoning that if he saved her first, she might reach Angela in time to help her. He didn't have the time or the inclination to examine his motives more closely.

He adjusted his aim, ready to take another shot as Bravo lifted a bloody hand from his thigh to reach for his rifle. Vega was coming toward the fallen man from the opposite direction, so a missed shot on Wu's part might hit her. He cursed, moving sideways to get a better angle. Meanwhile, Vega reached Bravo in time to kick the weapon from his grasp.

Bravo immediately shifted his hand toward a pistol holstered on his belt. Vega picked up his rifle and smashed the stock into his face, knocking him flat. This time, Bravo did not get up.

Vega disarmed the unconscious man, collecting both his weapons as another shriek sounded from inside the main building.

Wu estimated that less than thirty seconds had passed since the first scream. Not long under most circumstances, but an eternity with trained killers hunting them.

He pivoted and ran back toward the nine o'clock window where he and Vega had climbed out minutes earlier. Peering inside, he saw that the operator code-named India was in a standoff with Flint, each aiming a gun at the other.

A scan of the rest of the room brought his heart to a shuddering stop.

Angela was pointing her pistol at a man Wu didn't recognize who was crouched behind Tace, one hand wrapped around the boy's upper arm while the other held a piece of cloth. Tace held perfectly still, his widened eyes rolling upward toward the rag poised just above his head.

"Don't shoot," Angela called out to Wu. "Or the cloth will drop."

The rag was damp, and the man holding it wore gloves. Angela clearly believed it posed a threat to her son. Wu concluded the fabric must have been soaked in some sort of toxin. Judging by what had been used on Dr. Wallace aboard the cruise ship, it could be transmitted through the skin.

Angela's warning alerted the man to Wu's presence outside the window. He shifted his gaze from Angela to confront Wu. "Look what I found on my way from the helicopter."

So the man had flown in with the team but wasn't dressed in tactical gear. This must be Alpha, the one coordinating the attack, which had gone off the rails thanks to Vega, and now he was here to salvage the operation.

Wu kept his response measured. "Let him go."

The man Wu now thought of as Alpha shook his head. "I'm giving the orders, and you're all going to toss your weapons to me." He flicked a glance at the cloth and added, "By the way, there's no antidote."

Wu took this as confirmation of his prior assumption. He could not shoot Alpha without endangering Tace.

Angela laid her gun on the altar and raised her hands. "I'll go with you. Just leave my son here with Agent Wu."

Another shake of the head from Alpha. "I'm taking both of you."

The response told Wu all he needed to know. The child would be used as leverage against the mother. A five-year-old child could serve no other purpose for their operation. Once Alpha loaded Angela, Tace, and their wounded onto the helicopter, the Black Hawk would doubtless return, this time using Hellfire missiles to demolish the encampment entirely. This far out in the desert, there would be no witnesses, no collateral damage, and therefore no need to hold back.

An investigation would provide enough information to identify their bodies, but there would be precious little evidence left to connect their deaths to anyone in particular.

Alpha shouted his next threat loud enough to be heard outside. "That goes for you too, Vega. Toss your weapons in through the window, then go around and walk inside through the front door with your hands up."

Wu had lost sight of Vega. He had no way to communicate with her. He recalled a time when she'd quoted from the Ranger's Creed.

"Surrender is not a Ranger word."

No way was she going to follow Alpha's orders . . . but what the hell would she do?

CHAPTER 60

Dani pressed her back against the outer wall beside the three o'clock window. Foxtrot and Echo, both now dead, lay on the dry, cracked earth at her feet. She had a rifle slung across her back, a knife in her boot, and a Glock in her hand.

While a voice she didn't recognize issued demands from inside the chapel, she'd checked the weapons she'd taken off Bravo, stashing his pistol in the rear of her waistband. She ignored the shouted commands, unwilling to relinquish weapons that could be turned against her colleagues or the Peraltas.

Not for an instant did she believe this band of murderers intended to spare Tace, who would become a liability once they got what they wanted. Even if they didn't kill him outright, they would keep him alive only to hurt him to control his mother.

As long as she had breath in her body, that wouldn't happen.

Her heart ached for brave little Tace, who whimpered but didn't cry. She sent up a silent prayer that his courage would hold out, because things were about to get a hell of a lot scarier.

"You've got five seconds, Vega." The newly arrived stranger's voice carried through the smashed-out window beside her.

"Five."

She edged closer to the window frame and saw India's profile as he stood at the center of the chapel locked in a standoff with Flint. The detective had risen to his feet to hold him off while behind the altar with Angela.

Wu had entered the chapel through the nine o'clock window directly across from her. His anger was palpable as he pointed his weapon at something behind India. Craning her neck, she spotted the stranger, also in the middle of the space, crouched behind Tace.

Dani swallowed the obscenities rising to her mouth. Anyone who used a five-year-old as a human shield—while looking the child's mother in the eyes—deserved whatever came.

"Four."

There were two enemy combatants left, neither of them facing her, and each focused on one of her colleagues, leaving her a slight opening to surprise them. But only if she moved fast.

She waved her free hand to signal Wu, Flint, and Angela without drawing anyone else's attention. After making eye contact, she pointed at India, then held up her index finger, then pointed at herself. *I'll take out India first.*

Next, she pointed at the stranger and raised another finger, then pointed at herself. *I'll neutralize the stranger second.*

"Three."

Angela's eyes widened a fraction, and Dani worried one of the men would notice and turn to see what she was looking at. Dani tapped her temple, indicating she had an idea. This was not a reckless shoot-out.

When Angela continued to stare, frozen in fear for her son, Dani closed her hand into a fist and placed it over her heart. *Trust me.*

Angela's gaze returned to the stranger, and Dani took it as consent to follow her lead.

Some would call it foolhardy, others risky, and still others insane, but their only chance to save Angela and Tace involved sacrifice. And she was the only one in a position to sacrifice herself.

"Two."

Desperate times . . .

She raised her Glock from low-ready position, took careful aim, and squeezed the trigger.

With precision gained through tens of thousands of rounds fired through various weapons over the years, her shot hit its mark and India collapsed to the floor after a lethal shot through the neck.

She instantly shifted her sights onto the last man standing. Now alone and surrounded, he might listen to reason.

Instead, he'd moved the damp rag closer to Tace's head. "Stay back."

The lower half of the cloth dangled from the man's hand. Shooting him would make it drop onto Tace's face.

Still standing outside, Dani holstered her Glock. She couldn't shoot her way out of this situation, nor could she reason with a hired killer. She could think of only one resolution to this nightmare scenario.

She signaled Wu, pointing at him, then at her mouth, then at the stranger.

Either he would understand her silent message or he wouldn't.

But one way or another, this would end in death.

CHAPTER 61

Dani waited. Everything depended on the connection she'd formed with Wu. She saw the instant his eyes registered comprehension.

Wu turned his attention to the man holding Tace. "I'm putting my gun down." He bent to lay his Glock on the floor. "No one else needs to get hurt."

"Kick it over here."

Dani had hoped her boss would understand that she needed him to use talk as a distraction, but Wu had come up with a gambit that monopolized the man's attention far better.

"Okay," Wu said, placing the toe of his shoe against the edge of the pistol. "Be careful when you pick it up."

Dani leaped headlong through the window, avoiding the few remaining shards of glass poking up from the frame. Her body arced through the air, tucking into a somersault and rolling up onto her feet.

She'd done the maneuver countless times in training, but never with so much at stake. She used her momentum to carry her forward, where she latched onto the man's forearm, yanking the hand that held the rag to the side as she went.

He reflexively clamped his other hand onto Tace's arm with brutal force. The child was his only leverage, and he knew it.

While both of his hands were occupied, Dani executed her plan, using her free hand to slam her bladed palm into his throat.

He gasped for air, choking and sputtering. Still clutching Tace's arm with his left hand, the man's right hand instinctively flew to his throat.

The hand that held the rag.

Dani watched the wet fabric slap against the one area of the man's body not covered in clothing.

His grip loosened and Wu pulled Tace from his grasp. Angela rushed to her son, scooping him up in her arms. Flint pulled mother and son behind him, taking up a protective stance, ready to fend off a fresh attack from the stranger.

But the fight had gone out of the man, who slumped to the floor.

Dani kicked the rag that had fallen from his slackened hand away from his reach. It flew toward an overturned pew, where it landed with a soft *splat*.

She kneeled, careful to stay out of reach of the gloved hand that might still have residue from whatever was on the fabric. "Do you have a med kit handy?"

"Told you," he said. "No antidote."

She couldn't tell if his voice was raspy from the throat punch or if the toxin was already taking effect. She had asked the question because she couldn't trust him to tell the truth about either a poison or an antidote but felt no need to point this out.

She could tell by his expression that his threat had not been idle.

"How long?" she asked gently.

His clear blue eyes met hers. "Less than five minutes."

CHAPTER 62

Foley had never wasted time wondering how those he killed transitioned from life to death, nor did he concern himself with the prospect of his own eventual demise.

Until now.

He'd heard others say ridiculous things like, *"My life flashed before my eyes."* Such expressions had never made sense to him before. After all, how could you relive decades in the space of an instant? And yet . . .

His own personal highlight reel began in a ramshackle hovel in the Appalachian Mountains, where he'd arrived in this world as the seventh child of a couple who would have been denied permission to adopt a dog.

He rarely discussed his youth but, when pressed, said he was a smart kid who'd chosen his parents unwisely. Children in his neck of the woods didn't go to college to study philosophy. Or anything else, for that matter.

Instead, they went into trade. Mostly the drug trade and the sex trade. The ambitious ones aimed high, setting up illegal distilleries, grow operations, or meth labs in the dense forest where cops weren't likely to go. Some tried to get into organized crime, which had a ready-made distribution network with better job security. And medical. If you counted doctors on the take who asked no questions and worked out of a mobile clinic for cash.

Once upon a time, he'd been like all those other losers. That was what Karl Vaden called them.

"Life's losers, my boy," Vaden would say. "Poor bastards who will never know the taste of caviar, the luxury of a private jet, or the feel of a supermodel under them in bed."

Foley was hooked. What he found out only later, after years climbing the ladder into his boss's inner circle, was that the life he offered came at a price.

For someone like him, caviar never tasted as good as a hamburger, jet fumes made him nauseous, and supermodels never gave him a second glance. They only faked orgasms for the billionaires they were trying to snare.

He couldn't blame them. Some had backgrounds worse than his.

Then he met *her*. The one meant for him. Foley had never read a single line of poetry. Never believed in fate or love at first sight. He was in full control of himself.

But one look at her and his traitorous heart was lost.

She walked right past him, heedless of the fact that she had just obliterated his well-honed survival instincts, making her way to the pool. When she untied her wrap and let it slide from her bronzed skin, his pulse elevated to stroke level.

Who was this goddess?

The question had barely formed in his hormone-addled mind before it was answered.

"What the hell are you looking at?"

Foley spun around to face his boss, whose pinched features radiated anger.

He was uncharacteristically slow to respond. "What?"

Two beady eyes narrowed on his. "Why are you ogling my daughter?"

"I wasn't—"

"You damned well were."

"I didn't know—"

"Well, now you do." Vaden jabbed an accusatory finger at him. "Let me make something perfectly clear." He jerked a thumb in the direction of the pool. "I've raised my daughter to expect the best. Elite schools, exclusive neighborhoods, carefully curated friends. She's a thorough-bred." He scowled. "I will not breed her to a mule."

It had taken every bit of control to keep his composure. The boss had insulted his own daughter, referring to her as cattle raised to fetch the highest price at auction. Then he'd cut Foley down to size, comparing him to a lowly beast incapable of passing along its genes.

Foley was younger then. The comment had made him determined to prove Vaden wrong. He listened to recordings every night, practicing pronunciation until he lost all traces of what the boss had called his hillbilly accent. He took lessons in fighting and strategy from skilled members of Vaden's elite security team. He became fanatical in his devotion, eventually working his way to the top of Vaden's inner circle.

A year ago, he began to suspect that Gustavo Toro wanted to replace him. Savvy, tough, and handsome, Toro attracted everyone's attention, including Vaden's. Foley had felt vindicated when the boss learned Toro had double-crossed them by claiming he'd killed Dr. Castillo and disposed of her body.

As a stream of recollections continued to flow, Foley was treated to a review of the night he set Toro up to die in an ambush. He'd underestimated his rival, and the plan had backfired spectacularly when Toro decimated the tactical team. Foley had to hire a replacement squad, which Vega and her team had just eliminated, but that was no longer his concern.

As the most recent events in his life played out in excruciating detail at dizzying speed, a new awareness came over him. For the first time, the filter of his upbringing dissolved, and he saw the truth with total clarity. He realized Toro had been right to defy his orders, right to stop dealing with Vaden, right about everything.

With a new perspective, he also realized that when he died, Vaden would replace him within the hour, just as he did with the nameless supermodels he slept with or the domestic staff who tended his many properties. To a man such as Vaden, Foley was one of many inter-changeable minions put on this earth to serve his needs.

It didn't matter that Foley had tortured, maimed, and killed other human beings to further Vaden's interests. Or that he often risked his own life to protect him. Vaden took that as his due. But the loyalty went only one way.

In short, Karl Vaden was a user.

To Vaden, he would never be anything other than a country mule.

In that moment, Denton Foley decided he would no longer be a tool for his boss to use and throw away like so much trash. He'd use his last moments to make sure Vaden's last years were spent in the kind of hell to which Foley's own soul was surely bound.

CHAPTER 63

Wu kneeled beside Vega and looked down at the dying man. Before any other considerations, he was responsible for everyone's safety. "Is anyone else from your organization headed here?"

The man shook his head. "The only one left is the pilot. He'll stay with the bird. It's just south of here and powered down."

More than ever, Wu wished his sat phone would get a decent signal to warn FBI personnel from the Phoenix field office. Whether he trusted the man or not, the pilot wouldn't attack if he thought his team was still inside, and he couldn't fly away without taking the time to power up and check his controls.

He addressed his second concern, which was getting what information he could while there was still time. "What's your name?"

The question was met with a groan.

Realizing the man he'd come to think of as Alpha might hold back identifying information in an effort to shield his boss, Wu added, "I know you work for Karl Vaden."

He sighed. "Denton Foley."

Wu recalled the name somewhere in a long list of Vaden-Quest employees. This would serve as confirmation of what he and Director Franklin had discussed on the jet.

But he wanted more. Perhaps Foley would be willing to share. "What do you do for—"

"There's not much time," Foley said. "I want to make a confession."

Flint pulled a digital voice recorder from his pocket, stepped closer, and clicked it on. "Repeat your name."

"Denton Foley."

"Are you of sound mind?"

"Yes."

"Are you aware that you are dying?"

Foley shuddered slightly. "Yes."

"Do you wish to make a final statement?"

"Yes."

"Do you make this statement voluntarily?"

"Yes."

A seasoned homicide investigator, Flint knew how to take what the courts referred to as a dying declaration. A person's comments could be entered into evidence as an exception to the hearsay rule if they knew they were dying and made them freely.

"Go ahead, then," Flint said quietly.

"I've worked for Karl Vaden for fifteen years. I've committed more crimes than I can count on his orders. The last person he told me to kill was Richard Sterling. I made it look like suicide."

Ordinarily, Wu would have asked him for details, but he wasn't sure how long Foley had, so he let him continue.

"Vaden sent me to Exmyth to clean up. I deleted dozens of files from their server." His face reddened as sweat beaded along his hairline. "I didn't just purge the files, though. I sent copies of everything to a secret cloud account Vaden doesn't know about." He glanced from Flint to Wu. "Before I flew out here, I got into the Vaden-Quest database and sent copies of hundreds of financial transactions to the same place. It's all there. Everything you need to nail that arrogant prick."

Wu kept his question brief. "Why?"

"Toro's video was a wake-up call." He studied them. "You guys don't know that Vaden and I were watching you in the vault at the

Toltec Hotel. The assistant manager, Ethan Polk, backdoored us into the security cam system." He glanced at Vega. "Nice codebreaking."

Vega tensed but said nothing.

He kept his eyes on her. "By the way, you should know I've been following your movements with Tracker Dust."

Vega had used all sorts of advanced tech in the field, but her furrowed brows indicated she hadn't heard of Tracker Dust.

Foley elaborated. "One of our subsidiary companies has a lab specializing in bleeding-edge chemical research. They're the ones who made that toxin." He glanced at the rag draped over the nearby pew.

Wu figured the lab was also the source of whatever substance was on the card that had driven Dr. Wallace to jump off the cruise ship.

"Tracker Dust is a powder that's invisible to the eye but gets deep into the fibers of any fabric it touches. I don't know the details, but it's got tritium isotopes."

The color drained from Vega's face. "Isotopes?"

"Tritium is a radioactive isotope, but you're not in any danger," Foley said, obviously reading her alarm. "The new tech can follow its signature over long distances."

Vega didn't look convinced. "How do you know I'm not in danger?"

"Remember Polk helping you with your bag?"

She nodded.

"He wasn't being nice." Foley's words began to slur. "His gloves were coated with the stuff. The small amount transferred onto your bag wouldn't cause an issue. Not unless you chewed on the material, anyway."

Wu didn't appreciate the dark humor, but at least he now knew how their adversary had stayed a step ahead of them after their trip to Las Vegas.

And how they had located the wilderness retreat. Wait. That part didn't make sense.

He asked Foley, "We haven't been able to get a decent signal out here in the desert. How did you track us?"

Foley made no response. His breathing grew labored.

And then the answer came to Wu, bringing a wave of dread. "You spoke to Father Ramirez?" When Foley merely nodded, he asked, "And Sanjeev Patel?"

Another nod. "I feel hot."

"They wouldn't just offer up our location," Wu said. "What the hell did you do to them?"

Foley's eyes drifted shut. "Burning up." His face, now bright red, glistened with perspiration. "Guess I'd better get used to it." His eyes drifted shut.

Denton Foley was done answering questions.

CHAPTER 64

Dani's own fear for Father Ramirez and Patel was mirrored in Wu's grim expression.

"I agree with you," she said to him. "They wouldn't have volunteered any information about us. We have to get back to the church."

Everyone understood her meaning. Now that they had Angela and Tace, they could leave the wilderness retreat.

Except for the Black Hawk nearby armed with who-knew-what. Out in the open desert, they'd be completely exposed to an airstrike.

"We need cover," Wu said, apparently thinking along the same lines.

She had already come up with a different idea. "Or we need to disable their bird."

Wu gave her a sharp look. "How?"

"Wait here," she said, still working out the details in her mind. "I've got a plan."

Wu moved to block her path as she headed for the door. "Let's hear this plan of yours."

"I'm going out on recon over the ridge," she said. "I've been around Black Hawks and their pilots enough to know where to shoot to disable them." She unslung the rifle from her back. "With this, I won't have to get anywhere close to take out the tail rotor."

Wu gave it some thought, then turned to Flint. "Stay here and guard Angela and Tace."

Flint moved closer to Angela, who gazed up at him with admiring eyes.

"Let's go," Wu said to her. "I've got your back."

She started to object, then paused. In the past, she would have insisted that she could take care of the situation more effectively on her own. But now, as she looked at Wu, she no longer saw an administrator in the corner office.

She saw a true partner. One she would trust with her life. Without another word, she turned and walked out the door.

Wu fell into step beside her as they headed toward the ridge at a steady pace, but neither spoke. They couldn't risk being overheard during their approach.

When they finally neared the crest of the ridge, Dani came to an abrupt halt. Wu stopped and looked her way.

She pointed to herself, then at the ridge. *I'm going up there.*

Next, she pointed at him, then down at the ground. *You stay here.*

He shook his head. *No way.*

She put a hand on her hip. *Yes way.*

He upped the ante by crossing his arms. *I'm the boss.*

She raised a brow. *Not in this situation.*

He dragged a hand through his hair. *You're impossible.*

She smiled. *I know. Deal with it.*

Silent argument over, she turned and lowered herself into a tactical stance. After moving close to the top, she got down on her knees and put her left hand on the ground. Carrying the rifle in her right hand, she crawled forward. At the very peak, she went down on her belly and inched ahead just enough to peer over the crest.

The Black Hawk was exactly where Foley had said it would be, giving her confidence that the rest of his statements were also true—or at least not total bullshit. The pilot was leaning against the outside of the cabin, smoking a cigarette.

He had a pistol on his belt, but he'd be more likely to scramble for cover than engage with an unseen enemy who was actively firing on him.

She assumed a prone shooting position. Propped on her left elbow for stability, she spread her legs wide to brace for the recoil and caressed the trigger with her right finger. Looking through the scope, she made slight adjustments until she was satisfied with the distance, windage, and trajectory. She put the crosshairs on one of the rear propeller blades, which were considerably smaller than the massive main rotors.

The high-powered round should be sufficient to destroy or damage the blade enough to prevent it from turning. If the pilot tried to start the bird, she would take out another. And another.

Breathe in.

Take out the slack on the trigger.

Breathe out.

A smooth and steady pull of her finger.

She was rewarded with the satisfying *crack* of snapping metal and the sight of a hunk of shrapnel flying away from the helicopter's tail.

The pilot's cigarette dropped as he grabbed his gun and darted under the craft, scrambling for cover. His head whipped this way and that, trying to find the source of the attack.

Wu's commanding voice boomed out over the space between them. "FBI, drop your weapon and put up your hands!"

The pilot froze. After a long moment, he dropped his pistol on the sandy ground and came out from under the helicopter with both hands in the air.

She and Wu were walking forward to take him into custody when the sound of another Black Hawk reached her ears. Had Foley's last words been a lie?

CHAPTER 65

Dani raised a hand to shield her eyes from the midday glare as she squinted up toward a fast-approaching fully outfitted attack helicopter in the sky.

Foley had told them no one else was coming to back up his team, but then again, the man was a career criminal and a killer. His dying declaration had been filled with hate and anger against his boss, and Dani was certain he'd hurt or killed Father Ramirez and Patel. Why not take out a few more cops before he left this world?

Just to make things even more fun, she and Wu were in the process of making an arrest when the helicopter appeared in the distance. Their would-be prisoner, a Vaden-Quest pilot, was currently standing with his hands up beside his disabled helicopter. Had he managed to transmit a distress signal to his cohorts?

Wu followed her gaze. "You watch the bird," he said. "I'll deal with the pilot."

She would have to divide her attention, monitoring the incoming air unit and the arrest. The pilot might take advantage of the distraction to dive for his gun, which he had tossed on the ground moments ago.

She walked alongside Wu, but kept glancing up, unsure if they were about to be strafed again or if Patel had gotten word to the Phoenix field office before Foley and his cronies showed up at the church.

She pushed away the thought and focused on the immediate problem. How could she get a better look at the approaching threat? She considered her options. Using the rifle scope as a monocular was out. She'd have to aim the weapon at the incoming helicopter, drawing fire no matter who was inside. Removing the scope to hold it up to her eye was also a bad idea. If the craft turned out to be hostile, she'd be vulnerable while she reattached it and sighted in the weapon.

Wu zip-tied the pilot's wrists while Dani scooped up his discarded gun. She took a protective stance in front of both men, covering them from the potential threat of the incoming helicopter. She held her rifle in low-ready position, prepared to shoulder it at the first sign of trouble.

Moments later, she got a better view. The breath left her body in a huge sigh. "It's a gloss-black UH-60." She glanced over her shoulder at Wu. "HRT."

The FBI's elite Hostage Rescue Team deployed in Black Hawks painted a shiny onyx color to distinguish them from the military's green ones. The message had gone out, and it had gotten to the right people.

Wu gave her a wry smile. "We could've really used them about twenty minutes ago."

They all watched team members rappel down from the helicopter on fast ropes and jog to them.

"SAC Wu?" the lead operator called out.

Wu stepped forward to give them an overview of the situation. It wasn't until she overheard him talking that she learned there were two dead and two wounded subjects on the floor of the helicopter's cabin. Those must be the first four she'd shot while they were rappelling down.

Wu made no mention of her involvement, and she realized he was taking care not to say too much . . . at least until the inevitable investigation from the Office of Professional Responsibility, when they would all have to give a highly detailed account of their actions.

The HRT leader, who had introduced himself as Supervisory Special Agent Demarco, signaled one of his team to take custody of the pilot while a medically trained operator tended to the wounded and two others checked the helicopter for weapons, devices, or outgoing communications.

Dani waited impatiently while HRT personnel secured their location. She was about to ask the question she dreaded most when Wu beat her to it.

"Did anyone go to Our Lady of the Sacred Heart Catholic church in Apache Junction?" Wu said to Demarco. "We have reason to believe the priest and one of our analysts may have been hurt."

"They're okay," Demarco said. "We found them tied up in the parish rectory. They were roughed up a bit, but the EMTs didn't find signs of lasting injury, and they both refused transport."

"What happened?" Wu asked sharply.

"According to your cyber analyst, a SWAT team arrived soon after you left. They'd tracked you to the church somehow but lost the signal. They wanted your location."

Dani's gut clenched. Foley had called it Tracker Dust, but it meant she'd been the one who led a hit squad straight to the church—and eventually to Angela and Tace.

"They didn't give up the info," Demarco went on. "But the team managed to get the signal back. They were going to kill both of them, but when the priest said a prayer or something, they just tied them up and left them." He turned to Dani. "The analyst wanted me to tell you that your brother saved them."

"What?" She could not make sense of her personal and professional worlds colliding at such an odd moment.

Demarco lifted his palms in a shrug. "He said he'd explain it to you later. We were running short on time and had to get our asses out here." He glanced at the pilot. "Although it seems like you've got everything under control."

Wu said, "Speaking of which, we have two vehicles, but there are four more dead and one wounded over at the wilderness retreat that need transport."

Meaning he'd rather not haul them in the SUV while they drove back to the church to get Patel and check on Father Ramirez.

"The PFO has vehicles coming," Demarco said. "They're a little behind us."

The Phoenix field office was nearly two hours from their current location, depending on traffic. Dani was grateful a helicopter had been dispatched, but a question nagged at her.

"How did the HRT get involved?"

Every FBI field office had a nonstanding SWAT team consisting of field agents who performed tactical duties in addition to their regular investigations. The Hostage Rescue Team, however, was the Bureau's most highly trained tactical unit. On a par with special forces units in the military, the HRT was full-time and based at Quantico, with rapid-deployment capabilities anywhere. Calling them out required special authorization.

"Director Franklin hit the red button," Demarco said, frowning. "No idea how he was aware of any of this, though."

Dani and Wu exchanged a knowing glance, but neither commented.

They spent the next fifteen minutes walking back to the retreat, filling in Demarco and the remaining HRT members who weren't detailed to the helicopter.

With time to think, Dani recalibrated her previous thoughts about Foley. He hadn't been able to bring himself to kill Father Ramirez or Patel. He was the shot caller, which meant he hadn't allowed the others to do so either.

She'd never know what he'd been thinking at the church, but she was with Foley when he died. In a moment of clarity, he realized Vaden had been using him for years—and he wanted revenge.

Whatever his true motivations, she believed in her heart Foley was telling the truth about wanting his boss to go down.

She could only hope that indicated he was also telling the truth about the tritium isotopes on her duffel bag not causing her any harm. Either way, she'd have the damned thing incinerated first chance she got.

They made it to the retreat to find Flint standing guard in front of the altar. When he saw them, he called out to Angela, who rose from where she and Tace were hunkered underneath it.

Angela led Tace by the hand, taking him out from behind the bullet-pocked stone. "Now would be a good time," she said to Flint.

Perplexed, Dani watched as Flint smiled down at the boy and extended a hand. Without hesitation, Tace let go of his mother's hand to take Flint's, and the two walked to the far end of the chapel.

Angela waited until they were out of earshot—but still in view—before turning to face Wu. "While we were waiting, I asked Mark to look after Tace for a few minutes when you got back."

Dani barely had time to register that Angela had called the detective by his first name before she bit her lip and continued. "It's time I told you and your agents the truth."

CHAPTER 66

It was one of those times when Wu did not appreciate being correct. He'd suspected Angela was holding out on them, but they'd been too busy fighting for their lives for him to confront her.

Now that the immediate threat was over, he wanted answers. "Several people died today, and people I'm responsible for were nearly killed protecting you. It's about time you leveled with us."

Angela winced. "I'm sorry. I wanted to say something, but I didn't know who to trust."

"Toro trusted the FBI. That's why he sent us. He was protecting you too. That should've been good enough."

"I know. I've just spent so many years living in fear that hiding and lying became a habit."

This woman was clearly traumatized. Concern for his team was making his words come out harsher than he'd intended.

He gentled his tone. "Why did you disappear, and why is Karl Vaden spending a fortune to send his private army after you?"

Angela glanced over at Flint and her son, who were still on the far side of the chapel. Tace was giggling at something the detective said. Her gaze shifted to Vega, and then to the HRT personnel standing in a row beside her. Angela was stalling, but he gave her time. Whatever she was about to relay must be painful.

Finally, she blew out a sigh and began her story. "At Exmyth, I was assigned to a team working on advanced propulsion technology. Dave Easton, Mort Wallace, and I were getting close, but we couldn't manage a breakthrough. Eventually, I told them about my dissertation involving gravitational field theory for my PhD in quantum physics, and Dave suggested I review my notes. Maybe something completely out in left field would make a difference."

Looking at Angela now, in blue jeans and a T-shirt with her hair tied back in a ponytail, it was hard to remember she was formerly Dr. Tina Castillo, a brilliant scientist. Wu hadn't studied physics since college, and he'd been exposed only briefly to quantum physics, but he would try to keep up.

"I had an idea about how to generate graviton fluctuations and shared it with my team. My hypothesis required a whole new line of budgeting and additional time to test, so we took it to Richard Sterling." She shook her head. "I had no idea he was getting funding from VQE."

He supposed that, as a scientist, she was more interested in conducting research than who paid for it. At least, until she learned it was Vaden-Quest Enterprises.

"The next day, I was pulled from my team and ordered to relocate to California to work directly for Karl Vaden at his headquarters. Like everyone else, I knew who Vaden was and wanted nothing to do with him or his company."

So far, this conformed with what they'd learned from their investigation in Denver. He couldn't tell where this was going but sensed her growing tension.

"I refused to go. That's when Vaden sent Gustavo Toro in."

When she trailed off, Wu knew they'd arrived at the sticking point. The part of her story that didn't add up. Keeping his tone neutral, he prompted her to go on. "Why would he send someone to kill you if he wanted you to continue your research?"

Although he wouldn't put it past Vaden to have someone murdered to prevent others from benefiting from their work, the potential for his own profit would be a bigger motivator. Dr. Castillo's death would be a last resort.

Her eyes slid away. "Toro came to convince me to cooperate. I pretended to change my mind about going to California, but I was only buying time to go back through my research and make modifications. No one would be able to replicate my results from reading my notes."

He factored this in. "So after a while, Vaden got tired of waiting, or he realized you had no intention of moving to California?"

She nodded. "That's when he sent Toro again. This time, he was supposed to beat me into submission or kill me." She lifted her chin, meeting his eyes. "I still wouldn't go."

"But Toro didn't follow orders," Wu said, turning the problem over in his mind. "He didn't beat you into submission or kill you. And when you refused to cooperate, he helped you escape. Why would he risk his reputation, his career, and even his life for someone he barely knew?"

"Because I *gave* him a reason. Something more important than his own miserable life."

He considered her response. She had emphasized the word "gave." What reason could she have given him? And what would be more important than his own life? Suddenly all the pieces fell into place, and he understood her deception—and why she'd kept it up.

Her brows furrowed in thought. "The strange thing is, I could never figure out what Toro was thinking. I studied complex problems for a living, but he was a complete mystery to me."

CHAPTER 67

Five years earlier
Denver, Colorado

Gustavo Toro had never killed a woman.

Perhaps that made him old-fashioned. Or maybe sexist. He wasn't sure, but somehow it didn't feel right. Whenever he'd been sent to deal with a woman, he'd used charm rather than violence. But this time, he'd been ordered to hurt Dr. Tina Castillo until he broke her spirit. Failing that, she would have to die.

He stood outside the door to her apartment, dreading what came next. The only reason he'd taken the job was because he knew that asshat Foley wouldn't have any problem hurting her.

Toro resolved that if he couldn't change her mind, he would make her death quick and painless.

If he could bring himself to do it.

He rang the doorbell and waited.

She yanked open the door. "What do you want?"

He stepped over the threshold without waiting for an invitation. "Came for a chat."

She backed up into the living room area. "Get out."

"Not until we talk."

"I've got nothing to say to you."

She reached behind her and snatched up a lamp. With surprising speed she threw it directly at his head.

He dodged it easily and put his hand out in a calming gesture. "What's gotten into you?"

She let out a derisive snort. "Interesting choice of words." She glanced around and spotted a ceramic mug on the coffee table.

He got there before she did and grabbed her wrist before she could reach it. "I just want to have a conversation," he lied.

This wasn't going well at all. If he couldn't get her to listen, he'd have no choice in how this ended.

Her eyes narrowed to slits. "I know why you're here."

Did she?

She tried to pull away, but he held on to her wrist. She glared up at him. "Karl Vaden sent you to force me to work for him."

Well, she was half right.

"But I won't go. I don't care what you say. You're a liar."

"You want the truth?" He decided to appeal to her logical side. "You're coming with me when I leave. I'll either take you to California or bury you in the woods somewhere far outside the city."

Her mouth opened, then closed again. "Y-you're supposed to kill me?"

"If you don't cooperate."

She stared at him for a long moment. "I knew you were a lowlife, but I never understood exactly how low you'd go."

The remark should have made no difference, but it stung. He hardened his features, not allowing her to see any reaction. "The choice is yours."

"I'm not going." She straightened. "I will never work for that man. Ever."

He squeezed the hand that was still wrapped around her wrist. "Ouch!"

He eased the pressure but didn't let go. "Don't force me into a corner."

"I'm not forcing you to do anything. You came here freely. And you did it for money, not because you have to."

She really had no idea how things worked, so he explained. "If I didn't come, someone else would. Someone a lot less . . . understanding."

"Understanding?" She glanced at his hand still holding her. "You call this understanding?"

"Compared to the alternative."

He could practically see the wheels turning as she eyed him in silence. Assuming she was making peace with the fact that she would have to come with him, he waited her out.

After a full minute, she spoke, her voice unexpectedly quiet. "I'm pregnant."

He was still processing the new information when she added, "With your child."

His mind raced back to their time together three months earlier when he'd first come to see her. Vaden had expected him to use force, but as always, he'd charmed his female target instead.

And then, as always, he'd left.

In his many previous encounters, this had never happened before. Had his normal precautions failed? It didn't seem possible. "Are you sure?"

"I took five home pregnancy tests. I'll take another one for you right now if you want."

A new thought occurred to him. "How do you know it's mine?"

She used her free hand to slap his face. Hard.

"Hey!"

She'd pulled her arm back, ready to deliver another blow. He caught her other wrist and pinned both hands to her sides.

It had been a stupid question. She was a total academic. The type who could probably count the number of dates she'd ever had on one hand. If he was being honest with himself, her loneliness was probably the reason she'd fallen for him so fast. He felt her body tremble and realized she was crying.

Shit.

She didn't fight him when he pulled her into his arms. He held her for a long time while he came to grips with his new reality. He couldn't hurt her. He couldn't kill her. And he now agreed with her decision not to go anywhere near Karl Vaden.

He stood there in silence, coming up with a plan to double-cross one of the most ruthless and powerful men in the world. A man who had nearly inexhaustible resources at his disposal. A man who made it his business to destroy anyone who betrayed him.

In that moment, Toro knew a bullet would come for him one day. His only goal was to keep the next one from finding Tina Castillo and his child.

CHAPTER 68

Present day, Friday, October 11
Sacred Heart Wilderness Retreat

Dani let out a long, slow breath when Angela finished her story.

Like Angela, Dani had never truly understood what was in Toro's heart, but she had learned that there was much more to the man than she'd first thought.

"I was so angry at him back then," Angela said. "I never took the time to thank him for all the things he did, and I should have. I know he never loved me, but he did love Tace. And he risked his life to protect us." She looked forlorn. "I haven't felt safe since he died."

Dani reached out to clasp Angela's hand in silent solidarity. She noticed the men around them looking at their joined hands, but no one commented. Perhaps they understood that a bond had formed between the two women whose lives had been touched by Toro.

Dani turned to Wu and raised an expectant brow. If he didn't offer the Bureau's protection, she would offer her own.

"I can make arrangements," Wu said. "You'll have all the security you need." He paused. "And a new identity."

Her cover as Angela Peralta was blown. Wu had the kind of authority needed to get the US Marshals involved, wrapping Angela and Tace into WITSEC while they investigated Karl Vaden and his empire.

When the day came for her to testify against him in court, she had to be alive and unafraid to do so.

Angela gave Wu a watery smile. "Thank you." She drew in a ragged breath. "There's more you need to know." She released Dani's hand and took a moment to compose herself. "Toro kept evidence against Karl Vaden, VQE, and everyone else who hired him."

This was the treasure trove of evidence Toro had dangled in front of Director Franklin in the video that had started them down this path. Desperate as she was to get back to the church to check on Patel and Father Ramirez, Dani had to hear more about Toro's stash.

"It's hidden under the floorboards in the kitchen of my house," Angela said. "There's a one-terabyte flash drive with bank records, recordings of phone calls, emails, texts, and digital files with terms and agreements. Everything's in a mini safe with material from each crime scene in labeled plastic baggies. Toro called it his 'insurance.'"

Wu turned to the HRT leader. "An agent is posted on Angela's property. I want HRT there, too, until we can get evidence techs to collect it all."

After their initial search of the house hadn't turned up Toro's stash of evidence, or any sign of Angela, an agent had stayed behind to make contact in case she returned.

"I'll warn the agent and get backup rolling as soon as we have a signal," Demarco said. "But Vaden could have already deployed personnel to that location."

He was right. While they'd been engaged in a shoot-out in the desert, Vaden could have sent a different hit squad to go through Angela's property.

"By now, Vaden knows we have Angela," Dani said. "With no other leads, her house is a logical choice for a closer look."

"It won't matter if he finds the evidence and destroys it," Angela said, drawing everyone's attention. She grasped the gold necklace mostly hidden by her T-shirt and began tugging it out. "I got scared. What if there was a fire or a burglary? What if they captured us and I needed to bargain for our lives? So I made a copy." She held the chain up to show them an oval-shaped medallion. "It's hidden in here."

Dani looked closely at what was unmistakably a religious medal, but she didn't recognize the saint on the front. "Who's that?"

"Albertus Magnus." Angela smiled. "Also known as Albert the Great. Patron saint of scientists."

She should have known. "Can I see it?"

Angela released the clasp and handed over the necklace. "The drive is embedded in the back. Toro's evidence is in one file, but my real notes—not the ones with the messed-up numbers—are in another file with my name on it. There's also a third file made by Toro. It's a message for Tace. I never tried to open it, so I don't know what it says." The sadness returned to her eyes. "I was planning to show it to Tace when he turns eighteen, but I'll check it out first to make sure Toro didn't say too much about how he made a living. That's a legacy nobody wants."

CHAPTER 69

Our Lady of the Sacred Heart Catholic Church
Apache Junction, Arizona

Dani hurried through the church and crossed the courtyard behind it, desperate to get to the rectory.

She and Wu had joined the HRT in their Black Hawk, which took less than fifteen minutes to get from the retreat to the large parking lot in front of Our Lady of the Sacred Heart.

Within ten minutes of takeoff, Demarco regained a signal. Dani was relieved when the agent posted at the Peralta property reported that no one had approached the house. Tactical personnel and evidence techs from the Phoenix field office were on the way. Another loop closed, tightening the case against Vaden.

Flint had volunteered to drive Angela and Tace in her car, while agents from the Phoenix field office reclaimed the SUV they'd loaned to the contingent from New York.

Despite reassurances from Demarco, Dani wanted to see Father Ramirez and Patel for herself. During the flight back, Wu had taken full responsibility for what had happened to them. She disagreed. As the one with the most tactical training, she was answerable as well.

She opened the rectory door and nearly collided with the priest, who was standing directly behind it.

"I was just on my way to the sacristy to prepare for the healing service," Father Ramirez said.

She took in the livid red mark on his cheek and his swollen left eye. "You should add a prayer for yourself."

He rested a hand on her shoulder and looked into her eyes. "I'm fine."

Her attempt at humor had not fooled him in the slightest, but he had other concerns. "What happened to the men who questioned us?"

There was no way to sugarcoat it. "Only two of them survived, Father."

He bowed his head, and Dani realized he was praying—she assumed for their immortal souls. She wasn't sure how much his intercession would help but respectfully waited for him to finish.

When he looked up, the priest's eyes were filled with compassion. "I believe their leader stopped them from killing us."

Dani had wondered about that. "Agent Demarco told us you said a prayer."

Father Ramirez nodded. "Divine intervention saved us."

Patel made his way from the living room to the foyer where they were talking.

Wu moved past her to examine the analyst. "You're limping."

Patel waved the observation away. "Compared to what could've happened, I'm friggin' dandy."

Wu wasn't amused. "Why didn't you let the paramedics take you to the hospital?"

"I told you I'm fine." When Wu narrowed his eyes, Patel added, "Sir."

Before she had gotten to know the boss, she would've thought he was being stern with Patel. Now she understood that he truly cared for those he worked with and held himself accountable for their safety.

Father Ramirez cleared his throat. "I'll check back with you all after the service. You can stay here," he said, offering them privacy.

When the door closed again, Dani asked Patel the question that had been burning in her mind. "What happened, and how did my brother play a part in it?"

She and Wu both listened as Patel gave a harrowing account of their treatment at the hands of Foley's men. Patel had accessed a program he and Axel were developing to see if he could use it on their current investigation when there was banging on the rectory door. He managed to hit the audio transmit button and toss the laptop under the sofa before a team of operatives barged in. When he described how Axel had gotten on a video chat with Director Franklin, Wu looked like he could use an antacid.

"Let me get this straight," Wu said when Patel finished. "You're working with an outsider on a computer program for the Bureau?"

Patel was quick to explain. "We're creating algorithms for enhanced predictive analysis." He glanced at Dani. "Axel got the idea from Vega's pattern-recognition skills and his own obsession with mathematical sequences."

Wu gave his head a small shake. "As soon as we get back, I'm going to make it my business to recruit him. It's bound to be safer than having him on the loose with the kind of skill set he has."

"Already gave him an application." Patel grinned. "He turned twenty-one a few months ago."

"Hold on a sec." Dani held up a hand. Her head was spinning with all the new information. Why had her brother held out on her about something so important? He'd be hearing from her. Soon. But she had another concern as well. "Axel is a kind soul. You can't give him a gun and expect him to use it on people."

"Hello?" Patel crossed his arms. "Have we met? I'm not exactly the violent type either. Axel can be an analyst like me."

"We'll take that up later," Wu said, changing topics. "Right now, we need your tech skills. Angela Peralta gave us a flash drive to review."

Within minutes, they were sitting around a rustic wooden-plank table in the kitchen. While Patel booted up the laptop he used for suspicious material, Dani pried the edge of the Saint Albert the Great medal Angela had given her to dislodge a tiny drive. She put it in Patel's outstretched palm.

When three folder icons appeared on the screen, Wu pointed at the one on the left marked Evidence. "Open that one first."

The folder opened to reveal rows of documents, spreadsheets, and pdfs.

"This is going to take a long time to get through," Patel said, clicking on a document labeled Clients.

It was a list of names and dates going back fifteen years. Dani recognized a few names, but judging by Wu's muttered expletives, he was familiar with most of them.

"I'm going to need the biggest task force we've ever had," he said. "And it'll have to be set up in a SCIF."

"Let's see what else is here," Patel said, closing the document. "This looks interesting." He opened a spreadsheet titled Colonel X.

Dani sucked in a breath. This was the code name of the man she had gone undercover with Toro to investigate months earlier. "None of the colonel's clients are here."

Wu nodded. "He never told them who had hired him. This is just a list of dates, locations, and payments, but it should be enough to connect some dots."

Dani agreed. The low-hanging fruit would be the document with the people who had hired Toro directly before he began working for the colonel in addition to his own clients. But working backward through the spreadsheet, they could probably figure out enough to put names to those individuals as well.

Patel closed the sheet. "Let's hope Toro came through on this one." He clicked open a document titled VQE.

And yes, Toro had literally and figuratively gotten the receipts on Karl Vaden and his company. They were scanning through what he had accurately described as a treasure trove of data when a knock at the rectory door interrupted them.

Wu opened it to find Angela on the threshold. Flint stood beside her, cradling a sleeping Tace in his arms. The boy must have dozed off during the drive from the retreat. Dani had never seen this side of the rugged NYPD homicide detective, but he looked very natural as he walked past them to lay the boy gently on a sofa and cover him with a crocheted blanket.

They reconvened in the kitchen, gathering around the wooden table where their conversation wouldn't wake Tace, who was clearly exhausted from his recent ordeal.

"Have you had a chance to look at the files?" Angela asked Dani as soon as they were settled. "I'm hoping there's all the evidence you need to nail Vaden, but I've also decided it's time I heard whatever Toro had to say."

Patel had already taken the precaution of closing all the open files. He looked at Wu expectantly.

Wu regarded Angela thoughtfully. According to what she'd told them, Toro had hidden the evidence in her house. He made sure she could access it, which she had done in order to make a copy of the digital material for herself. She could have watched Toro's video at any time—something he would've known. So Toro didn't have a problem with her seeing what was there.

The question was, Did Wu?

Dani trusted Angela not to share anything Toro said. Especially since doing so would only endanger her son's life more. Besides, she would probably need to corroborate some of what was said or provide additional details to help the investigation going forward.

Wu gave a curt nod to Patel, who clicked on the video file, angling the screen so they could all bear witness to Toro's last words.

CHAPTER 70

Five months earlier, Thursday, May 9
The Peralta property, Apache Junction, Arizona

Toro propped the camera on the dashboard of the ancient VW Bus and settled himself against the macramé hemp seat cover. He'd parked outside so Angela and Tace couldn't hear what he was about to say. Aware this would be his farewell, he decided to begin with business before moving on to what was sure to be the most difficult speech of his life.

"The first part of this message is for Director Franklin. I'm not sure if this will count in a court of law, but here goes."

He raised his right hand. "I solemnly swear that everything I am about to say is the truth, the whole truth, and nothing but the truth."

He was trying to cover all his bases. There was no way he could print out an official statement and get a notary public to witness his signature. This video would have to do.

He pictured a team of Feds finding the lockbox after following his trail of clues. After all, if they hadn't succeeded, they wouldn't be watching him now.

"When you—or the agents you sent—opened the lockbox, there was stuff in plastic baggies along with the flash drive. The baggies have physical evidence that will prove what's on the drive, which includes a money trail for every financial transaction, recordings of conversations, and my notes from each contract."

He started at the beginning.

"The oldest cases go back fifteen years. I was freelancing then. I could claim I needed money to pay for my mother's kidney transplant, but that would be bullshit, and I've sworn to tell the truth."

This was harder than he'd thought it would be, and he was just getting started.

"I wanted fast cash, fast cars, and fast women. You know, the good life. By the time I learned better, I was in too deep to get out. The first time I was hired to terminate another fixer, that's when I knew how my own life would end one day. Sometimes, it sucks to be right."

A soft, humorless laugh escaped him.

"That's also when I started keeping financial records, recording phone calls, and saving texts. At first, all the data was on an encrypted flash drive, but then I started collecting stuff from each job to prove the digital evidence was legit. Nothing like DNA to back up your story." He paused. "I kept everything in my apartment in Monaco."

The Feds would be wondering how the evidence ended up in Angela Peralta's house, but he'd get to that later.

"The only info that's missing is the names of the colonel's clients. You'll have to figure out who they were, but I took as many notes as I could."

The FBI had tens of thousands of employees. It was one of the reasons he'd chosen them. They should be able to fill in the blanks with what he provided. He changed the subject to the person he wanted them to start with. How far had their investigation gotten now that they'd found his stash of evidence? Better to lay out the facts than risk any doubt.

"I've only shared half the reason I made it so difficult to find the evidence. Now I'll tell you the rest."

He leveled a steady gaze at the glowing red dot below the camera's lens.

"Obviously you've found Angela and Tace Peralta. She can explain how we met and why I helped her go into hiding. But she has no idea that she's the reason I cooked up the whole treasure hunt scheme."

He heaved a sigh.

"First, I'll explain why her last name is now Peralta. I wanted her to have a safe home to raise Tace and no financial worries. I'd saved a nest egg under the name Miguel Peralta and paid cash for some land near the Superstition Mountains. I'd been fascinated with the Lost Dutchman since I was a boy. If I lived long enough—and didn't end up in prison—I planned to retire and search for the mine. Once I realized that wouldn't happen, I changed the deed and gave the property to Angela and Tace. I also set up an anonymous trust for them, so nothing could be traced back to me."

He paused a moment as the truth hit him. His boyhood dreams hadn't come true, but maybe Tace's would. He refocused his thoughts, moving on to the day that had changed everything.

"Last March, I drove to Apache Junction to visit Tace. I missed the little guy. When I walked to the front door, I heard a man's voice shouting inside. I went around the side and looked in the window. Some asshole was in the living room with Angela. Before I knew what was going on, he punched her in the face."

The memory still filled him with rage.

"I ran back to the front and used my key to get inside. By the time I got to them, he had Angela by the arms and was shaking her like a rag doll. I jerked the fucker around and cold-cocked him. He went down like the sack of shit he was."

He made no effort to hide his satisfaction.

"Angela was hysterical. She was supposed to pick Tace up from kindergarten in five minutes. I told her I'd have a talk with the dude—she said his name was Alan Hooper—and tell him not to see her again."

He remembered her wary expression, but she asked him no questions, so he told her no lies. No need to get her in trouble when the Feds watched this video.

"Truth is, I had other plans. I stuffed Hooper in the trunk of my car and hauled his ass out into the desert. I got him out and gave him a chance to take me on in a fair fight."

He felt his lip curl. "Like most men who beat women, he was a wuss. Blubbered like a baby. I made sure he got everything he dished out before I snapped his neck. Dumped his carcass into an abandoned copper mine. I'd tell you where to find the body, but I honestly can't remember exactly where it is. Maybe someone out there cares enough to give Alan Hooper a proper burial, but I couldn't find any sign of it when I researched him later. Let's put it this way—nobody was looking for him. Nobody called the media. Basically, nobody gave a damn."

Good riddance.

"The incident with Hooper worried me, though. It was the second time Angela had let her guard down and seriously misjudged a man. The first being me, of course. But now things were different. She had Tace, and I couldn't risk someone like that hurting my son. I'd been keeping tabs on them, but one day I wouldn't be able to."

That would be the day when his past finally caught up with him, which must have happened for the FBI to be watching this video. It felt weird to think of his life in the past tense when he was still living it, but this was what planning was all about. Contingencies, and more contingencies.

"That's when I decided to relocate the evidence I'd collected from Monaco to Angela's house. I'd helped her escape a kill order once, and if her cover was ever blown, she'd need that info as leverage. But if I died, she'd have no legal right to get into my apartment and take the stuff. She needed the stash handy, but where no one else could find it."

He recalled explaining all this to Angela, who didn't want any part of it. He stayed in Arizona more than two weeks, making his case, finally convincing her the evidence might be her only bargaining chip if Vaden ever discovered she was alive—and that she had a child.

"In late April, I left for Monaco to put everything in place. Over the next week, I made two videos and gave the first one to my local lawyer. Then three days ago," he glanced at his watch to check the date, "May sixth, a man named Denton Foley called me with a contract for Simon Buckwald. The order came from Karl Vaden himself, and I've got recordings to prove it. Like me, Vaden and Foley use burners, but you can ID their voices."

He didn't waste time explaining who Foley was. Everything was in the digital files.

"The next day, Foley sent a private jet to fly me to the States, which meant I could wear my Kevlar vest and hide the evidence in the inner pockets. I never took it off, which was lucky because I was ambushed the night I went to do the job. If you go to Buckwald's cabin in the woods, you'll find evidence of a gun battle and a bunch of dead guys. The bodies will be gone, of course. Vaden sent in a cleanup crew, but they couldn't get everything. I don't know the names of the men on the hit squad, but you can check your missing persons files for DNA matches, because I sure as hell spilled a lot of blood that night."

He couldn't recall the body count, but it had been high.

"When I contacted Foley later, he claimed Buckwald must've been paranoid and hired extra security. I pretended like I believed him. But Foley's lie told me he was acting on his own and Vaden hadn't green-lighted me."

At least not yet.

"I'd already planned to put the second video in the vault at the Toltec, but I had to take extra precautions in case Foley was suspicious." He gestured around him. "I bought this beater VW Bus and drove it to Angela's house. When I'm finished with this video, I'll put it with the rest of the evidence and hide it under the kitchen floor. Then I've got one final piece of business here in Apache Junction. After that, I'll head back to the Toltec before anyone knows I left."

He looked into the distance at the Superstition Mountains. "I spent most of my life chasing money. Now I know there's another type of treasure that's far more valuable than gold."

A weight descended on him as he continued to the second part of the video.

"I'd never thought I would leave anything but pain and misery behind when I left this world. To be honest, maybe I wasn't so different from that asshole Alan Hooper. Would anyone give a shit when I was gone either? But then I got to spend time with Tace, and for the first time, I felt . . ." His voice caught and he couldn't finish the sentence, so he said, "I'd do anything for that boy."

Why couldn't he bring himself to say the words out loud? Was it because he'd never heard them himself?

"Man, that kid did it right. He had his dad's looks and his mom's brains. He was strong and brave for such a little guy. Had a kind of seriousness about him too. An old soul in a young body. I don't know. I sound like all those sappy dads I used to laugh at, only now, I get it."

And he did get it. Like an arrow to the fucking heart. He swallowed the lump in his throat and moved on.

"That reminds me. I knew I couldn't raise my son, but I asked Angela to let me name him. She agreed, but I never explained why I called him Tace. The next part of the video is for him. I'm hoping he'll see this when he's old enough. Not sure when that'll be, but I trust Angela to know."

He paused in case Angela wanted to edit the video so Tace would only see this part of it.

"Hi, mi'jo. I'm your dad. I'm not sure if you remember me, but I was the amazingly handsome guy who used to come visit when you were little." He chuckled, lightening the somber tone. "We used to play games like hide-and-seek. Remember the time you crashed your tricycle and skinned your knee? I told you to rub some dirt on it and get back on the trike. And damn if you didn't."

He'd been proud of his boy for refusing to accept defeat, or letting fear stop him. That kind of inner strength would serve him well in life.

"I'm going to tell you something my own dad never told me." He looked at the camera intently, willing his son to feel the sincerity of his words. "I'm proud of you, mi'jo. No matter what happens, never forget that."

One of the reasons he hadn't intended to have a child was because he was afraid he'd be just like his old man.

"I've got a shit ton of regrets, but the biggest one is that I couldn't be the kind of father you deserved. I was able to give you a roof over your head, financial support, and some protection, but the fact that you're watching me now means I failed you. Again."

His throat tightened with emotions he barely understood. The next part was going to kill him, but he said it anyway.

"I had to find someone else I could trust with your safety. The sad truth is that I haven't known any honorable men in my life. I'm ashamed to admit that I had to put my faith in a stranger, but he's the most honorable man I could find who also has the power to protect you. I hope like hell I made the right decision. If not, well, it's one more thing I screwed up."

He had used every resource he had to look into Thomas Franklin. Fortunately, there were hundreds of news stories about the FBI director. On top of that, Franklin had been vetted and approved by the US Senate. With above-top-secret security clearances and adversaries constantly looking for dirt, the man had to be clean enough to squeak. He also had a reputation for taking no bullshit—an essential quality when going after someone like Karl Vaden, who would try to bribe, extort, or threaten his way out of trouble.

"Enough about me," he continued. "This is about you, and it starts with your name. There's a meaning behind it." His next words come out in a broken rasp. "My time with you was short, mi'jo, but I treasured every moment we had."

And then he finally shared the secret he'd kept from everyone—even his son's mother. "Tace is short for Tesoro," he said quietly. "Because to me . . . that's what you are."

CHAPTER 71

Dani held Angela while she softly wept.

"I never knew," Angela whispered against her shoulder. "He told me the reason he chose to use Peralta, but I thought Tace was a family name or something."

Dani realized Flint and Wu were silently watching. She was grateful to them for waiting, even though they probably wondered what "Tesoro" meant. Who said cops weren't sensitive?

The thought reminded her that Toro had shown remarkable sensitivity as well. It was difficult for her to fathom that someone who dealt in death could value life so highly.

Then again, maybe the ever-present reality of mortality gave him a different perspective. Life was short . . . and then you died. Make the most of the time you have on this planet.

"What's a tay-sorrow?" Flint asked, mangling the pronunciation of Toro's beautifully accented Spanish.

Dani smiled. "It means treasure."

She waited while the implications sank in.

Wu closed his eyes and leaned back. "So the hunt was for us to track down Toro's treasure . . . his son."

Angela lifted her head from Dani's shoulder. "And to protect him," she said. "We used to talk about it. If anyone found out Tace was his son, they'd hurt him to control Toro or take revenge on him."

Dani refrained from mentioning that she was certain Foley had intended to use Tace to control Angela. She could see why Toro had reluctantly kept his distance from his son, despite his evident love for the boy. Any detectable relationship would put Tace in danger.

"Speaking of which," Angela said, turning to Wu, "you mentioned a new identity earlier. I want to get as far from here as possible now that Vaden and his cronies found us. In fact, I'd like to go back home."

"To Denver?" Wu asked.

"To New York City, where I grew up." She darted a glance at Flint. "Seems like the right place to start over." Her gaze shifted to Dani. "I have no relatives there since my parents died, but maybe you could be Tace's madrina."

Dani felt a rush of emotion. "I'd be honored to be your son's god-mother." She grinned. "And my family will be there for both of you."

"Good, because I'd like to talk to your mother about her art. That drawing she made makes me want to get back into the lab," Angela said. "Changing light and sound wave frequencies alters the movement of subatomic particles. I want to use harmonics to align them."

Dani pulled out her creds and handed Angela the scrap of artwork. "So that's why you kept staring at this."

Angela took the paper reverently, her focused attention reminding Dani of Axel when he was faced with a complex computer problem. She smiled at the thought. A scientist would fit in with her relatives just fine.

Wu's mind was apparently still on the video. "I wonder what Toro meant when he said he had one last piece of business in Apache Junction."

She recalled the cryptic comment but couldn't make sense of it. "Knowing Toro, it could have been anything."

At first, she assumed it was something criminal, but he seemed to have undergone a change of heart. If so, what was so important that he would delay his return to Las Vegas?

A faint groan came from the living room. Tace was stirring from his nap. Without another word, Angela rose and handed the drawing back before heading for the sofa to check on her son.

Wu leaned in, speaking in an undertone. "I'm not sure I should've let her see the whole video."

He looked worried. He'd been responsible for the decision to share the recording with Angela.

Dani stuck with the facts. "She could've watched it anytime. Besides, she'll see it eventually when this whole mess goes to trial."

"The question is," Flint said, "When will Tace get to see it?"

Dani had started to offer an opinion when Wu's sat phone vibrated loudly enough to interrupt the conversation.

"Wu here." He paused to listen. "Yes, sir." He glanced at Patel. "Sending it to you now."

He disconnected. "That was Director Franklin. You need to upload all the files to him right away." He paused. "Franklin says it's urgent."

CHAPTER 72

Vaden-Quest Enterprises HQ
Los Angeles, California

On the verge of failure, Karl Vaden was about to pull off his greatest success. Thomas Franklin was offering him a way out. If this worked, he would be untouchable.

To his knowledge, and he had plenty, no one had ever gotten such a highly placed official in their pocket. The kind of power, protection, and prestige having someone of Franklin's caliber behind him was invaluable.

Vaden chuckled to himself as he pulled into the deserted parking lot. This was like something out of an Oliver Stone movie, but he was intrigued enough to listen. Truth be told, he wouldn't have left the VQE headquarters building for anyone except the director of the FBI.

Two hours ago, Vaden was in his office, watching a satellite feed of the operation in the Sonoran Desert going to shit. One operative after another had fallen. He couldn't see what went on inside the large building in the center of the church site, so he had no clue what became of Foley. And frankly, he didn't care.

Foley was what he termed a "useful idiot." Like his operatives, members of his various strike teams, Assistant Director Hargrave, and Gustavo Toro. On second thought, Toro could be better described as a useful weapon. One that could be wielded to great effect, then discarded when it no longer served a purpose.

When Agent Vega shot the tail of the helicopter, Vaden had seen enough. He turned off the video feed, poured himself a double, and sipped it while he figured out his next move.

He assumed the Feds would soon find whatever evidence Toro had preserved for them. Vaden's attorneys were good, but he couldn't count on them keeping it all out of court. So he would have to make damn sure there wouldn't be anything to corroborate whatever was there when they came to his door with search warrants.

Decision made, he poured another measure of scotch and tossed it back before embarking on a methodical search through all his databases, files, and records. He began a seek-and-destroy mission for anything incriminating. Sadly, this was not something he could entrust to his admin staff, who were mostly in the dark about the full extent of his business dealings. They would ask a lot of inconvenient questions about why they were purging documents, and they would also make excellent witnesses for the prosecution that they did so on his orders.

Then he recalled his tech-support specialist and smiled. There was another kind of useful weapon. Vaden interrupted his search to place a call.

Straight to voicemail.

Frowning, he sent an urgent text.

No response.

He sat back and thought. It's possible that his tech guy had also watched the sat feed. If so, he was probably on a flight overseas by now. Which was where Vaden himself should be, but first he had business to finish.

He was just getting back to his task when his cell phone buzzed with an incoming text from an unknown number.

WE'RE CLOSING IN. YOU HAVE AN ESCAPE CLAUSE, BUT NOT
FOR LONG. LET'S TALK. MEET ME BY THE NORTH ENTRANCE OF
WHALEN PARK IN 30 MINUTES. COME ALONE. – #13

It had taken him a full minute to recall a comment he'd made to
Thomas Franklin years ago, right after he was confirmed by the Senate
to serve as the Bureau's thirteenth director.

*"There were twelve before you, and there'll be plenty more after you, but
I'm not going anywhere."*

Vaden had meant it as a dig, implying that he would carry on,
business as usual, no matter who was in the Hoover building.

He and Franklin had a history. The first time he'd seen Special
Agent Franklin many years ago, Vaden had been a mere vice president
of acquisitions at another company. The quintessential G-man in his
Hoover blues and starched white shirt, Franklin led a team of agents on
a raid of the corporate finance department.

Vaden had skated that day, and he'd used the opportunity to take
over the company when most of its board went to prison. Franklin had
tried to snare him years later without success.

Their current relationship could best be described in terms of
mutual grudging respect. So why was he reaching out now? In the
past, principled people had come to him with similar offers when their
circumstances changed. Was Franklin facing a frightening diagnosis?
Perhaps his wife or one of his children? Whatever had brought the
director to him, Vaden would leverage it to the hilt.

The unknown number on the caller ID seemed like it came from
a burner phone. The cryptic message contained a warning, but hinted
there was a deal to be made.

Vaden had glanced around his office. There was a lot more work
to do, but if Franklin was offering an escape clause, maybe he wouldn't
have to demolish decades of work. If he left immediately, he could get
there in time.

He decided there was no harm in hearing what the director had to say. If it wasn't to his liking, he was no worse off. He followed the instructions, waving away his chauffeur and walking past his limo to get into his Lambo, a favorite toy. During the drive over, he thought he'd figured out what Franklin wanted.

The FBI director had power, but not money. Vaden, on the other hand, had enough money to buy power.

So that would be the exchange they would make. They would hammer out the details after coming to an agreement. He relaxed when he pulled into the abandoned parking lot. Only one other vehicle was there, an Escalade, but silver rather than the government-issue black. This would be Franklin's personal ride, then. Like Vaden, the FBI director had a security detail and a driver. And, like Vaden, he must have dismissed them from this meeting.

His confidence was further bolstered when he walked into the park and saw Franklin sitting on a bench by himself. He realized the director of the FBI had access to all kinds of tech and could be recording the meeting, but he had tech of his own.

"Cards on the table," he said by way of greeting when he sat beside Franklin. "I just activated a signal-jamming device."

Franklin pretended to look hurt. "I go to all these extremes to meet with you alone and you think I'm wearing a transmitter?"

"It's not that I don't trust you." He shrugged. "I don't trust anybody."

Vaden's jammer also prevented him from receiving any communication, but he couldn't imagine anyone more important to speak to than Franklin at this moment. Everything else could wait.

He opened with his biggest concern, which was his own personal situation. "Your text mentioned an escape clause?"

Franklin nodded. "Your situation is . . . not good. But there are still options open to you."

So there were still alternatives, even though Franklin made it sound like he didn't have much choice. He wasn't sure if things were really that bad or if this was a negotiating tactic. Either way, it didn't pay to haggle under these circumstances. Franklin, damn him, could name his price.

"What are my options?"

Franklin looked thoughtful. "You can surrender to me right now, or you can try to make a run for it and get tackled by the Hostage Rescue Team."

At first he was shocked. Then, taking in Franklin's deadpan expression, he got the joke and laughed.

Franklin joined in. "I'm not kidding, Karl."

The laughter died and he studied Franklin's face. There was no trace of amusement.

"Don't fuck with me, Tom." He lowered his voice. "I know where you live, where your children go to school, and where your wife likes to shop."

Franklin's eyes hardened. "Keep talking. You're adding more years onto your sentence."

He shot to his feet and looked down at Franklin. "How about I put a bullet in your brain right now and leave?"

Franklin casually lifted his hand and raised an index finger.

Lasers cut through the air. Vaden looked down to see ten red dots painting a tight circle on the center of his chest.

He glanced back up to meet Franklin's steady gaze.

"It's over, Karl."

"No!" His world was tilting on its axis, spinning out of control. He forced the pulse pounding in his ears to slow. He had to make Franklin see reason. "I can buy you anything you want. I can make your wildest dreams come true. I can—"

"Maybe someday you'll understand," Franklin said quietly. "I don't care about those things."

He wanted to grab Franklin's lapels and shake sense into him but didn't dare. "Then what?"

"Justice," Franklin said. "Pure and simple. No one is above the law. Not me. Not you."

The air rushed out of his lungs as the reality of his situation crashed in on him. He'd been outmaneuvered by one of the few people on the planet he couldn't threaten, coerce, or buy. In a perverse way, he was glad Franklin hadn't sent one of his agents to make the arrest.

"Why the ruse?"

Franklin stood. "While we've been talking, teams of agents are executing search warrants at your main facilities. They're at your headquarters now seizing your computers."

Realization hit him with the force of a physical blow. Franklin and his agents had assumed he would know they were coming and start destroying evidence. They could access blueprints and see that his headquarters was basically a fortress where a warrant service could end in a standoff or a hostage situation. But Franklin understood he was the only person who could have lured Vaden away from his building during a crisis.

The old dog had apparently wanted to hunt one last time.

He scowled at Franklin. "When my attorneys are finished with you, the President will ask for your resignation."

Franklin looked supremely unconcerned.

It was an idle threat, and they both knew it. Vaden's life was essentially over. He would doubtless spend the rest of his days in a cell, powerless and alone.

Because deep in his heart, in the darkest places he never took out to examine, he knew there was no such thing as friendship. No such thing as honor. No such thing as love. There was only power.

And he had just lost it all.

CHAPTER 73

Wu felt awkward sitting at the head of the conference room table, but Director Franklin had insisted that he lead the after-action debrief.

To make matters worse, he was unfamiliar with everyone in the room except Vega and Patel, who sat to his left. He knew the agents who headed the LA field office by reputation but hadn't worked with them before. Forty minutes ago, they had joined the director to hear what the search of VQE headquarters had yielded.

Which was every bit the treasure trove Toro had promised.

He would have told Franklin that his ruse to get Vaden away from the building had probably saved thousands of documents, but he didn't want to sound like a kiss-ass, so he'd simply laid out reams of evidence, each piece more damning than the last.

While he wouldn't publicly praise those above him, he fully believed in giving recognition to those who worked for him.

"Analyst Patel and Agent Vega were invaluable," he said in conclusion. "They worked seamlessly getting through the firewalls to access and decrypt loads of hidden files before anyone could remotely wipe the system."

They reacted differently to the weight of everyone's gaze. Patel stared down at the table, while Vega looked straight ahead without any show of emotion, as if sitting at attention. It was clear neither enjoyed the spotlight, so he moved on, asking for questions.

The Bureau's Los Angeles facility was headed by Assistant Director in Charge Kiesha King, who was the first to speak. "Vaden had a private tactical team in Arizona shortly after you arrived. Did you find out how they knew to go there?"

King was sharp. She'd landed on the part he'd attempted to gloss over.

Franklin cut in, saving Wu from mentioning ADIC Hargrave's indiscreet comments at the Pentagon. "We're currently reviewing that," he said in a tone designed to end further discussion.

"What about the operatives from the cruise ship?" King asked. "Did we ever catch up with them?"

In response, Wu turned to Patel. "Can you bring up the relevant video clip?"

Patel shot him a questioning look but made no further comment as he navigated to one of the more recent encrypted files they had found on Vaden's computer.

Wu narrated as an image of the Caribbean Sea filled the wall screen. "This was taken by a VQE operative posing as a fisherman during the search for the two passengers known as Ursula and Paul Cole. As you can see, he drops a transponder into the water to signal them to swim to him. They must have had a receiver so they could locate a rescue boat that would evacuate them from the area if they had to jump overboard."

Only the man's right hand was visible as he kept what must have been a phone camera focused on the water. In the distance, two divers broke the surface and swam toward his boat in earnest.

The man bent to pick up a three-gallon plastic bucket by its handle. One-handed, he propped the rim on the boat's railing and tipped it.

A wave of blood gushed out, along with chunks of mutilated fish, raw beef, and chicken parts, staining the water red.

"Foley forwarded this video to Vaden," Wu said. "We believe Vaden ordered the man to chum the water and wanted proof that the two operatives who had caused him so much trouble had been disposed of."

Before the swimmers could get close to the boat, dorsal fins were cutting through the water like guided torpedoes headed straight for them. Wu signaled Patel to stop the video, sparing the other agents the grisly sight that would burn in his mind for years to come.

One of the LA field agents who had assisted on the search looked as if his breakfast wasn't sitting well, but he rallied to pose an unrelated question. "What about the man Toro killed in the desert back in March?"

"Alan Hooper," Wu supplied. "We did some checking, and none of his living relatives had seen him for years. We spoke to a distant cousin who didn't seem concerned that we might never locate his remains."

Sadly, Toro had been right about the man.

Director Franklin spoke next. "Is there a status update on Karl Vaden?"

Wu glanced at Patel, who had been monitoring communications from the Assistant US Attorney's Office.

"AUSA just met with his attorneys," Patel said. "He'll be arraigned tomorrow." The corner of his mouth went up. "Several VQE employees have asked for appointments. It's a stampede to see who can cut a deal first."

That made sense. Vaden was the kind of leader whose loyalty was only to himself. The people around him would know their boss was the type to push the blame onto them and deny knowledge of their actions. Their best bet was to look out for themselves, because they were well aware Vaden sure as hell wouldn't.

"What about the investigation into Toro's list of clients?" King asked. "Karl Vaden is the biggest name, but there are plenty more."

Wu was about to respond when the director got to his feet.

"The investigation will be split into two dedicated task forces," he said, addressing the room at large. "The one dealing with Vaden and VQE will be run out of this field office in LA. The other task force will take on the rest of the list and will be based in New York."

This was news to Wu. He wondered if he would have to relocate to LA or if Franklin wanted him leading the charge in New York. He wasn't sure how he felt about moving.

Franklin checked his watch. "I've got to fly back to Washington tonight." He glanced at King. "Choose the members of the LA task force and provide a roster to me tomorrow." He shifted his gaze to Wu. "I need to speak to you privately. Let's go for a walk."

All eyes turned to Wu. The director hadn't been smiling when he made the invitation, which was actually an order. Was he being taken out to the woodshed?

CHAPTER 74

Dani waited for Wu and the director to leave the room before rounding on Patel. "What the hell were you thinking?"

His eyes widened. "What are you talking about?"

As if he didn't know. "I need to talk to my brother—the guy you've been recruiting on the down-low." She gestured toward his laptop. "Can you set up a comm link?"

Patel sent an alert to Axel before turning to Dani. "He really is brilliant. I couldn't pass up the opportunity when he approached me."

As he'd no doubt intended, Patel had reminded her that the secret collaboration had been Axel's idea. That didn't let Patel off the hook, and she would deal with her brother after making that clear.

"There are some things you don't understand about Axel. He had a hard time growing up, because other kids—and even some adults— couldn't understand him. I did what I could to help, but it was hard on him when I left for the military. He's all grown up now, I get it, but at times when I look at him, I still see that little boy I left behind."

"You won't be leaving him behind this time," Patel said. "You can help him start a whole new phase of his life. And that's exactly what it is—*his* life, not yours."

He rarely discussed personal business with her, so the fact that he did now added weight to his words.

The comm link flickered to life. Her brother's startled face filled the screen. "Hi, Dani," he said, quickly recovering. "Didn't expect to see you."

"You backdoored the FBI director's secure comm link without authorization. I figured that deserved a video call."

His cheeks reddened. "You have to admit, it was kind of a cool idea."

She rolled her eyes. Of course it was cool. It was pure Axel. "I'm glad you got through to him, and I'm proud of you for thinking on your feet in an emergency. My only problem is all the sneaking around you've been doing."

He gave her an indignant frown. "Are you kidding? You sneak around for a living. And you've been doing it for years. Consider this my first covert mission."

"First?"

She knew about his application to the Bureau but was curious to hear about it directly from him. How much had been his idea versus Patel's?

"I'm not a badass like you, but I'd like to use what skills I have to serve my country and to help people. Is that so hard to understand?"

"Of course it's not. It's just that I worry about you."

"When we were kids, Dad was away a lot and Mom couldn't always take care of us." He glanced away, no doubt recalling their mother's fragile state. "So you stepped in. When I was hurt or scared, you were the one I ran to. But I'm not a kid anymore, and you still need someone to watch over and protect." He regarded her thoughtfully. "You should seriously consider having niños of your own. You'd be a great mom."

"Yeah, I'd be ideal in a postapocalyptic hellscape. Not so much in the suburbs."

"You sell yourself short, Dani. Besides, there's someone else who needs a mama bear to look out for him."

The image of Tace Peralta's big brown eyes as he reached up to take Detective Flint's hand flashed through her mind.

Axel grinned. "Patel told me you're going to be a godmother."

She started to question him, then stopped. Sometimes, plausible deniability was a good thing.

She had reached out to Axel with an agenda in mind, but the conversation had taken an unexpected and unsettling turn. She had never imagined herself with a family of her own, but Axel's heartfelt words made her wonder.

She pushed the thought away. Years ago, she had loved and lost someone who would have been up for the challenge of dealing with a woman who was also a warrior and protector.

Would fate ever see fit to give her another chance?

CHAPTER 75

Wu appreciated the cool night air fanning his face. He would have enjoyed it more if he weren't strolling through the grounds around the LA field office building beside a man who had total control over his career.

It didn't help that Director Franklin hadn't cracked a smile, or uttered a word, since they'd exited the building.

It was pure torture, but Wu maintained a respectful silence. Franklin would speak when he was ready.

Finally, Franklin said, "Assistant Director King will oversee the investigation into Vaden in LA. I'm not sure who's going to run the task force in New York."

Wu nearly missed a step. Franklin had told him he would be in charge of it all. His parting comment to ADIC King meant he'd taken away half of the responsibility, and now it seemed he was taking away all of it.

"Is there a problem, sir?"

"Yes." Franklin came to a halt. "And it's you."

Wu's mouth went dry. He turned to face the director. Only then did he see the faintest hint of amusement crinkling the corners of Franklin's eyes.

"You're messing with me, aren't you?"

"You should get used to my sense of humor," Franklin said. "Most people don't think I have one." He resumed walking. "I'm going to promote you to assistant director. At issue is where to put you."

To say Wu was shocked would be a massive understatement. This was not how promotions occurred in a government system. Sure, he'd filed the necessary paperwork last year, but he assumed he'd be in his current position for years before an opportunity came up.

Then again, the head of any large agency was given a great deal of latitude in how they handled the job.

"Thank you," he offered, aware it sounded weak considering the extraordinary nature of what Franklin had confided. He thought he understood the nature of Franklin's problem. "I wasn't aware of any openings."

Assistant directors were high up among the executive ranks of the Bureau, and slots didn't open often.

"Dan Silverman just put in his papers," Franklin said. "He's moving to a quiet cove in Maine to write crime novels."

Silverman headed the Washington field office, the only location besides the NYFO and LAFO with an assistant director in charge. Now Wu understood the director's comment about getting to know his sense of humor. The director's office was in the Hoover building on Pennsylvania Avenue, less than a ten-minute drive from the WFO.

"I try to avoid forcing things on people," Franklin continued. "Especially not those I intend to work with closely."

Was he offering Wu the option to turn the promotion down? He felt like he was missing something important.

"What are my options, then?"

Franklin stopped again and turned to face him. "Assistant Director Hargrave made a grave error in judgment at the Pentagon. The data you recovered from Vaden's communication convinced me he hadn't intentionally compromised the investigation or endangered anyone." He heaved a world-weary sigh. "I've seen it before. Hargrave knew he'd gone as far as he could in the Bureau, and he wanted to set something up for the future. He'd set his sights on Vaden, and he was far too eager to prove himself useful."

Wu had seen it too. "Hargrave overshared. Unfortunately, he seemed threatened by me and did what he could to put me in a bad light every chance he got."

"He was right to feel threatened," Franklin said. "Without even trying, or knowing you were doing it, you made him look subpar by comparison."

That had never been Wu's intention, but he didn't argue the point. His days of covering for Hargrave had come to an end.

Franklin continued, "What most people don't understand is how much damage a leader who puts his own self-interests first can do." He paused. "I offered him the chance to retire rather than face a formal investigation."

It had been a kindness. Hargrave had dedicated more than a quarter century to the FBI, and he would be allowed to keep the pension he'd earned if he left quietly.

When Franklin raised an expectant brow, Wu got his meaning. "You're considering me to fill Hargrave's spot." He made it a statement.

"It's a tough choice," Franklin said. "I'd like you in Washington close to me, but you were born and raised in New York. You still have family there, and you'd probably jump at the chance to run the NYFO your way."

It was like the director was reading his mind. "Of course, sir, but—"

"But there's another consideration," Franklin cut in. "Agent Daniela Vega."

Wu didn't trust himself to speak. He recalled Hargrave's accusations in Franklin's office, and his own vehement denials—had they been overly vehement?

The director would not have offered him a promotion if he believed there was any truth to Hargrave's smear campaign, but had he spotted some chemistry?

Franklin gave him a knowing look but made no further comment.

The cool breeze had vanished, leaving Wu hot under the collar.

He changed the subject. "You want me in DC, so why are you putting New York on the table?"

"Because you might want to stay near family, friends, and colleagues," Franklin said.

Wu got his meaning. If he stayed in New York, Vega would be strictly off-limits, but if he moved to Washington, she wouldn't be in his chain of command. He would be free to find out if there were any future possibilities with her.

"You've got a bright future ahead of you, Steve." Franklin narrowed his eyes. "Tread carefully."

The director was putting him on notice. If he wanted to be with Vega, he had to leave her. But as long as he was still her boss, he couldn't ask her out, or pressure her to find out how she felt about him before he made his decision.

Franklin eyed him closely. "Life is full of risks. You have to choose which ones are worth the gamble."

CHAPTER 76

Dani was reviewing computer files with Patel when Wu and Director Franklin returned to the conference room. She studied their expressions and body language. She detected no overt hostility, but there was an undercurrent of tension she couldn't read. When neither man made a move to sit, she and Patel instinctively rose.

Wu appeared to be lost in thought as he stood across from her.

Director Franklin addressed the group. "When Gustavo Toro sent me the video, he promised it would be a tough case. He wasn't exaggerating. He also recommended I put my best agents on it. And that's exactly what I did." He glanced around the room. "A simple 'thank you' seems insufficient for people who put their lives on the line in the pursuit of justice."

Mention of Toro brought their last encounter to mind, along with everything she had learned about him over the past few days. She had come to understand him in an entirely new light. When they first met, she thought of him as nothing more than a ruthless killer with no moral compass. Now she knew differently. Toro was a complicated man who had lived by his own code.

She would do everything in her power to help his son. And when Tace was grown, if he ever asked her about his father, she would tell him the unvarnished truth, hiding nothing, because he should understand every part of who his father was.

The director shook each of their hands, ending with Wu. Still gripping his hand, Franklin pulled Wu in close and murmured something Dani couldn't make out.

She was alarmed when Wu's gaze fell on her as he muttered a low response. If she didn't know better, she'd think they were discussing her.

Franklin straightened and turned to Patel. "I'd like you to fly back with me to Washington. You can demonstrate the program you and Axel Vega are designing. I'll arrange for you to meet with the deputy director in charge of technology first thing in the morning."

Dani's jaw went slack. Before she could recover, Franklin had turned his hawklike eyes on her. "Our nation faces daily cyber threats that include espionage, terrorists, ransomware, and more. They're growing in complexity. The Bureau needs people like your brother . . . and I intend to recruit him."

She had no words. Axel's mind did indeed work differently than most. She was so grateful someone in such an esteemed position appreciated his raw talent.

Patel tried to hide his excitement, failing miserably. He snapped his laptop shut and walked out ahead of the director, who cast a meaningful glance over his shoulder at Wu before closing the door behind him.

Now alone in the nearly deserted building, Dani took the opportunity to study her boss. It had been a long day, but she wasn't sure if the lines on his face were a sign of fatigue or concern.

"What's going on, sir?"

A hint of annoyance flickered across his features for an instant, then disappeared. "Hargrave's going to retire early."

She was too tired to be diplomatic. "I'm assuming the director gave him an ultimatum."

Wu nodded. "Hargrave wasn't serving the public anymore—only himself." He paused. "Franklin offered me his spot."

This should have been fantastic news, so why did he look troubled? Something else was at play. Rather than congratulating him, she said, "And?"

"And there's also an opening for an ADIC at the WFO."

She waited for him to elaborate, but he didn't. "So he's giving you a choice?"

Wu nodded and took a step closer, his eyes boring into hers. "I chose Washington." He seemed to want to say more but was holding back.

"Congratulations, sir."

"Don't call me 'sir,'" he responded sharply. "My name is Steve."

Years of military service had conditioned her to address commanding officers by their rank or using sir or ma'am. She couldn't imagine referring to the colonel in charge of the Ranger regiment as Joe or Sam, or whatever. As an assistant director in charge, Wu's position was every bit as far from hers as her former colonel's had been.

"Steve," she said, testing the sound of his given name. It seemed . . . intimate.

He smiled down at her. "The decision has a lot of consequences professionally and personally. I've always wanted to head up the NYFO and run it the right way. It's a dream job for me."

"Then why go to DC?"

"The director's taken an interest in me. I'd be close to him, but far from everyone in New York." His gaze took on an intensity she'd never seen before. "The express train makes the trip in under three hours."

He made no further comment. Silence filled the space between them as she considered his words. And then, with the sudden realization of cracking a code, she decrypted the hidden message he was trying to convey.

She remembered his expression when she'd insisted on using herself as a decoy at the wilderness retreat. And when Bravo had nearly shot her. And when Captain Skála had pulled her from the path of a speeding forklift and held her tight against him.

She also recalled her own thoughts about him at the hotel. He was handsome and refined. The exact opposite of a girl from the Bronx who was more comfortable in the barracks than the Ritz. To her, someone like him had seemed unattainable.

And that was precisely why she had never noticed the subtle signs. In his current position, however, she was equally unattainable. Forbidden fruit.

The realizations crashed in on her in a matter of seconds. When his gaze softened, she knew he'd read the dawning awareness on her face. He took another step closer, and his scent, now familiar, surrounded her.

He had made two things clear. First, this was goodbye. Second, they would be only a short train ride apart. He could not come out and ask, nor could he initiate any physical contact. He could only stand there, a silent plea in his eyes, and wait for her response.

Any potential future they might have was in her hands.

She had taken his strong presence for granted. When he left for DC, he would take a piece of her heart with him. Her father and then Holt, her first love, had done the same. How much more could there be left? She had made a huge mistake by not confessing her true feelings to Holt before he died. Fear had tied her tongue, and her silence had haunted her ever since.

Could this be her chance to banish the ghosts of her past?

She stood on the edge of a cliff, unsure if she should take a leap of faith. Life offered no guarantees. They both could have died many times today. She had to find the courage to say what she couldn't years ago, or she'd always regret it.

She lifted her hand and placed it on his chest. His stoic expression gave nothing away, but she felt his heart race under her palm.

"There's something I have to tell you, Steve." She gave him a slow smile. "I've always liked trains."

EPILOGUE

The following morning, Saturday, October 12
Our Lady of the Sacred Heart Catholic Church
Apache Junction, Arizona

Father Ramirez walked into his study in the rectory holding a cup of strong, hot tea. He had placed the mug on his desk and leaned forward to open the curtains and let in the morning sun when movement caught his eye.

He peered into the courtyard to see a man and woman standing under the wide canopy of a mesquite tree. The man gently pulled the woman against him and kissed her. She raised her arms to wind them around his neck.

Smiling, the priest twitched the curtains closed. He had known Angela Peralta since her arrival in Apache Junction five years ago and had regularly kept her and her son in his prayers. He'd often thought Tace could use a father figure, but no one had seemed right.

Until a New York City homicide detective came to town with a group of FBI agents. Some would call it a miracle, and he'd agree.

When Tace fell back to sleep in the rectory last night, Angela and the detective had stayed up to watch over him. It seemed they had also formed a bond.

Earlier this morning, Father Ramirez had been preparing a homily for that evening's Mass when Angela asked him to hear her confession. Not only had she wanted to unburden herself, but she also felt he deserved to know all the circumstances that had nearly cost him his life.

He had listened in rapt attention to a wild tale of a former identity as a cutting-edge scientist, the hit man sent to kill her who helped her go into hiding instead, and the greedy business mogul who hired a murderous crew to hunt her down. She'd also shared that the hit man, Gustavo Toro, was Tace's biological father.

He might have suspected she watched too many thriller movies, but the men who had come to his parish yesterday, and Detective Flint's account of the shoot-out at the wilderness retreat, convinced him she was probably downplaying her story, if anything.

Angela wanted to move back to New York, where she was from. She had asked Agent Vega to be Tace's godmother and hoped to get to know her family. What he'd just seen in the courtyard told him there were other reasons for moving across the country. There would be plenty of comfort and protection for her there.

He reflected on Special Agent Dani Vega, a complex woman who carried many secrets. He wondered what Dani had said the last time she'd gone to confession. She had taken several lives yesterday in the defense of others. He'd heard about her military background as well and hoped she was at peace.

The notion reminded him of a confession he'd heard five months ago, back in May. When Angela told him her story, Father Ramirez was certain the person who had come to him in search of absolution was Gustavo Toro—something his vows prevented him from disclosing.

Toro had said he could not stop killing because it was part of his profession. Father Ramirez now knew precisely what that job had been. But it was more complicated than that. Toro lived by a code. Somehow, he knew in his heart that Toro had died by that same code.

Father Ramirez regretted that he'd been unable to grant him absolution that day, but there was something he could do for him now.

He sank to his knees, crossed himself, and recited an intercessory prayer for the dead. "Eternal rest grant unto him, O Lord, and let perpetual light shine upon him. May his soul, through the mercy of God, rest in peace. Amen."

The troubled person in the confessional months ago had not minimized the damage he'd done. Had not pleaded his case. Had not made excuses.

Instead, he had explained his situation in the starkest terms. The taking of life was no small thing, and Toro felt the inescapable weight of his deeds.

According to Angela, he knew his days were numbered and made elaborate plans to care for his son. Nothing brings clarity like the prospect of death.

Father Ramirez was unaware of the details, but knew he was dealing with something profound that day. *"I sense deep pain and remorse."*

Toro's response came out as a whisper. *"You have no idea, Father."*

True enough. He'd never been a contract killer, but he understood people, and he could tell Toro's heart was breaking. He'd come for absolution but left unfulfilled. Had there been a chance for redemption before he died?

Father Ramirez heaved a weary sigh and got to his feet. Some things he would never know. As he rose, a ray of sunlight filtered through a slit between his office curtains. He let the golden beam play across his face and smiled. Perhaps his prayer had been answered.

Perhaps Gustavo Toro had finally found peace.

ACKNOWLEDGMENTS

My husband, Mike, has been incredibly supportive through all my endeavors. The best partner and friend anyone could want, he is my rock.

My son, Max, brings me joy every day. How blessed I am to play a part in his journey.

So much more than an agent, Liza Fleissig shares my vision and makes miracles happen. Her advice, support, and outstanding professionalism have been life changing for me and many others.

My other agent, Ginger Harris-Dontzin, is always in my corner. Her sage advice, timely intervention, and unswerving support have helped me on many occasions.

The men and women of the FBI work without expectation of fame or fortune. They dedicate themselves to upholding their motto, "Fidelity, Bravery, Integrity." A special thanks goes out to Ret. Special Agent Jerri Williams, who shares their stories in her award-winning *FBI Retired Case File Review* podcast.

To create a fictional story with an authentic feel, speaking to those who were there is imperative. Former FBI executive Lauren C. Anderson, who served in New York City, was generous with her time and considerable expertise. Any liberties taken in service of the plot or mistakes made are my own.

Executive editor Megha Parekh, my acquiring editor, has been with me throughout my journey with Thomas & Mercer. Her strong advocacy, continued support, and keen instinct for story have made all the difference. Always ready to discuss new ideas, her creative collaboration has been invaluable.

My developmental editor, Charlotte Herscher, put her impressive talent toward making this story better. Her incisive observations, well-thought-out critiques, and sharp eye for detail kept me on track through many iterations of the manuscript.

The amazing team of editing, marketing, and artwork professionals at Thomas & Mercer is second to none. This story is particularly complex, and Andrea Nauta, Jon Ford, Ashley Little, and James Gallagher worked with me tirelessly to double-check each component of the unfolding mystery. I am incredibly blessed to have such talented professionals by my side.

ABOUT THE AUTHOR

Photo © 2016 Skip Feinstein

Wall Street Journal bestselling and award-winning author Isabella Maldonado wore a gun and badge in real life before turning to crime writing. A graduate of the FBI National Academy in Quantico and the first Latina to attain the rank of captain in her police department, she retired as the Commander of Special Investigations and Forensics. During more than two decades on the force, her assignments included hostage negotiator, department spokesperson, and precinct commander. She uses her law enforcement background to bring a realistic edge to her writing, which includes the bestselling Nina Guerrera series (optioned by Netflix for a feature film starring Jennifer Lopez), the Dani Vega series, the Veranda Cruz series, and the Sanchez and Heron series, coauthored with #1 *New York Times* bestselling author Jeffery Deaver. Her books are published in twenty-four languages. For more information, visit www.isabellamaldonado.com.